A Rool

Madison followed Park
where he could pretend t
fake smiles until they rea
around, red-faced and angry.

"That was bullshit out there today," he said through clenched teeth. A thin sheen of sweat covered his red forehead. "I just got a call from a buddy at campus security, asking if it's true this might be a homicide. Then I got a call from a guy in homicide asking the same thing, and wondering why he didn't know about it. Look, I don't care if you blow off Rourke or me. That's annoying, but it don't matter. But you're a lab tech, not a homicide detective. If you want to be a homicide detective, I'll tell you what you do: You go to the police academy, you work your ass off for ten, maybe twenty years, pass a bunch of exams every couple of years, and kiss the right asses at the right times. Then maybe you can be a homicide detective. And then maybe someone will give a crap what you have to say about what some goddamn coed thinks about a very cut and very dried overdose case that a lot of people want wrapped up quick..."

Body Trace

A C.S.U. INVESTIGATION

D. H. Dublin

BERKLEY BOOKS, NEW YORK

THE BERKLEY PUBLISHING GROUP
Published by the Penguin Group
Penguin Group (USA) Inc.
375 Hudson Street, New York, New York 10014, USA
Penguin Group (Canada), 90 Eglinton Avenue East, Suite 700, Toronto, Ontario M4P 2Y3, Canada
(a division of Pearson Penguin Canada Inc.)
Penguin Books Ltd., 80 Strand, London WC2R 0RL, England
Penguin Group Ireland, 25 St. Stephen's Green, Dublin 2, Ireland (a division of Penguin Books Ltd.)
Penguin Group (Australia), 250 Camberwell Road, Camberwell, Victoria 3124, Australia
(a division of Pearson Australia Group Pty. Ltd.)
Penguin Books India Pvt. Ltd., 11 Community Centre, Panchsheel Park, New Delhi—110 017, India
Penguin Group (NZ), Cnr. Airborne and Rosedale Roads, Albany, Auckland 1310, New Zealand
(a division of Pearson New Zealand Ltd.)
Penguin Books (South Africa) (Pty.) Ltd., 24 Sturdee Avenue, Rosebank, Johannesburg 2196,
South Africa

Penguin Books Ltd., Registered Offices: 80 Strand, London WC2R 0RL, England

This is a work of fiction. Names, characters, places, and incidents either are the product of the author's imagination or are used fictitiously, and any resemblance to actual persons, living or dead, business establishments, events, or locales is entirely coincidental.

BODY TRACE

A Berkley Book / published by arrangement with the author

PRINTING HISTORY
Berkley edition / September 2006

Copyright © 2006 by The Berkley Publishing Group.
Interior text design by Stacy Irwin.

ISBN: 0-425-21239-4

BERKLEY®
Berkley Books are published by The Berkley Publishing Group,
a division of Penguin Group (USA) Inc.,
375 Hudson Street, New York, New York 10014.
BERKLEY is a registered trademark of Penguin Group (USA) Inc.
The "B" design is a trademark belonging to Penguin Group (USA) Inc.

PRINTED IN THE UNITED STATES OF AMERICA

10 9 8 7 6 5 4 3 2 1

DONNA LAMOTT raised her hand to knock a little bit harder on the door to room six of the Alpha Alpha Gamma sorority house. Just as her knuckles were about to make contact for the third time, the door to room five opened instead.

Valerie Chirelli's head poked out. "For Christ's sake," she said coldly, leaning against the doorjamb, "if it's that important, just go on inside."

Chirelli looked rough, like she'd been partying all night. There were big bags under her bloodshot eyes. Nothing too unusual there.

"But if you knock on that door one more time," Chirelli continued, "you'll be spending the fall semester in a wheelchair."

Donna smiled acidly as Valerie retreated into her room, and opened up the door to number six.

The first thing that hit her was the smell. The windows were open, but even so, there was something unfamiliar mixed with the smell of Beth's paints—a sickly sour stench hanging in the stifling heat.

Ashley Munroe was slumped over her desk, wearing a typically indecent, short pink robe. There was a pool of vomit next to her face. Donna stepped closer and saw that Ashley's robe was soiled. A dark, mustard-brown stain was seeping out from underneath her. A puddle of something that looked like urine had collected on the wood floor under her chair, and some of it had soaked into the rug.

Donna made a face. "Oh," she murmured distastefully.

She stepped forward, trying to see if Ashley was breathing, but before she could get close enough, she noticed Beth's easel and canvas toppled onto the floor. The palette had rolled across the room, leaving a trail of yellow and orange paint.

She took another step forward, and for the first time, noticed Beth, wearing black pajamas, awkwardly kneeling on the floor in front of her sculpture project. Donna had seen her working on that project before, though she'd be damned if she had a clue what it was supposed to mean. The installation consisted of a dozen or so ceramic pylons, most about a foot high, the tallest maybe two feet. They were three-sided, undulating, and slightly twisted. Each one tapered to a point. When Donna had seen them before, the figurines had been a dark, greenish black, but now half of them were redone in oranges and reds, not unlike the canvas on the floor.

The way she was kneeling in front of her little statues, Beth looked like she was praying. The figures seemed to be gathered around her, almost as though they were listening.

With an unnerving feeling that she was disturbing something between them, Donna cleared her throat once, then again, louder.

That was when she noticed a small, dark red object on the back of Beth's neck. It looked like she was wearing a red spiked collar—but with only one spike? And in the back? Donna shook her head with disdain.

"Beth," she said loudly, reaching out and giving her shoulder a little push. But there was no response.

"Beth," she said again, annoyed.

Donna leaned over, hoping to catch Beth's attention. But when she did, she saw that her eyes were closed tight. She seemed to be sucking on the top of one of the figurines.

"Come on, Beth, stop it." She gave her another shake.

With a soft, wet, sucking sound, Beth's head started to sink down, as if she were devouring the statue. Suddenly Donna noticed that the bauble on the back of Beth's neck had grown into a four-inch spike, glistening with blood, protruding obscenely from under her jaw.

Donna's mouth quivered noiselessly as she realized what she was looking at.

The new colors on the pylons weren't paint at all, but a garish mixture of blood and vomit. Pieces of yesterday's corn were plainly visible on the carpet between the figurines, where the splattered vomit mixed with the blood that had soaked down the front of Beth's shirt and pooled around her knees.

As Donna stood there staring, a fly came in through one of the torn screens in the windows and landed on one of the sculptures. Almost instantly, it was joined by three or four others. Donna felt faint, nauseous, but still she was unable to move or make a sound. Her breaths were shallow, short, and rapid. Somewhere in the back of her mind it occurred to her that she was going into shock.

The sound of the flies in the otherwise quiet room was soon joined by another noise. It was that same wet, sucking sound as before, but quieter now, and sustained.

Donna bent closer, watching with horror and fascination as Beth's head slowly, almost imperceptibly, slid lower. The blood-covered spike emerged just as slowly, growing out of the back of her neck.

Unable to stop staring, Donna was only inches away when she was startled by a sickening, cracking, tearing noise, like a drumstick being torn from a turkey. Beth's jaw seemed to unhinge, and blood suddenly flowed freely from her nose and mouth. The skin on her neck tore open, and she finally sank to the floor.

Donna watched Beth's descent in silent horror until her eyes focused on the floor. That's when she noticed the puddle of Beth's blood had grown, and that she was now standing in it. That's when Donna LaMott began to scream.

CHAPTER 1

THE HEAT shimmering on the tarmac had been visible
through the airplane's windows, but as she stepped out
onto the top of the exit staircase, the feel of it still took
Madison Cross by surprise. It was a force that resisted
her, almost physically pushing back. She paused, actually
considering turning around and getting back on the plane,
wondering for the thousandth time what she was doing
back in Philadelphia. But the grumbling surge of weary
travelers waiting to get off propelled her forward and
down the portable stairs.

It was a short walk across the tarmac and into the terminal, but by the time she reentered the air-conditioning, her
clothes were damp with perspiration. The pilot had warned
them about the heat, of course, but the reality of it was still
jarring. Madison couldn't help wondering how long it
would take her to get reaccustomed to the Philadelphia
summer.

She collected her bags as if in a trance, then kept
walking through the terminal and back outside. The taxi

stand wasn't quite as hot, but the exhaust fumes from the buses and cars seemed to hang right in front of her.

As she settled into the back of a cab, the driver turned and asked, "Where to?"

Madison realized she wasn't sure. She had planned on checking out her apartment before heading to work, but the plane had sat on the runway for more than an hour in Chicago and now she was running late. She stared at her watch and tried to figure out whether or not she had time to drop off her bags and freshen up.

She was subletting a condo she had never seen from a second cousin she had never met. All she had was an address in Old City, a key, and an alarm code. She closed her eyes and tried to calculate how long it would take to get there, get inside, get cleaned up, and get to work.

When she opened her eyes, the cabbie was still looking at her, clearly exasperated.

"Center City," she said with resignation. "Police Headquarters."

He stared at her uncomprehendingly.

"The Roundhouse. Seventh and Race."

The driver nodded and hit the meter. "Accident on the expressway. Gotta take I-95."

"Whatever." She closed her eyes and sank into the backseat.

Just a few weeks earlier, Madison Cross had it all figured out: graduating first in her class from the University of Washington School of Medicine, nice but unremarkable boyfriend, great residency lined up at Stanford—all of it far, far away from Philadelphia.

Now she was back. Alone. And instead of a residency at Stanford, she was about to start a job she knew nothing about in the crime scene unit of the Philadelphia Police Department.

What the hell was she thinking?

* * *

PHILADELPHIA'S CRIME lab was located in police headquarters. The building was officially called the Police Administration Building, but everyone called it the Round-house. While not actually a circle, The Roundhouse was rounded—a sinuous, concrete form built in the optimism of the early sixties, when architects were allowed to have some fun. To Madison, the building represented a golden age before she was born, before the turbulence and trouble that hit the city in the late sixties and persisted for the next twenty-five years. It was actually something of an architec-tural landmark, but it had come to be taken for granted by the city's inhabitants.

The cab pulled over on the Race Street side of the build-ing, a common mistake. A broad courtyard stretched in front of an open and welcoming main entrance on Race, but, in what probably should have been taken as a bad omen, the front entrance had never actually been used. Be-fore the building was even finished, the powers-that-be de-cided Race Street had become too much of a highway to locate an entrance there. So they barricaded the front door and put up a couple of small signs redirecting visitors to the back entrance.

As the cab drove away, Madison stood on the sidewalk for a moment, appreciating the building's dramatic curves, feeling a little better about her decision to come here. Then she sighed and walked around the block, through the small parking lot, and past the half dozen smokers out back.

Inside, she signed in at the desk. She'd been here many times as a guest when she was a kid, but this was her first time as an employee. Or as an adult, for that matter.

Studying the directory on the wall, she suddenly felt enveloped by a nebulous cloud of foreboding. Quickly she realized it was actually cheap cologne. Lots of it.

She turned her head slowly and was greeted with the cocky grin of a self-assured redneck.

Philadelphia had a side that was cosmopolitan and international, open-minded and tolerant, but it only extended so far. Not far enough, she thought to herself, to include this guy.

"How 'bout I help you find what you're looking for?" he asked, in a twang that sounded more Alabama trooper than Philly PD. He wasn't bad-looking, but the twinkle in his eye looked like it had been well practiced in the mirror, and he seemed to think he was a few pounds lighter and a few years younger than he actually was. Definitely not her type.

"No, thank you," she said, followed by the smile that said, "Don't take this personally, but I have absolutely no interest in you whatsoever." It had taken years to perfect that smile, but by the end of her freshman year at the University of Michigan, she could use it to deter the drunkest, horniest idiot, usually with no hard feelings.

But not this guy. He took a step closer. Madison instinctively made a mental note of where his instep was in relation to her heel.

"Don't be like that," he cooed. "I know this place like the back of my hand. Let me help you."

Now she was getting annoyed, as much at herself for not finding Lieutenant Cross on the directory than at him for being . . . him. After all, the damn thing was in alphabetical order. But the stranger's persistence had her flustered.

The seconds passed. She could feel him staring at the side of her head, sense him opening his mouth for whatever the third stanza was in his standard repertoire. Then she found it: Lt. D. Cross, room 302. Third floor.

"No, thanks. I've got it." She gave him the same smile, thinking repetition might help drive home the message.

"Well, maybe—"

"I don't think so," she said, cutting him off.

As Madison turned and walked to the elevator, she could feel his eyes on her. She resisted the impulse to hold her briefcase over her rear end just to keep his gaze away from it, a gaze that lingered on her as she waited for the elevator, as she got in, and as she turned around. Though she fought the urge to look at him, peripherally she could see him still staring, slowly nodding his head appreciatively. As the doors closed, all she could do was remind herself that every city had its own special breed of dog.

The elevator let her off in front of a small desk and a small woman in a uniform and sergeant's stripes.

Madison squared her shoulders. "Lieutenant Cross, please."

The woman looked her up and down, blatantly appraising her. "Down the hall and to the right," she said, keeping the results of the appraisal to herself. Madison didn't bother to ask, either—she knew how worn and weary she must have looked. Why make two enemies on her first day?

As she neared the end of the hallway, she could hear David Cross's voice—a booming, businesslike baritone that seemed to be taking issue with someone or something.

". . . And I don't expect things to be half done," he was saying. "We start the job, we do the job, we finish the job. That's how we solve cases. And that's how we keep our heads above water. Come on, Elena, you know that."

The hallway opened onto a large room tightly crammed with desks, filing cabinets, and lab tables covered with microscopes and other equipment. On the far wall, a row of doors led to other rooms with what looked like more specialized equipment.

Lt. David Cross was standing and talking to a small

Hispanic woman sitting behind a desk. Her face was
striking in a hard kind of way, and her dark eyes burned,
but didn't look away from his. She obviously didn't like
what he was saying, but she was listening.

Also listening nearby was another woman with reddish-
blond hair and a sprinkling of freckles. She seemed like
she'd heard this speech before and was waiting patiently
for the tirade to finish. As her eyes started to roll, they
caught Madison's, and she gave her a little smile.

Madison smiled back, somehow surprised to see any
women here, much less two of them. In fact, the only man
she saw was huddled over a microscope, quietly studying
whatever it was magnifying and ignoring the verbal ex-
plosion on the other side of the room.

He was tall, with dark, curly hair and glasses. His fingers were long and nimble, but they looked strong. When
he adjusted the microscope, Madison noticed they were
unadorned.

For a second, Cross looked right at Madison, but he
didn't react. He seemed to be winding down, and he took
a seat on the desk next to the woman he'd been talking to.

"So you'll get it done today, right?" he asked quietly.

The woman named Elena nodded and looked down.

Cross clapped a large hand on her shoulder and gave
it a quick squeeze before he stood. There didn't seem to
be any awkwardness in the room over what had just happened, which made Madison wonder if it was a common
occurrence.

Cross motioned for Madison to step forward. He patted an empty desk and whispered, "Here's your new
home," as he handed her an ID.

"Okay, everyone, I'd like you to welcome a new member of the team, Madison Cross, who will be joining us as
a technician."

Madison scanned the faces of her new coworkers, suddenly feeling very vulnerable. The woman who had smiled at her looked more guarded now, and the one Cross had just been admonishing, Elena, was practically glaring.

The guy at the microscope turned around and looked at her with the faintest of smiles. He was extremely handsome, in a bookish kind of way. His glasses had very thin wire rims. Madison briefly wondered what he'd look like without them.

"Ms. Cross just graduated first in her class from the University of Washington School of Medicine," Cross continued, thankfully rescuing her from that daydream. "She's certified in DNA analysis, she's interned at the CDC, and she's studied forensics and pathology. We're lucky to have her. I know you'll make her feel very welcome and help her in any way."

Turning to Madison with a professional smile, he said, "Okay, Ms. Cross, I'd like you to meet our team."

He started with the woman with the freckles and worked his way around the room. "Melissa Rourke, crime scene investigator." Polite wave. "Elena Sanchez, chemical analyst." Polite wave.

He turned to the other side of the room. "Aidan Veste, chemical analyst." Polite wave and a small, sympathetic smile. She caught herself smiling back a little more than she needed to. Aidan looked down as Cross continued. ". . . And Tommy Parker, crime scene investigator."

Madison did a quick head count, wondering if she'd missed somebody. Then she realized Cross was gesturing to someone standing behind her. She turned around and saw the good ol' boy from the lobby, wearing lots of denim and that same arrogant smile.

Cross looked back and forth between Parker and Madison. "What . . . ?"

Parker's smile widened. "We already met."

Cross looked down and muttered, "Oh, shit."

With his head still down, he looked up at Madison with the first hint of familiarity. "That's seldom a good thing," he mumbled out of the side of his mouth. He quickly raised his head and clapped his hands. "Great," he continued. "I guess we're all ready to get to work, then."

He pulled a slip of paper out of his pocket and held it far enough away so he could read it. "We've got two bodies over at the University of Pennsylvania. Couple girls in one of the sororities."

At the mention of the word "sororities," one of Parker's eyebrows twitched upward.

Cross scanned the room. "Rourke, why don't you take Ms. Cross and go have a look."

Veste went back to his work.

Parker looked put out.

Rourke took the slip of paper and grabbed her handbag from the back of her chair. "Come on," she said genially. "I'll drive."

Madison was falling into step alongside her when Lieutenant Cross called from the door to his office. "Actually, Ms. Cross," he said, "could you step into my office for a moment before you go?"

Rourke smiled. "I got to grab a couple things anyway," she said. "I'll meet you back here in a five minutes."

By the time Madison had doubled back, Cross was inside, but his door was still open. She glanced around before she entered, but no one was paying any attention except Parker.

"Close the door," Cross said as she walked in. As soon as it clicked behind her, his arms opened wide. His face spread into his best proud-Uncle-Dave smile, the one he saved for special occasions.

"How's my girl?" he said, crossing the distance between them and wrapping her up in his big arms.

Madison's eyes grew moist. It took her a few seconds to force down the lump in her throat, but she finally managed to croak "Hi, Uncle Dave."

He pulled away from her, holding her at arm's length. "Maddy girl, look at you." His eyes were moist, too, and it suddenly hit her how much he must have been missing her. "It's great to have you here." Then he grew solemn. "Now . . . are you doing okay?"

"Yes," she replied quizzically. "Why?"

"Well, you sounded in quite a state when you called. Is everything okay?"

It was true, Madison had been upset when she called him two weeks earlier. Life had seemed to be going just right, when suddenly she had realized somehow it was all wrong. She broke up with her boyfriend and backed out of her residency.

When she called her uncle in desperation, he had offered her a job in the crime lab.

On an impulse, she had accepted.

"I'm fine," she said. "I just . . . I don't know. I guess I just realized I wasn't going where I wanted to go. And I guess I missed home, too." She smiled in an effort to keep her eyes dry. "So thanks for the job, and for . . . well, just thanks."

He waved his hand dismissively. "With your training, your instincts, we're lucky to have you here, Maddy. Or should I say, Dr. Cross."

She cringed. "Oh, God."

"What is it?" he said, confused.

" 'Dr. Cross . . .' Look, I know I finished med school, but not my residency. Until I do, I'd just as soon you didn't . . ."

"Okay. I understand. No more 'Dr. Cross.' "

She smiled. "Thanks."

Cross put both hands on her shoulders and gave her a little shake. "Now, you go help solve some crimes. They're a good bunch we've got out there. You can learn a lot from them." He grinned. "Probably teach them a thing or two, as well, eh? Now go on."

She felt like she had back in high school, when Uncle Dave found her hiding on the school's back steps, wracked with self-doubt and insecurity an hour before tip off of her first basketball game. It was just after she'd moved in with him and Aunt Ellie, a year or two before her dad finally disappeared for good, but long after he had crawled into a bottle to stay. Nearly ten years after her mom was killed.

When he found her, he sat down beside her and just started talking. To this day, she couldn't remember more than a word or two of what he said, but when he was done, she was ready to take on the world. She had a great game that night, and a great season. Ever since, she'd been able to draw on that memory when she needed strength.

Madison leaned forward and gave him a peck on the cheek. "Thanks."

He winked at her. "None of that in front of the troops, now, okay?"

She winked back at him and turned to go.

"Oh, and Maddy . . . ?"

She turned back.

"Your aunt Ellie is dying to see you. She wants to know if you can come for dinner tomorrow."

"That'd be great."

CHAPTER 2

MELISSA ROURKE drove a Chevy Tahoe, and she drove it at speeds that were highly inadvisable unless you had a close affiliation with the Philadelphia Police Department. The University of Pennsylvania was several miles from the crime lab, but the way Rourke drove, there wasn't much time to chat.

"First in your class, huh?" Rourke said over the sound of the air conditioner as they accelerated up the Vine Street Expressway. She shook her head. "If you don't mind my asking, what the hell are you doing here?"

Madison laughed nervously. It was a very good question, one she herself had been working unsuccessfully to answer. "Seemed like the right thing to do."

Rourke shot her a sympathetic, almost pitying glance. "You know it probably wasn't, right?"

"Yeah." Madison laughed again, looking out the window at Thirtieth Street Train Station as they crossed the river and merged onto the Schuylkill Expressway. "I know."

They took the South Street exit and started wending their way across the Penn campus.

"I had a cousin who went here," Rourke explained. "She lived in one of the other houses, Kappa Kappa something, I don't know. The place we're looking for is right up here, on the left."

They bounced along for a moment, silent except for the hum of the air conditioner, until Rourke snorted. "So you already met Parker, huh? How did that go?"

Madison rolled her eyes. "Probably about how you'd imagine. I was looking at the directory in the lobby and he asked if he could help me. Then he asked again. And again. It was fine, he just wouldn't let it go, you know?"

"Oh, I know." Rourke laughed. She looked over at Madison. "But you don't have to worry about Tommy. I mean, Tommy is . . ." She paused. "Well, it sounds like you already know what he is. But you don't have to worry about him, okay? Apart from anything else, he's a damn good investigator."

Rourke pulled over to the curb and slammed the gearshift into park. "Anyway, a bunch of us are getting together for a beer tonight. You should come out." She turned to look at Madison's face. "I don't know if Tommy'll be there."

"Thanks, but I have a feeling I'm going to be pretty beat."

ALPHA ALPHA Gamma was a large stucco house, nondescript except for the Greek letters nailed to the second-floor balcony.

Two squad cars were parked out front next to three of the little campus security vehicles. An ambulance was pulling away slowly with its lights off. Another one was parked with its rear doors open, a distraught-looking young woman perched on the back step being comforted by two paramedics. She was draped in a foil blanket despite the oppressive heat.

On the side of the road, a handful of uniforms and campus police gathered idly. A man in a suit fidgeted beside them, looking nervous, hot, and uncomfortable. Not far away, a small knot of sorority sisters stood sobbing and comforting each other.

Rourke showed the uniforms the ID that hung from her neck. "Where are they?" she asked without breaking stride. Madison stayed close behind, holding up her ID as well.

"Second floor, front," one of the uniforms replied. "Room six."

The guy in the suit gave his face a quick wipe with a handkerchief and fell into step beside them. "Harold Smith, university external affairs," he said.

Rourke climbed the front steps and walked through the entrance in silence. Madison followed her lead.

"The thing is," Smith continued as they approached the stairway, "the university is concerned that an incident like this does not get portrayed in the wrong light."

Rourke slowed halfway up the steps, messing up the rhythm of the entire trio. Madison almost stepped on Smith's heel.

"And what light would be the 'wrong light,' Mr. Smith?" she asked acerbically.

Smith smiled anxiously. "I know this is a delicate matter, and the university hopes you will appreciate that fact. We would just like this whole thing concluded as quickly as possible, and with a minimum of embarrassment to the university and the city."

Rourke resumed her pace. "Gotcha," she said sarcastically.

As she reached the door to room six, Smith close on

her heels, she pointed to the patrolman standing next to the door. "Possible crime scene," she said flatly, stopping Smith in his tracks.

The uniform stepped aside as they approached.

Rourke gave him a slight nod. "What've we got, Eddie?"

He shook his head. "I don't know, Rourke. You tell me." He looked at his notebook. "We got an Ashley Munroe at the desk and a Beth Mowry on the floor."

Rourke paused inside the room. Then she pulled out her camera and started taking pictures from every conceivable angle.

Madison hesitated for a moment at the threshold. She'd grown up with police and police work all around her, but this was the first time she'd ever been a part of it. Steeling her nerves, she took a deep breath and stepped through the door.

The room was hot and it was hard to breath, in no small part because of the thick stench that hung in the air—like an unflushed toilet, only worse. Two windows were open, their screens torn and sagging, but they seemed to offer no breeze at all. A third window held a big air conditioner that appeared to be brand new. Madison couldn't believe it wasn't on; another reminder of how long she'd been away from the Philadelphia summers.

Madison's next breath caught in her throat as she spotted the bodies.

One of them had long, honey-blond hair and was slumped over a desk. She wore a very short pink robe made of a thin, shimmery synthetic that seemed to be wicking up the mixture of feces and urine that spilled out from under her body and puddled under her chair. Her head was turned to one side, and her hair cascaded over the desk and hung off the edge.

The papers and books scattered across the desk were

flecked with the vomit that pooled in front of her face and dripped down onto the floor. Flies buzzed around her, taking turns lighting momentarily on the vomit and excrement before flying off.

On the other side of the room, a girl with short bleached hair was kneeling, crumpled over what looked like a dozen small stone spikes. The carpet around her was wet with blood.

Madison gasped and looked away when she saw the girl's face, but knowing that Rourke and Eddie were probably watching her, she forced herself to look back. The girl's mouth was stretched taut around the base of one of the stone spike figures, and at least twelve inches of it protruded through a ragged hole in the back of her neck. Her face was swollen and distended, and her jaw looked unhinged, like a snake eating an enormous egg.

Two flies crawled across the bloody length of stone that jutted through the girl's neck.

Madison let her gaze linger long enough so that the strength of her stomach would be beyond dispute. Then she stood and stepped back, taking a survey of the room.

Beth Mowry's black pajamas were smeared with paint—the same yellows, oranges, and reds as the garish canvas lying on the floor a few feet away. There was a smell of paint in the air, but with the windows open and the intense competition from other smells, it was almost undetectable. A trail of vomit led from the girl back to the canvas. Some was even splattered across it, looking almost like part of the picture, some kind of gruesome trompe l'oeil.

Rourke had stopped taking pictures, but when Madison looked over at her, she resumed, slowly circling each of the girls, snapping away. When she finished the close-ups, she stepped back a few feet and took some more.

Madison studied the surrounding decor, as much to

look away from the carnage as anything else. It didn't lack
for feminine touches but was more functional than frilly.
The walls and woodwork were off-white and looked like
they had been painted dozens of times without ever being
stripped.

The room itself looked old, but everything in it was
new and expensive. Each side of the room had a bed and
a desk with a new, expensive-looking notebook computer
on it. There was an iPod on one of the bedside tables and
a flat-screen TV on one wall.

Rourke was in the corner, talking to the uniform, Eddie, who was reading from his notebook. She motioned
for Madison to come over.

Madison stepped gingerly across the room, carefully
avoiding anything that might be considered evidence, or
that might get on her shoe. As she neared, Eddie turned
and busied himself on the other side of the room.

"So what do you think?" Rourke asked, looking at
Madison expectantly.

She sighed. "It's terrible."

Rourke closed her eyes, summoning patience. "No, I
mean what do you think? What do you think happened?"
She held out a pair of latex exam gloves. "Have a closer
look around. Just try not to disturb anything."

Madison gave each of the bodies a brief examination,
checking the skin, the eyes, the hands. She peered once
again at the girl impaled on the spike, but she couldn't see
much with the object still lodged in the wound.

When she was done, she straightened up. "Well, this
one obviously has massive trauma, through the mouth and
out the neck. The other one has needle marks, one arm and
one leg, but they don't seem fresh." She paused. "Pupils
are dilated on both of them."

"So?" Rourke prodded.

Madison paused again. "What did Eddie have to say?" she asked, in part to buy herself time to think.

Rourke looked dubious, but she flicked through her notes and started reading.

"Roommates, found by one of their classmates about an hour ago when one didn't show up for class. Both apparently cramming for finals, or 'crits' in the case of the artist over there." She shrugged again and put away her notes, looking up at Madison with the same expectant look.

"Right." Madison thought for another second. "Well, let's see. Other than the . . . trauma . . . neither of them showed any bruising that I could see. No broken fingernails or signs of struggle. They both vomited, suggesting maybe they ingested something. Both had dilated pupils. You said they were cramming for finals or . . . what was it? Crits?"

Rourke nodded. "Critiques. It's like finals for art students. The faculty reviews their work for the semester. Apparently, this one was supposed to have some pieces finished up for today."

"Right. Okay. Well, that wound is pretty horrific over there, but with no other signs of struggle, it could easily have been some kind of accident. So they're cramming, they ingested something . . . My first thought would be some kind of amphetamine. Could have been an overdose, I guess. Maybe that one just fell while she was getting sick."

Rourke nodded appreciatively. "Bingo. Very good. Eddie found this on the floor." She held up a plastic bag containing about a dozen pills. "I don't recognize them. Any ideas?"

Madison furrowed her brow. "Yes, I think so." She frowned, thinking. "I'm pretty sure it's a drug called methylphenedrine."

"Methylphenedrine? You mean Ritalin?"

"No, Ritalin is methylphenidate. This is new."

Rourke looked vaguely impressed. "What is it?"

"It's one of the newer ADD drugs. Still an amphetamine, though, like Ritalin."

Rourke shook her head sadly as she looked at the two girls. It was the first sign of emotion she had shown since arriving. "Kids start taking this drug in grade school, by the time they get to college, they're taking it as a study aid to help them stay up all night. Then they start snorting it, shooting it up. It goes from medicine to study aid to dangerous party drug." She sighed, nodding at the two dead girls. "And then this."

"I knew abuse like this was getting more common," Madison said, "but I think this type of fatal overdose is still rare."

"One of the unfortunate perks of this job; you get to see a lot of things that are rare." She shrugged. "Who knows, maybe this stuff is just stronger."

"Yeah, maybe."

Smiling sweetly, Rourke handed Madison a pair of specimen bottles and a few wooden tongue depressors. "Welcome to the team." She pointed toward the vomit. "I need you to collect some samples of the . . . emesis." She nodded over at the girl on the floor. "Try to get some that isn't tainted with blood. And be careful not to get any on the outside of the jar; you'll be glad you did."

Madison smiled graciously and bent to the task.

As she was screwing the lid onto the first jar, she heard Rourke muttering, "Aw, Jesus Christ. Now what?"

Madison looked up to see Tommy Parker standing at the doorway, grinning. He whistled appreciatively. "Yikes. What a fucking mess."

Rourke marched over to him. "What the hell are *you* doing here?" she asked, sounding distinctly annoyed.

Madison turned her head slightly to listen in.

"Hey, Newbie," Parker said over Rourke's shoulder. He nodded at the bottle of vomit in her hand. "You having fun yet?"

Rourke poked him hard in the ribs. "Hey!" she said sharply, getting his attention. "Focus. What are you doing here?"

"Ouch! Damn, woman, that hurt."

"Again," Rourke said. "You. Here. Why?"

"Don't worry, I'm not moving in on your case." Parker leaned forward and lowered his voice. "Downtown got a call from the university. The president's office. Apparently, the mayor sits on the alumni board, and he's getting on Lieutenant Cross to finish this quick. *Quiet* and quick. The lieutenant asked me to stop up here and let you know."

"Already? Jesus. That was fast." Rourke snapped off her gloves. "Well, they're in luck. There's a shitload of blood and a hell of a mess, but for all that, it looks like a pretty straightforward overindulgence in study aids." She handed him the bag of pills.

He held the bag at arm's length, turning it around to look at it from several different directions. "What is it?"

"It's called methylphenedrine," Madison replied.

"Methylphenedrine?" He wrinkled his brow. "What's that, Ritalin?"

"Similar. It's newer."

"Hmm. Must've been a lot of it." He bent his head to study the girl impaled on the floor. "How the hell'd she do that?" He looked over at Eddie, grinning like he was about to make a wisecrack. Then he shook his head, thinking better of it. "Whatever."

Eddie looked disappointed. "So, you guys just about finished up?" he asked, hooking a thumb over his shoulder. "They want us to seal the room and get rid of the blinkie lights, so we don't have an audience when the meat wagon gets here."

Rourke nodded. "Yeah. We're going to need toxicology and the ME's report, but I think we're done with the room." She turned to Madison, who was finishing up her specimen collection. "You almost ready?"

Madison stood, putting the lid on the second jar. "I guess so," she said dubiously.

Rourke sighed. "What?"

"I don't know, it's just . . ." Madison tilted her head. "One thing bothers me about the methylphenedrine overdose."

Rourke and Parker waited impatiently for her to continue.

"It's the fact that there's two of them."

"What do you mean?" Rourke asked.

Madison shrugged. "I mean, one would be a rare occurrence, right? But two of them? What are the chances of that?"

Parker shook his head. "Maybe it's one in a million. But, hell, in greater Philadelphia you got, like, five million people. So what?" He turned to Rourke. "Come on. Since I'm here, I might as well give you a hand."

"But neither of them called for help or anything," Madison continued.

Parker put down the case he was packing. He was obviously starting to get annoyed. "What?"

"It's just strange. Your roommate collapses and you don't call for help?"

Rourke shrugged, starting to look annoyed, too. "People act strange when they're strung out on drugs, okay? It's just one more reason they're so bad for you," she added condescendingly. "Now come on, let it go."

Parker shook his head, laughing and swaggering across

the room. "C'mere, Newbie," he said, waving her over. He stopped next to the canvas.

Madison reluctantly walked up next to him.

"Come on," he said, waving her closer. "I won't bite."

She gave him a look like she didn't quite believe him.

"Okay," he said, crouching down about a foot or so. "That girl is what, five-four? Something like that, right?"

He turned with one eye closed and looked along his arm, which was pointed in the direction of the girl on the floor. "Okay, this is where she was, that's where she is, and over there's where she was going. Bingo. Look over there. What do you see?"

Madison tried hard not to roll her eyes, complying as good-naturedly as she could.

Just past Beth Mowry's body, on the other side of the sculptures, was a small bookcase. Sitting on the top shelf, almost in a direct line from the easel, past the girl on the floor, was a silver cell phone.

"See? She *was* going to call for help," he said patronizingly. "Feel better about it now?"

Madison could feel her face getting hot.

With his head turned partially away, Parker snickered and pretended to try to hide it from Madison while at the same time making a face at Eddie.

Rourke looked away, too, trying not to smile.

Now Madison was starting to get annoyed. "No, come on, think about it. Even if she *was* trying to call for help, she was already vomiting. It's not like her friend was in the bathroom or in bed not feeling well; she got sick at her desk and passed out. So this one starts vomiting before she can even call for help? Okay, maybe you're okay with one-in-a-million odds, but these two must have gone down within a couple minutes of each other."

For half a second, Parker and Rourke paused,

momentarily considering what she had said. But then Madison continued, "It just doesn't make sense."

Her voice seemed to snap Parker out of his brief rumination.

"Sense?" he said, shaking his head with a derisive grin. "It never makes sense. Jesus, Newbie, you got pills, puke, and pupils, the overdose trifecta. It's. An. Overdose." He laughed, looking around to make sure Eddie was paying attention. "Hell, I'm about to call the overdose textbook people so they can come down here and take a picture of this fucking mess." He laughed again and resumed packing up.

Madison shook her head stubbornly. "I still don't think . . ."

"Madison!" Rourke barked. "Jesus, that's enough!" She snapped closed the case she had been packing and held it out to her. "Here. Take this down and put it in the car."

CHAPTER 3

WHEN MADISON reemerged into the daylight, she saw that the security vehicles and all but one of the squad cars had left. The gaggle of mourning sorority sisters had relocated onto the front porch, their subdued chatter continuing uninterrupted as they parted to let Madison through.

She eased the heavy case onto the ground. As she opened the back of the truck, she heard a small voice behind her.

"Are you with the police?"

Madison turned around to see a petite, preppy-looking woman with shoulder-length, light brown hair. "Kind of," she replied, wiping the sweat off her forehead with her wrist. "I'm with the police crime lab."

"So they think there was a crime?" the girl asked, a tinge of excitement in her voice.

"Well . . . It's probably just a drug thing, but when two healthy young people die like that, something's usually not right."

"So you think they were *murdered*?" Her eyes went wide.

Madison cringed at the girl's words. "I didn't say that." She looked around her to make sure neither Rourke nor Parker were in earshot. "Why?" she asked quietly. "Do you think someone may have wanted them killed?"

"Oh, my God." The woman's eyes went even wider as she clapped a hand over her mouth. "You *do* think they were murdered." She turned and scurried back to the group.

"Wait!" Madison cried, "They probably weren't murdered. . . ." But it was too late; the group gasped collectively as it listened to the sensationalized version of their exchange.

Madison turned back to the car. "Shit, shit, shit," she muttered as she maneuvered the large black case into the back of Rourke's truck.

When she turned around, someone else had wandered up, a pale, thin, angry-looking woman with a frozen coffee drink in a tall cup. "I know some people," she said.

"What?" Madison said wearily, leaning against the back of the truck.

"People who had a reason to harm Ashley. I know some. A lot." She laughed scornfully. "Don't get me wrong, I'm not surprised she OD'd, if that's what happened. Whatever it was she was taking, I'm sure she took plenty. I'm just saying a lot of girls didn't like Ashley. Plenty of guys, probably, too."

Madison kept listening, but didn't respond.

The girl took a long sip of her drink. "Ashley was a whore. She ruined relationships by the dozen." Another sip. "She'd break a girl's heart taking her guy, then she'd dump him and break his heart two weeks later."

She laughed bitterly. "And every Neanderthal loser with a penis between his legs would line up to be next.

She just did it to Gary Swinson, what, like two weeks
ago. He was such a mess, Ashley got a restraining order
against him."

She squinted over Madison's shoulder and then ducked
her head down. "Oh, my God, there he is, the poor
chump."

Madison turned around to look. Halfway up the block,
a skinny kid with dark hair was sitting on the steps outside another house.

"That's just outside the fifty yards he had to keep between them," the girl observed. "Mmm, mmm, that is a
shame."

Madison couldn't see the boy clearly, but he was sitting on the steps with his elbows on his knees. His head
drooped from his neck. She could barely make out red-
rimmed eyes staring blankly from under thick, black hair.

"I guess it doesn't sound very sisterly, but . . ." The
woman shrugged. "Frankly, I'm not all that upset about
Ashley Munroe being dead. And I bet there's a lot of girls
who will sleep better tonight knowing they don't have to
worry about her."

"You said you wouldn't be surprised if they OD'd. Did
they do a lot of drugs?"

"I don't know if it was a *lot*," she said with a shrug. "But
they definitely did some, and it was more than a little."

"Do you know where they would have gotten them?"

She sipped her drink as she thought about it. "There's a
guy named Craig Williams or Wilson or something. Lives
over on Baltimore Avenue. I know they go over there
sometimes."

"Thanks."

She laughed again, sadly this time. "Still, the whole
thing's kind of hard to believe. And it sure is a shame
about Beth and all, but it's kind of ironic, too, you know?"

"How do you mean?"

"Well, you know, just . . . the poor little rich girl, starving artist, has everything she ever wanted, and now this."

"Beth had money?"

"Only about as much as God. Of course, it was all in a trust fund or something, but her brother bought her everything she ever wanted. It gets hot, boom, he shows up with a new air conditioner. Crits are coming, he says, 'throw away that cheap Dick Blick paint.' He actually throws it away himself, which pissed her off, actually. But then he shows up with a new set of Swiss paints, Lascaux, a new easel, new brushes, a new smock, the whole setup. He bought her that Thunderbird out there. She got sick of her Mini Cooper, boom—he gets her a Thunderbird. That girl did not want for anything. Except maybe a better class of friend."

"What do you mean?"

"I mean most of her so-called friends just hung out with her so she'd drive them around in her cool new car or let them watch that big TV in front of that giant air conditioner. But, man, did she mope around." She raised her eyebrows and hugged herself against a chill that Madison couldn't feel. "Of course, I guess she won't be moping around anymore."

AS MADISON returned to room six, Rourke and Parker were just finished packing up, quietly muttering to each other. Madison was sure it was about her.

Just as she walked through the door, Eddie called out, "Hey, look at this!" He pulled a coffee can out from under one of the beds. "Shit!" He pulled out a bundle of cash almost as wide around as the can itself.

Eddie flicked through the wad, then looked up at the ceiling for a second, calculating. "Maybe fifteen grand here."

"Yeah," Madison said. "Apparently, Beth was loaded."

Rourke, Parker, and Eddie all looked over at her.

"The artist," she pointed. "Beth. One of her friends said she was rich."

Parker looked down.

"Who were you talking to?" Rourke asked.

"Just a couple of the girls. They came up to me and started talking."

Rourke's eyes bulged slightly. *"They?"*

"What did you tell them?" Parker asked.

"I didn't tell them anything," Madison said defensively. "I just listened . . . and I told them it almost definitely was not a murder."

"Jesus Christ," Parker muttered, not quite under his breath.

Eddie turned to Rourke and Parker. "You guys need to keep your people under control."

CHAPTER 4

PARKER STALKED out of the room, shaking his head and muttering obscenities.

Rourke had been pretty annoyed as well, but after the ME's office had taken away the bodies, she still offered to buy Madison lunch. They ended up in an Indian place on Fortieth Street that Madison had been to once, years before. The samosas were good and the talk was small and when they finished eating, Rourke wiped her mouth and leaned forward on her elbows. She smiled awkwardly. "Sorry about . . . back there. I know this is your first day. But . . . well, it *is* your first day. Some of us have been doing this for a long time now."

"I'm sorry," Madison said, "it's just—"

Rourke put up a hand. "Hold on. Don't you guys have a saying in med school, about when you hear hoofbeats?"

"Think horses and not zebras."

"Right. Well here, it's like, think dead horses before you think dead zebras. Those girls had all the signs of an OD. The vomit, the pupils . . . The pills were right there, new pills at that. And the other thing looked just like an accident." She tapped the side of her head. "Horses."

Rourke paused, then smiled. "The other thing is . . . we work in the lab and at the crime scene; we're not homicide detectives. You keep stepping on toes like that, rightly or wrongly, and you're going to make a lot of enemies fast. Okay?"

The waitress brought them their coffee and the check.

Rourke flapped a pack of Splenda between her thumb and forefinger. "So," she said as she tapped it into her coffee. "What else did they say?"

"Who's that?"

"The girls outside the house."

Madison smiled sarcastically. "I don't know; am I still in trouble?"

Rourke sipped her coffee and smiled, but didn't answer.

"Right." Madison gave her arm a nervous little scratch, wondering how to play it. "Well, they said a lot—at least one of them did. She said this Ashley girl was a bit of a slut. Said she liked to steal boyfriends and then dump them a week later. Not the most popular girl in school. Except, I guess, among the guys she was currently sleeping with."

Madison bit her lip, thinking about what to tell her next. "One guy she broke up with a couple of weeks ago apparently took it pretty hard. Ashley got a restraining order, which to me would seem like a possible—"

"Sh-sh-sh!" Rourke threw up a hand, her eyes rolling up under her lids. "Please don't start with the 'M' word. Accidents don't have motives, and this is an accident. Go on. What else did she say?"

"Just that, and the fact that Beth, the other girl, was extremely rich. Trust-fund rich."

Rourke gulped her coffee and nodded. She thought for a second, then took another gulp. "You done?" she asked, standing.

Madison nodded, taking a last sip of coffee before rising out of her seat.

Rourke swung her handbag over her shoulder. "We're going to stop in at the ME's office."

THE STERILE glare off the tiles and the not-quite-hospital smell of the hallway were well known to Madison.

It was not generally a pleasant sensory combination, but she was grateful for the familiarity—it made her feel like she was back in her element. Still, it crossed her mind that a trip to the morgue right after lunch might be some kind of test, see if her stomach was up for the job.

Rourke led the way through the corridors and down a flight of stairs to a set of heavy swinging doors.

The ME looked to be in his mid-fifties; he was at least forty pounds overweight, and balding. His face and his torso seemed to slope outward at the same angle: flat at the top, but swelling dramatically at the bottom. His clothes looked rumpled, and the hair that encircled his head stuck out in random directions.

Madison had seen similar grooming habits in other pathologists and wondered if working in a windowless basement with a bunch of dead people made it impossible to make an effort in the morning.

He looked up at them and grunted, which Rourke apparently interpreted as an opening for an introduction.

"Frank Sponholz, Madison Cross, our new technician. Madison, this is Frank Sponholz, our ME."

Sponholz grunted again.

"What have we got, Spoons?"

On the table in front of him lay Ashley Munroe, minus the pink robe and the vomit she'd been wearing before. She was extremely beautiful, even with the discoloration where the side of her face had rested on the table. Even dead on a slab.

Somehow, seeing her here didn't bother Madison as much as it had at the sorority house. Out of her room, out of context, she seemed more like a cadaver in med school, and less like a person who had been cramming for finals the night before.

On the next table behind him was another body, still covered with a sheet.

"I haven't opened either of 'em up yet, but there's a couple of interesting things you might want to see first."

Rourke rubbed her hands together. "Whatcha got?"

He thought for a second. "Well, I'm sure you already noticed the pupils, substantially dilated on both of them."

They both nodded.

"Okay. Now this." He turned around and whipped back the sheet covering the second body, revealing the ruined face on the body behind him. ". . . This is a hell of a wound." He cackled. "I mean, I've seen a lot, and I've seen worse, but this is a good one, all right."

With the statue removed, the wound looked even worse—larger and more traumatic, if that was possible. Beth's jaw was dislocated, and the tissue around it sagged open. Her mouth was a gaping, crooked hole the size of a softball.

"Looks like she pitched forward onto it," he explained. "Appears to have been vomiting at the time: the tip of the implement she fell on had traces of emesis under the blood."

He took out a small flashlight and shined it into the cavernous hole in the girl's face. "The tip went through the back of her mouth on one side . . . virtually severed the jaw muscles and connective tissue there . . . nicked the carotid artery. I bet it wasn't fun, but at least she went quick."

He turned back to the other girl, rubbing his nose with his forearm. "And speaking of fun . . . this one's got track marks, left arm and left leg. Nothing too unusual there, especially in a suspected overdose."

He snickered. "She's also got a tattoo on the upper right thigh, ugliest damn thing I ever saw."

He tugged the skin of her thigh, pulling it to reveal the tattoo, which had been hidden by her other leg.

It was ugly, all right—an ugly little troll, bowlegged and muscular, with wild hair and a beard. He seemed to be holding his tail. It looked vaguely Egyptian.

"Cute," Madison said.

"Yeah, that's what I thought."

"What does it mean?"

"What does it mean?" Spoons laughed. "It probably means she got drunk one night, and that it's a lot easier to get a tattoo than to get rid of it."

THE CRIME lab was quiet when Madison walked in. Rourke had dropped her off, saying she had to run a couple of errands. Madison was grateful to have a moment to herself.

She plopped into her chair with a long, loud sigh and leaned back, letting her head hang over the edge. "Madison Cross . . . what the hell were you thinking?"

"That bad?" asked a voice behind her.

At the sound of Aidan Veste's voice, Madison almost slipped off her chair.

"Oh, shit. Sorry. I thought I was alone."

"It's okay." He smiled. "How was it out there?"

She shrugged. "I don't know."

"First days can be a bitch."

"Now you tell me."

"Actually, the rest of them can be pretty bad, too."

They both laughed.

Aidan opened his mouth to say something else, but what Madison heard next was Tommy Parker's voice bellowing, "Hey, Newbie! We need to have a chat."

Parker had just walked in. He was motioning Madison over to the opposite side of the room.

"Excuse me," she told Aidan casually, trying her best to mask her apprehension.

He leaned toward her as she walked past. "Don't take any of his shit personally."

Madison followed Parker to the far side of the room, where he could pretend they had some privacy. He was all fake smiles until they reached the corner. Then he turned around, red-faced and angry.

"That was bullshit out there today," he said through clenched teeth. A thin sheen of sweat covered his red forehead. "I just got a call from a buddy at campus security, asking if it's true this might be a homicide. Then I got a call from a guy in homicide asking the same thing, and wondering why he didn't know about it. Look, I don't care if you blow off Rourke or me. That's annoying, but it don't matter. But you're a lab tech, not a homicide detective. If you want to be a homicide detective, I'll tell you what you do: You go to the police academy, you work your ass off for ten, maybe twenty years, pass a bunch of exams every couple of years, and kiss the right asses at the right times. Then maybe you can be a fucking homicide detective. And then maybe someone will give a crap what you have to say about what some goddamn coed thinks about a very cut and very dried overdose case that a lot of people want wrapped up quick."

His voice had started out quiet, but now it was practically a roar. Madison braced herself against the force of it, trying not to betray the fact that it was having an effect.

"Until then," he continued, his voice slightly more under control, "try sticking to your own goddamn job. That is, of course, once you learn what the fuck that is."

"Come on, Parker, lay off," Veste said, walking up behind them. "It's her first day, for Christ's sake."

Sanchez walked into the room and yelled over, "Yeah, Tommy. Take a pill, man. I can hear you all the way down the hall."

"Fuck off, Veste," Parker snapped. "We're having a conversation here that needs to be had."

Madison put up her hand between them. "Thanks, guys, but I'm okay." She turned to Parker. "Are you just about finished?"

Parker stared at her for a moment. "Yeah, I guess I am."

She flashed a blatantly artificial smile. "Well, I'll try not to let it happen again, okay then? How's that?"

Parker shot her an icy glare and stormed off into the hallway.

Aidan waited a second before tilting his head close to hers. "You okay?"

Madison smiled. "Yeah, I'm okay."

For a second it seemed as though neither of them could think of anything to say, yet neither wanted to turn away. But the moment ended when Detective Cross walked into the room. "Ms. Cross, could you come into my office, please." He spoke without breaking his stride.

Madison and Veste shared a smile before she headed toward Cross's office. As Veste was headed back to his desk, Madison heard Sanchez telling him, "Down, boy."

CHAPTER 5

CROSS WAS sitting behind his desk, sifting through papers and moving them around as if he were looking for something. Or organizing something. Or pretending to look busy.

He cleared his throat without looking up. "Close the door," he murmured. "Sit down."

Cross ignored her for a minute after she sat. He seemed to have aged in the six months since she'd seen him last—not a lot, but enough so that he was looking more like her father. They were identical twins, but she'd never thought of them that way. Her dad had always looked older.

Now that Uncle Dave was catching up, the resemblance was striking.

When his papers were positioned pretty much how they had been when he started, he looked up at her. He seemed to smile despite himself.

"It really is good having you here," he confided.

She smiled. "Thanks."

He leaned back in his chair, returning to official mode. "So. How did it go out there today?"

"It was very . . . interesting. Let's say I learned a few things."

"Good, good. Because at this point"—he seemed to be choosing his words—"learning is what it's all about."

Madison waited for him to continue.

"It's good that you trust your instincts. It is. And I don't particularly care if you step on some toes now and again, especially when you're right. But these guys know what they're doing. They do. Even Parker. He can be an ass, but he knows his stuff. And there's a lot they can show you. So at least until you get a little bit of time in, don't just disregard them, okay?"

"Okay." Madison knew she had just received the kinder version of a Detective Cross ass chewing.

"I also heard something about you interviewing witnesses. What was that about?"

Madison was amazed at how quickly word got around. "No, I didn't interview any witnesses. I was loading the car and a couple of the dead girls' friends came up and just started talking to me. I didn't ask any questions. Not really."

"I see. The thing is, sure, the turf issues can get the other divisions riled up. But apart from that, when something ends up in court, who said what to whom and when, and after what warning, and with or without a lawyer present, all that comes into play. By all accounts this incident was just an unfortunate accident, but I've seen some very simple cases get quite messy. And I've also seen some very guilty people walk because of simple mistakes when interviewing witnesses or defendants."

He furrowed his brow. "Okay," he said. "That's it."

* * *

THE LAB had filled up since Cross called her into his office, and Madison felt conspicuous as she walked back into the room. Parker gave her his redneck sneer, but nobody else even looked up. She plopped down at her desk and checked the clock: 5:25.

Rourke was clearing her desk, getting ready to go. "Hey, Elena," she called over to Sanchez. "You coming out for that beer?"

"Pass," Sanchez shouted back. "Got home stuff tonight."

"Come on," Rourke cajoled, wiggling her fingers at her like casting a spell. "Icy cold beer . . . frosted glass."

Sanchez looked at her watch, did some mental arithmetic. "Yeah, I guess. Maybe one. I got to pick up Charlie at the sitter's by 7:30."

"Aidan, you up for a beer tonight?"

"Uh, sure," he said without looking up from his computer. "Yeah, I could go for a beer."

Rourke yelled out, "Hey, Parker, you coming?"

"I don't think so," he yelled back in a friendly, sarcastic tone.

On her way out, Rourke stopped at Madison's desk. "You sure you won't come out? Icy cold beer in a frosted glass?"

"You know what? Maybe I will." As she gathered her bags, she mumbled to herself, "I might even get something stronger."

THEY ENDED up splitting pitchers at a tiny after-work dive a couple of blocks away on Second Street in Old City.

Madison still had her suitcases with her, and she stacked them in the corner behind the table. It felt odd bringing her bags with her to the bar—not to mention the fact that she hadn't been to her new home yet. But it felt good to blow off some steam, and she thought it was a good idea to socialize with her new workmates. At least she had packed light.

Sanchez stayed for more than one. After the first round, her face softened and she actually laughed a few times. Rourke seemed to be on a personal mission to get her to relax: kidding her, praising her, drawing her out.

Madison was content to mostly listen, laughing at the old stories she'd never heard. Aidan was quiet as well, occasionally adding a critical detail to the stories he knew.

She caught him watching her a few times. He caught her, too.

As the laughter trailed off after one particularly hilarious anecdote, Sanchez turned to Madison.

"Okay, so seriously, girl, what are you doing back in Philadelphia? And working with us, of all things. I'd say, 'if you don't mind my asking,' but I've had a couple, so I won't." That got another laugh out of Rourke. "All these years, Cross has been telling us about the honors, and the internships at CDC, and the residency at Stanford. What the fuck are you doing here?"

Aidan's eyes were riveted on her. Rourke's eyes were checking out the guy behind the bar.

Madison laughed nervously. "I don't know. I guess, maybe . . . maybe I realized I wasn't doing what I wanted to be doing."

"And this is what you want to be doing?"

Madison shrugged. "I guess I'll find out."

Rourke rejoined the conversation. "I asked her the same question. She told me, 'It seemed like the right thing to do.' I told her, 'No, it wasn't.' "

Everybody laughed at Rourke's rendition of the

conversation, but they stopped short when she asked, "And didn't you have a boyfriend up there?"

Aidan looked away. Rourke added, "If you don't mind my asking."

When the laughter died down again, it got quiet. Get it over with, Madison told herself.

"I did," she said. "But . . . it was going nowhere. And I was going elsewhere, and . . . well, there you go."

Thankfully, the lull that followed ended when Sanchez looked at her watch. "Oh, shit, I got to go." She emptied her glass and put some money on the table. "Madison, welcome," she said with a quick smile. "I'll see you guys tomorrow."

"It's good to see her coming out," Rourke said after Sanchez had gone.

"She split up with her husband a while back," Aidan explained.

"He was a bastard," Rourke interjected.

"She's been raising her little boy, Charlie, by herself," he continued. "It hasn't been easy on her."

They were quiet for a moment, then Rourke finished her drink and made it official: "Well, I better get going, too." A few minutes later, they all headed out the door. Aidan helped Madison with her bags.

Outside, the evening was still warm. Aidan said he was parked close by and offered them both a ride. Rourke declined, said she was just up the block. She wished them good night, then headed up the street, leaving Madison and Aidan standing alone in front of the bar.

Aidan pointed at Madison's bags. "You need a ride."

"Yeah, I guess I do. Thanks."

He tipped his head up the block. "My car's this way."

As they walked up Arch Street, Madison leaned close to him. "You know," she said, "I appreciate you coming to the rescue with Parker today, but you didn't have to. I can take care of myself."

"Wouldn't doubt it for a second," he replied. "But . . ." He held up a finger to emphasize his next point. "Parker was being a dick."

She laughed. "Well, thanks, anyway."

"Here it is," he said, pointing to a silver Pathfinder.

They loaded the bags into the back and he unlocked the doors. Madison was relieved he didn't physically open the door for her.

"Okay," he said as he pulled out. "Where am I going?"

She gave him the address.

"What's the best way to get there? What?" he continued, quizzically, when Madison started laughing.

"I actually don't know. I've never been there."

He looked at her, incredulous. "Are you serious?"

"Yep. Sublet. It's my cousin's place. I don't even know her."

"So where is she?"

"Europe, I think. Teaching a semester abroad." She took out the address. "Wait, I think this is it."

He pulled over in front of an old stone building that looked vaguely like it might once have been a store of some sort. There were concrete steps up front and a ramp leading up beside them. A couple of the windows were dimly lit, but most were dark. The street was deserted.

"You sure this is it?" Aidan asked, looking around.

She checked the address again. "Yeah, I think so." She walked up the steps and tried the key. The front door opened.

She turned to him and shrugged. "This is it. Third floor."

He opened the back of the car and pulled out her bags.

As she put them on her shoulder, he said, "Here, let me help you with those."

"It's okay." She smiled. "I got it."

"Okay." He looked up at the third floor. "You sure you don't want me to come up?" He flashed a shy smile. "Just until you get the lights on and everything?"

"Now, is that really a good idea?"

"Personally, I think it's genius."

"It sounds very nice," she said, patting him on the shoulder. "But maybe I should wait until it's not my first day on the job."

CHAPTER 6

WHEN THE digital clock clicked to 6:59, Madison reached over and preemptively turned off the alarm. For an instant, she felt the confusion and disorientation of waking up in a strange place. It was not a sensation she was used to.

She shot up in a panic, but then saw her suitcases on the floor next to the door. It all came to her in a flash. Her cousin's condo . . . Philadelphia . . . working with her uncle at the Crime Scene Unit.

Her cousin's condo was clean, new and impersonal. The bedroom felt a bit like a hotel room, and the living room/dining room/kitchen areas were almost identical: white walls and beige curtains. The central air hummed quietly in the background.

Either her cousin had an unusually institutional sense of decor, or the place had come furnished, something that at other points in her life Madison would have considered unbearable. At the moment, she could see the appeal. It was the first bond of any kind she had felt with her unknown second cousin. The only evidence of another human having lived in the apartment was a dry, half-dead ficus tree sitting on the floor in what would have been a pool of morning sunlight, if the blinds had been open.

Figuring water would be the most urgent need, Madison filled a glass at the sink and slowly poured it into the pot. Four glasses later, the soil was barely moist.

She turned and opened the curtain, and the view caught her breath: three-quarters of the ample window were taken up with a spectacular view of the Ben Franklin Bridge. The stone foundation looked incredibly massive from this angle. The pale blue span, an immense wall on the near side of the river, arced like a seam across the sky, stretching into a thin ribbon where it ended in New Jersey.

Madison could have stood there for a long time, sipping her coffee and staring out the window. But she didn't have any coffee, and that was a problem.

She took a quick shower, got dressed, and decided to walk to work and try one of the coffee shops on the way.

Her cousin's place was on the eastern edge of the city, a few blocks up from the Delaware River, on the border between Old City and Northern Liberties. Just north and east of Center City, Old City was the area surrounding Independence Hall, Elfreth's Alley, and the Betsy Ross house, among other historic sites. It had been rescued from blight when Madison was very young. Now it was filled with expensive condos and art galleries.

The artists that helped save Old City had long since been squeezed out. Many of them had ended up in Northern Liberties, the next neighborhood north, which had once been a run-down neighborhood of former meatpacking plants. In recent years the artists had been followed by the shopkeepers, restaurateurs, and of course, developers.

Abandoned factories were turning into expensive lofts almost overnight, but the artists had yet to be completely driven out, and the neighborhood retained a palpable air of artsy quirkiness.

As she turned a corner a block or two away, Madison found herself standing in front of a tiny oasis at Second and Poplar, a corner lot transformed into outdoor seating for a tiny coffee shop called the Ground Floor. Round paper lanterns swayed in the soft morning breeze, hanging from the trees that kept the lot nicely shaded. A gravel path meandered between the tables.

The inside was small, but the people were friendly. Madison bought a large coffee and a scone and took them back outside. She thought about buying a newspaper, but she wasn't quite ready for news yet. Instead, she sat outside, enjoying the breeze and watching the people coming and going. The coffee was strong and rich and the scone was flaky and light.

For the first time since returning, she was starting to feel comfortable in Philadelphia. She sipped her coffee and considered the irony that when she finally felt at home it was in a neighborhood she barely knew.

She washed down the last of her scone, and bought a refill to take with her. As she left, she paused at the window, checking her reflection for crumbs. The scone, through no fault of its own, sank to the bottom of her stomach.

It took a second for Madison to notice it, but the guy sitting at the table in the window had his newspaper spread wide open. Splayed across the top was the headline "Two Found Dead in Penn Sorority" and under that, "Police Investigate Suspicious Deaths."

Madison pressed her nose against the glass, futilely trying to read further. Suddenly she noticed the same headline reflected in the window and whirled around to see a newsstand behind her.

"Shit," she said as she paid for a paper. "Shit, shit, shit, shit, shit."

Select words jumped out from the rest: suspicious . . . rumors . . . homicide . . . crime scene . . . cover-up . . . Murder.

She scanned the story, picking up more of the same. Amid the rumors that seemed to be swirling on their own accord were quotes from one student who had gotten her information from someone with the Philadelphia Police. Someone from the Crime Scene Unit. Madison.

Suddenly, the mild reluctance Madison felt about her second day on the job became an intense feeling of dread. But mixed in with the feeling was a sudden need to get there fast, to be there waiting when the shit hit the fan, to not walk into the middle of it.

Coffee sloshed out of her cup as she hurried up Arch Street. She dumped the cup in a trash can and broke into a run as a bus passed her. It slowed to a stop at the next corner, and she slipped on just as the doors closed.

The bus swayed and jostled too much for Madison to read the paper she had bought, but that didn't seem to be stopping anyone else—everywhere she looked, she was greeted by the same headline. Everyone on the bus had their noses buried in the juicy story.

It was not quite half past eight when she stepped off the office elevator. As she walked down the hallway, it was so quiet that, for a moment, she thought she was the first one there. But as she entered the crime lab, she saw that everyone was already there, and they were all reading the paper.

Parker was the first to look up when she walked in. He shook his head with disgust. Sanchez stared at her, expressionless for a moment. Aidan gave her a smile that tried to be supportive, but it came across as pitying. Rourke just looked disappointed.

As Madison started toward her desk, Lieutenant Cross

stepped out of his office. They glanced at each other awkwardly. Madison desperately hoped he could read the apology in her eyes.

Cross turned away from her, toward the rest of his team. Toward the people who worked for him for real, Madison thought, not just on some whim. He cleared his throat and held up the newspaper.

"I guess you all read the paper this morning." He smiled grimly. "The mayor did, and he's not very happy. More unhappy than usual. And the president over at the University of Pennsylvania is even more unhappy, not that it matters, except that it makes the mayor even more unhappy. And now the mayor is making the commissioner unhappy, too.

"So," he whacked the newspaper against the side of his leg a couple times. "This is how it's going to work. The commissioner asked me where things stood, and I told him it looked like an accidental overdose. He said until we could prove it *wasn't* a homicide, we have to investigate it like it was. He wants us to follow every lead, so no one can come back and say we were trying to hide anything."

Cross took a deep breath and lowered his eyes as he exhaled. "Until we can prove this was an accident, we're making this our top priority, okay?"

After an uncomfortable pause, the group muttered their assent.

"Rourke, Parker, and Cross. You were already working the case, you will continue to do so. Aidan and Elena will provide support as needed."

"I know how to prove it when it *is* a murder," Parker said. "How exactly do I prove that it wasn't?"

Cross smiled indulgently. "We just have to make sure that there's no possibility this turns out to be anything other than an accidental overdose—that we haven't neglected any reasonable angle."

"I thought they wanted this quiet and quick," Rourke said.

"That was then." Cross shrugged. "As it turns out, it wasn't quiet. Now it won't be so quick."

Madison tried not to take her eyes off Cross; she could feel Parker and Sanchez staring at her.

When Cross was done, he leaned slightly in her direction. "Ms. Cross, could you step into my office please?"

He was standing behind his desk when she walked in. "Close the door," he said.

She closed her eyes, too, preparing for the worst.

"How are you holding up, Maddy girl? Are you okay?"

Her eyes flew open. Guilt flared up inside her as she realized he wasn't going to lose his temper at all—he was actually going to be nice.

"I'm okay. I'm just sorry—"

"No, don't say it. I know. But it's okay. You just go out there and do your job. And be careful, okay?"

"Okay."

"Now, here . . ." He fished in his pocket and came out with a set of keys. "I know you didn't have a car in Seattle. I don't know if you made any arrangements, but here." He held out the keys to her.

"Uncle Dave! You didn't have to—"

"Shh!" He put up his hand. "It's nothing special. Actually, you might not even want it. It's from fleet sales. Surplus. A dark blue Crown Vic, of all things, and not even a very new one. It's parked in the back lot, in the corner. And technically, I haven't even bought it yet. The fleet mechanic said I could try it for a few days, then decide. He said it's a good car. A lot of miles left in it. You drive it for a few days; if you like it, it's yours with love from your aunt Ellie and me."

"Thanks."

"And don't worry about that other stuff. Someday I'll

tell you about my first day." He winked at her, though Madison noticed his eye didn't twinkle like it usually did when he winked. "Now, there's some paperwork for personnel on your desk. You're going to need to fill it out before the end of the day, okay?"

She nodded and turned to the doorway. As she left his office, she noticed Cross beckoning to Rourke to come in.

MADISON SAT in her chair and opened the thick manila envelope with RETURN TO HUMAN RESOURCES: ROOM 308 printed across it. As she thumbed through the tax forms and insurance papers, she saw Aidan walking over out of the corner of her eye.

"Shit," he declared solemnly, bending his head closer.

Madison turned her head to one side, momentarily confused. ". . . What?"

He knocked lightly on her desk and nodded knowingly. "It just kind of happens, you know."

Madison laughed quietly as he walked away, but as she turned back to her paperwork, she sensed someone else approaching.

It was Rourke, stone-faced. "C'mon," she said.

"What?"

"Going to the ME's office. See if Spoons has anything to help us out here."

CHAPTER 7

THEY DROVE in silence to the medical examiner's building and walked in silence when they got there.

Spoons grunted when they arrived. Rourke raised her eyebrows in greeting.

When Spoons saw Madison behind her, he laughed. "Hey, I hear you're a fucking celebrity," he said to her. "First day on the fucking job. I'm impressed."

Madison smiled warily—her temper was wearing thin, but the ribbing seemed good-natured.

Rourke was impatient with his levity. "All right, Spoons, toss us a bone here. Whatta ya got for us?"

"Well, not much." He picked up a clipboard and flicked through it. "They got the methylphenedrine, all right. Both of them." He looked up at them. "Not necessarily enough to kill thcm, though."

Rourke gave him a look. "Not necessarily, huh?"

Sponholz looked back at her without flinching. "That's right."

"It's not possible?"

He shrugged. "I guess anything's possible. Hell, they coulda been abducted by aliens or something, right? But I ain't putting it in my report, am I?"

"C'mon, Frank, work with me here. We could use a little help."

"I bet you could." He snorted. "You think I'm not already feeling some fucking pressure on this? You think my phone didn't start ringing as soon as that newspaper hit the goddamn streets out there?"

He laughed. "No, I'm not going to say it's an overdose, not conclusively. And it's not just because I don't want to be dragged through the fucking mud and sued by the manufacturer, although I don't. And it's not just because I don't want to wind up in the middle of the shit storm that's going to erupt if this does turn out to be something else, people yelling about a cover-up. Is it in the realm of possibility that someone could OD on this much? Sure, maybe, a bit of a stretch, but it's conceivable. But two?" He shook his head. "Fuck, no. You wouldn't sign off on that. You fucking know you wouldn't."

Rourke didn't reply.

"Look," Sponholz went on. "I'll keep looking for a cause of death until they tell me to stop, but I'm not going to sign off on that. So for right now?" He stabbed a finger at the report. "Inconclusive."

He turned to Madison. "Excuse my French."

"No fucking problem," she said with a half smile.

He snorted and shuffled back to his desk. "You guys think it's an overdose, I'll keep testing for that, but the way I understand it, you're supposed to be looking at it like a homicide now anyway, right? So, here." He held up a small evidence bag. "Maybe this'll help get you started on your merry way."

Rourke didn't say anything.

"What is it?" Madison asked.

"Pubic hair," Sponholz said proudly. "Dark and coarse. It definitely ain't one of hers. Found it mixed in with hers, but it don't match the snatch. Thought you might want to send it out for analysis, see if anything comes back."

"Okay, I guess," Rourke said grudgingly. "But I'm going to want tox screens on every drug known to mankind."

Sponholz laughed. "Are you kidding? Right now I'm running cocaine, codeine, and crystal meth. I'm almost done the letter 'C.' After that, I got the whole rest of the alphabet in front of me."

THE DNA lab was a small, equipment-filled room down a short hallway from the main crime lab. To Madison, it was a welcome hiding place, away from everyone else. And the fact that it was filled with equipment she knew how to use gave her battered self-confidence a much-needed boost.

Even so, when she placed the sample in the small microcentrifuge tube, she felt a wave of panic. The single hair rested on the surface of the medium for a moment, as if having second thoughts, before sinking, and Madison felt suddenly nauseous as she considered the possibility that she had just destroyed the sole piece of crucial physical evidence.

The hair seemed to dissolve almost instantly. Unfortunately, the next step was to wait. The sense of purpose and usefulness Madison had felt while preparing the sample disappeared faster than the sample itself did. Soon, Madison realized she was hiding, plain and simple, in the DNA lab.

She took a minute to straighten up some supplies. Then she poked her head out the door.

The lab was empty except for Rourke, sitting at her

workstation. The only sound was the quiet clicking of her typing.

Madison quietly walked to her desk, staring at the personnel forms she was supposed to complete. The way things were going, she wondered if she should bother. But she dutifully slid them out of the manila envelope and got started.

When she got to the part about any history of mental illness, she left it temporarily blank, thinking as she looked around that any questions regarding mental illness would be less a matter of history than of current events.

The question about whether she'd had mumps stumped her, and she wondered if her uncle would know. She looked up, trying to remember, and her eyes met Rourke's.

For a second, they stared at each other. Rourke's steely gaze held Madison's in place. After what seemed like an eternity, her face softened and she smiled, shaking her head.

Madison shrugged meekly. "Sorry."

"I know," Rourke replied. She seemed like she was about to say something else when her phone rang.

"Rourke, Crime Scene Unit," she answered. "Yes. Hello, Mr. Smith." She made a face for Madison's benefit, sticking her tongue out at the phone. "Yes, I was surprised to read about it in the paper, too." This time the face she flashed wasn't for Madison, but at her.

Madison looked down at her paperwork, but continued to listen.

"Is that so?" Rourke said, now jotting down notes on a pad. "And they were unable to reach him, huh? . . . Can you give me that address and phone number? . . . Right . . . Okay, well, we'll send someone out there to check it out, okay? . . . Okay, thank you, too, Mr. Smith."

Rourke disconnected the phone without putting down the handset.

Madison raised an eyebrow, questioningly.

Rourke ignored her, punching a number into the phone. "Yeah, hi, this is Melissa Rourke over at Philly C.S.U. Hey . . . Wondering if you can send me whatever you have on an Everett Munroe. Got out a month or two ago. Oh, really? When do you expect the system to be up again? . . . Yeah, I hear you. Well, could you send me whatever you have now? Then the rest when the system is back up? . . . Great. Thanks."

After Rourke hung up, she let out a sigh and fixed her eyes back on Madison. "Okay, this means nothing, okay? Absolutely nothing." She took a deep breath. "That was our friend Mr. Smith from the university. They tried to contact the girls' families to notify them of what happened. One of the girls, Munroe—the long blond hair, I think— listed her father as her only contact." She gave Madison a deadpan look. "The address and phone are Coffeewood Prison, in Virginia."

She paused as the fax machine beeped and started printing. "Except he got out two months ago, and they haven't been able to reach him at the forwarding address, which is in Philadelphia."

She paused again, clearly reluctant to continue. Before she did, she looked at Madison hard. "Like I said, this means absolutely nothing . . . but he hasn't checked in with his parole officer . . . and he hasn't updated his registration as a sex offender."

Rourke stared at her hard as she said it, as if daring Madison to reply. After a moment, she put down the phone and picked up her notepad and the fax. "I'm going to pay him a visit."

"I'm coming with you," Madison said, standing.

Rourke laughed and shook her head. "No, you're not. Chances are this won't have anything to do with any investigation; this is going to be telling some poor bastard that his daughter killed herself."

"I want to come anyway. I'm not doing anything here; I'm just waiting for the samples to amplify. Besides, it's all part of the job, right? How else am I going to learn?"

Rourke looked dubious. She held up a finger, her face stern. "Okay, here's the thing: You do not say a goddamn word, okay? Understand?"

"Absolutely."

"I'm serious. Yesterday was your first day. On your first day, you want to screw up—that's the time, and you did it and that's great. Get it out of your system. Second day is different. You understand?"

CHAPTER 8

THE FAX sat on the car seat between them, a picture of a thin, haunted-looking man with short graying hair. "Everett Munroe" was typed underneath it, and the words SEX OFFENDER in large block letters below that.

The address was a sagging row house in a particularly run-down section of Kensington. The front of the building was an enclosed porch that had been enclosed a second time in cheap aluminum siding. It buckled at the corners and drooped in the middle. In places, the siding was missing altogether.

The lights in the house were off and looked like they'd been that way for some time. There were no curtains in the windows and no furniture was visible in the dim light that filtered through from the windows in the back.

Rourke slipped her gun out of her handbag and into the back of her waistband. As she raised her hand to knock on the door, she paused and turned to Madison, whispering, "Not a single word, right?"

Madison nodded silently, and Rourke knocked hard on

the door. They both stepped back and waited a minute. Then Rourke stepped up and knocked again.

As she was stepping up to knock once more, a raspy young voice from beside them said, "If you looking for Mr. Everett, he gone."

The girl was about ten years old, African American. She was wearing matching shorts and halter top, made of faded yellow terry cloth.

"He left," she said around the finger hooked in the side of her mouth.

"Do you know where he went?" Rourke asked, turning to hide the square bulge in the back of her waistband.

The girl shrugged.

"How long ago did he leave?"

"I seen him at the market. He gave me a Scotty."

Rourke frowned, confused. "Where?"

"At the market."

"Where is that?"

The girl shrugged and tutted.

"So, he gave you a Scotty, huh?" Madison said with a smile.

The girl smiled back and nodded.

"What was that like?"

The girl thought about it for a moment. "It was good, I guess . . . but it was *really* hard."

Madison smiled to herself. A biscotti. "That market, was it outdoors? With lots of meat and fish and stuff? Right out in the open?"

The girl nodded again.

"Was it the Italian Market?"

The girl tutted again. "Yeah, that's what I said."

THE ITALIAN Market was a culinary landmark in South Philadelphia, an old-fashioned outdoor market selling mostly food, but all sorts of other goods as well. In the summer heat, it produced a distinct aroma that Madison had never quite gotten used to.

It took about twenty minutes to walk through the two dozen or so stalls and stores that comprised the market. At least half a dozen of the people working there had a distinct sex-offender-registry look about them, but none of them was Everett Munroe.

"All right," Rourke said, looking around her one last time. "I told Spoons we'd check in. Why don't we go do that now?"

"That's it?" Madison asked in disbelief.

Rourke gave her a look. "What, you want to just stay here and hope he shows up, on information from a ten-year-old? Or do you want to show his picture around, so every one will know the police are looking for the guy who just got out of the joint?" She turned to go, not waiting for an answer. "Come on."

"So what now?" Madison asked.

"What now?" Rourke shrugged. "We report him to the registry people. If he's not where he's supposed to be, they'll throw him back in jail and we'll tell him his daughter is dead. Right now, we go see what Spoons has for us."

They headed back to the car, but as they passed one of the stalls, with fish laid out on ice in wooden bins, Madison veered over to a kid with his hands full of trout. Rourke stopped and watched her impatiently.

The kid eyed her as she approached.

"I got a question for you," she said quietly. "I'm looking for a guy named Everett Munroe. Is he around here?"

A sloppy leer spread across his face. "Forget about that guy," he said, his eyes half closed in an attempt at smooth. "I got what you're really looking for, right here."

Half a dozen brutally emasculating responses crossed Madison's mind before she remembered the ID in her pocket. She smiled as she pulled it out.

"I'm sorry," she said sweetly. "You must have me confused with someone who's looking for a skinny little punk who smells like fish."

She held the ID up in the his face. "But I'm not. I'm looking for a guy named Everett Munroe. Do you really think it's a good idea to give me a hard time about it?"

Rourke looked on, amused.

As the kid took a step back, he seemed to shrivel and shrink. "Um . . ." He scratched behind his ear, thinking. "There's a guy named Everett, works weekends at Isgro's, the bakery, but he ain't there today."

As they headed back to the car, Rourke started laughing.

Madison growled in exasperation. "It's just too much with these guys sometimes. He's covered with fish. I'm asking about another guy. He starts hitting on me."

"You know that ID's not worth shit, right?"

"Tell that to Don Juan back there."

Rourke sighed. "Well, we can come back on the weekend and see if Mr. Munroe is here, but unless Spoons has something good for us, which I doubt, we're kind of running out of leads to chase. And it still looks like an overdose, no matter what Spoons says. Or won't say."

"Weird that it was methylphenedrine, and not something more common."

"Yeah, I guess," Rourke said. "Maybe we could try to find out where they got it."

Madison looked over at her, reluctant even to say it. "Craig Williams."

Rourke looked back. "Beg your pardon?"

"Craig Williams, or maybe Wilson. Lives somewhere on Baltimore Avenue."

Rourke just stared at her.

"I asked one of the girls at the scene," Madison explained. "She said she wouldn't be surprised if it was an overdose, so I asked if they did drugs and where they got them."

"And you just kind of left that out yesterday?"

"Sorry," Madison said sheepishly. "But at the time you didn't really seem to want to know."

Rourke took out her cell phone and pressed a few buttons.

"Kenny!" she said loudly, holding it up to her ear. "How are you, buddy? . . . I hear you. Listen, I'm working on something here with our new tech, and I'm wondering if you can help me out . . . Yeah, that's the one . . ."

Rourke glanced over at Madison, then quickly looked away. She laughed. "Yeah, that's the one all right . . . You know how it is . . . Well, anyway, I'm trying to find a drug dealer, guy named Craig Williams or maybe Wilson. Probably small time, and I think he's over on Baltimore. You got anything on him? . . . Yeah, I'll hold."

As they reached the car, Rourke cupped her hand over the phone and turned to Madison. "Kenny Jensen's a buddy of mine in narcotics. Usually pretty helpful in situations like this." Her attention jerked back to the phone as Kenny came back on the line.

"Craig Wilkins," she said, taking out her notepad. "That sounds right . . . 4591 Baltimore, got it. Great. What do we know about him?" She wrote a few more things in her notebook as she listened. "Beautiful. All right, Kenny. I owe you one, man . . ." She laughed. "All right, asshole, so I owe you one more, then . . . Right. Thanks, buddy."

Putting away her phone and notebook, she recited, "Craig Wilkins, small time, mostly pot. Busted once for possession with intent to distribute, pleaded down and got time served. Lives at Forty-sixth and Baltimore."

They got in the car and Madison looked at her expectantly. "So . . . ?"

"So, we go pay a visit."

CHAPTER 9

THE HOUSE Craig Wilkins lived in was a standard-issue, yellow-brick West Philly row house. It had probably once been a very desirable address, and it still was, in a funky, urban kind of way. Madison had been inside several of these houses—they all had high ceilings, ornate wood trim, beveled glass windows, and generous porches. Some had been restored to their old glory as spacious single-family dwellings, but most were divided into three, four, as many as seven apartments.

Wilkins's porch sagged visibly in the middle, a sag that grew perceptibly worse when they stepped up on it. One of the panes in the window looking out onto the porch consisted of three pieces of glass held together by duct tape.

Alongside the front door was a row of six doorbells. On a strip of masking tape beside the bottom one, the name "Craig" was printed in boxy, blue ballpoint.

Rourke pushed the button.

Half a minute later, they heard the click and screech

of a door opening somewhere inside. A shuffling noise approached and then a muffled voice announced, "I ain't got any. Come back tomorrow."

Leaning in close, Rourke said loudly, "If you ain't got any, then today's your lucky day. Open the door, asshole."

The curtain slid to the side, but the gloom inside was too thick to see anything but Craig Wilkins's fingers. "What you want?" he demanded.

"I want to ask you some questions," Rourke replied. "And you're going to open this door or I'm going to come back tomorrow, after you re-up, and then I'm going to come back every day after that, too."

After a series of clicks and scrapes, the door swung open. Craig Wilkins wore his hair in a large round Afro, and he had on a tie-dyed shirt, faded jeans, and sandals. Even though he was standing up on a step, Madison looked down at him.

"Craig Wilkins?" Rourke asked, holding up her police ID.

"Why?" he asked sullenly.

"Because I have some questions, dickhead. I'm not with narcotics, and I don't care about narcotics, but if you don't answer my questions, I can come back with some friends who *are* in narcotics. And after a second offense, you're not getting off with time served."

Wilkins looked past them, out the door. Apparently satisfied that no one was watching, he let them into the foyer.

"What is it you want to know?" he asked.

"I want to know what you know about Ashley Munroe and Beth Mowry."

"I don't know anything about them."

"Yes, you do. Ashley Munroe has long blond hair and you probably think about her when you're lying in bed at night, alone. Beth Mowry has short blond hair and kind of a pointy nose. They're in a sorority at Penn."

He rolled his eyes at Rourke's description of Munroe, but he clearly knew who she was talking about. "Yeah, okay. I know them. What about it?"

"Did they buy from you?"

"Why you want to know?"

"Just answer the question, asshole, or my friends from narc will come back and ask it for me. Only they'll have some other questions, too."

He puffed up his chest, trying to look big and tough. "Yeah, they buy from me sometimes."

"Okay, good. So how did you get hold of the methylphenedrine?"

He laughed nervously and took a step backward. "Look, I don't even know what that shit is, okay? Besides, you said this wasn't about no narcotics, now you asking me about sources?"

"What do they get from you, then?"

Wilkins took another step backward. "Look, I sell a little weed, is all, enough so I get a break on my own stash. I don't know what y'all are talking about."

"Where would they be getting speed? Ritalin, shit like that?"

"Look, I don't know nothing about all that—"

"Craig!" Rourke cut him off. "Stop it. I don't want to bother calling in favors, getting my friends to shut you down and send you back to prison. I don't care if you're just selling a little weed. I don't want to bust you, but I will, so just answer the fucking question."

Wilkins sighed deeply. "Dude named Ivan."

"Ivan?" Rourke said. "Is he Russian?"

"As much as I am." Wilkins laughed at that. "Black Russian, maybe."

"What does he sell?"

"All sorts of shit. Pills mostly. Speed, X, oxy."

"Where could we find him?"

Wilkins shrugged. "I don't know. He used to hang out at the park a lot, but I ain't seen him in a while."

"What's he look like?"

"Big black guy. Light skinned. Bald with a little goatee. I guess he does look kind of Russian, in a way." He laughed. "I never thought about it like that."

Clark Park was across Baltimore Avenue and down a block or two. It was a few acres of open space in the middle of West Philly, with grass, trees, and the odd sculpture, including—according to local lore—the world's only statue of Charles Dickens. The park was home to community fairs and festivals throughout the year, but on other days, you could find neighbors and students reading, playing Frisbee, drinking beer. And people selling drugs.

Madison and Rourke took a brief walking tour of the park but didn't see anyone who looked like Ivan. As they headed back to the car, Rourke called Kenny again and left a message.

WHEN THEY walked into the ME's office, Spoons was busy talking to a tall, wiry man, around fifty, in an expensive-looking suit. The tall man's head was bowed, nodding solemnly at what the ME was telling him. He looked up when they walked in, visibly shaken, his eyes and nose slightly pink.

Sponholz hurried over. "Negative on the cocaine, the codeine, and the Dexedrine," he whispered, ticking them off the fingers on his left hand. Then he switched hands. "Still working on dimethyltryptamine, Ecstasy, and ephedrine. This is the Mowry girl's next of kin, Vincent Mowry."

The man he'd been talking to sneezed violently, then wiped his nose with a tissue.

"Bless you," Spoons said loudly as he led them back to where Mowry was waiting.

Mowry looked over, still wiping his nose. "Thank you. Must be the dust."

Spoons swept an arm toward Madison and Rourke. "Vincent Mowry, this is Melissa Rourke and, uh, Maddy Cross."

"Madison," she corrected him. "Madison Cross."

Spoons rolled his eyes. "They're with the crime lab looking into Elizabeth's death."

"Crime lab?" Mowry said, looking suddenly perplexed. "I thought you said it appeared to be a drug overdose."

"We're pretty sure it was," Rourke said, soft and reassuring. "We just want to be thorough. Tell me, Mr. Mowry, did you have any idea that Elizabeth was using drugs?"

Mowry closed his eyes and nodded briefly. "I'm afraid so. I'd had my suspicions, but Beth always denied it. Then about two months ago, I received a call from the university Student Health Services. Beth had been found with a bag of pills by campus security—they fell out of her bag when she was showing her ID or something. Some kind of amphetamine. Ritalin, they thought. They called me.

"She seemed fine by the time I got down here, but she had obviously been taking something. I think it was Ritalin. She even admitted it to me, but she said she wouldn't do it anymore. She said she had learned her lesson. I believed her, and she seemed fine after that."

"I see," Rourke said sympathetically. When Mowry looked down, she shot Sponholz a look that said, told you so. "Well, thanks for you help, Mr. Mowry. We're sorry for the loss of your daughter."

Mowry opened his mouth, an awkward half smile tugging at the corner, "Actually," he said, pausing. "I'm Beth's brother. Her stepbrother, in fact."

"Oh." Rourke seemed taken aback.

Mowry smiled, like he was used to that reaction. "Our parents died some time ago," he said quietly.

"I'm sorry to hear that," Rourke said, still too taken aback to put her "sincerest condolences" expression back on.

Madison and Sponholz smiled the same understanding smile.

"Well," Mowry said, clasping his hands in front of him. "I'm sure you're all extremely busy. Thank you for your understanding, and for all your efforts."

AS SOON as the door closed behind Mowry, Rourke turned and said, "Okay, is it me or was that guy like ninety years old?"

Madison winced disapprovingly.

"No shit," Sponholz laughed. "He walks the fuck in, I'm like, 'I'm sorry about your granddaughter.' "

Madison stifled a laugh and shook her head.

"Oh, come on," Rourke protested, giving her a playful shove, "like you weren't thinking the same fucking thing!"

She snickered despite herself, because she *had* been thinking the same thing. "I'm just saying cut the guy a break. I mean he just ID'd his dead sister, and she died ugly, too."

"I'm only saying." Rourke held up her hands, defensively.

"You guys are brutal."

"Yeah, well, the job is brutal," Spoons countered. "Either you learn to be brutal, too, or you end up being brutalized."

"Amen, brother," Rourke said solemnly, leaning against the wall.

They were quiet for a moment after that. Abruptly, Rourke pushed herself upright. "Well, we better get going. C'mon, Madison. We'll check in later, Spoons. You keep working, all right?"

"When don't I work?" he laughed.

Rourke spun and walked out the door. Madison started to follow, but hesitated as she reached the threshold.

Spoons turned back to her. "What is it, kid?" he asked.

Madison gave him a slip of paper. "That's my number. Can you call me if you do find anything?"

"Yeah, all right. You got to learn not to get so involved," he told her. "But, yeah, I'll call you. Sure thing."

CHAPTER 10

THE STRAW-COLORED liquid in the pipette looked the same as every other sample Madison had ever analyzed, and for that she was grateful—it might be a new job, but it was still the same science. She emptied it onto the gel paper and applied the gentle current that would coax the individual DNA molecules of the sample into a genetic portrait of the person to whom they had once belonged.

"This came in for you," Cross had said, handing a bunch of papers to Rourke as they walked in. He barely glanced at Madison, still looking a little irritated. "What's it about?"

Rourke flicked through the pages of the fax from Coffeewood while filling Cross in on what they knew about Everett Munroe. Madison retreated to the DNA lab with her thermocycler and her tubes, relieved to have something productive to do that would keep her out of her uncle's way.

But the next step of the DNA fingerprinting process didn't take very long, and Madison was curious to read the fax. She picked it up on the way back to her desk and started reading. It made what seemed like a long story into a very, very short one.

Everett Munroe had been a schoolteacher and a widower. His wife had died in a workplace accident, leaving behind a small settlement. When his teenaged daughter, Ashley, ran away from home, the girl next door, Sara Oliver, began babysitting for his infant son, Eddie.

A month before the babysitter turned eighteen, one of the neighbors called the police and said Munroe was sleeping with her. He was arrested and convicted on two counts of statutory rape.

The babysitter's family asked for leniency, but the judge gave him five years anyway. His tenure at Coffeewood was not without incident, and he ended up serving the whole sentence.

Madison felt bad for the guy. Maybe there was a valid reason for the harsh sentence, but it seemed to be one of those cases where for one reason or another, the law had just gotten carried away.

As she kept reading, she could hear Rourke quietly explaining to Cross that Everett Munroe appeared to be in violation of his registration requirements.

"He's a sex offender?" Lieutenant Cross asked.

"Well, it was just statutory," Madison blurted out.

Cross and Rourke both turned to look at her.

"Excuse me?" he said.

"Well . . . Just that it was only statutory he went in for. With a seventeen-year-old, almost eighteen. Guy did five years, I assumed it had to be something violent—rape, assault, something like that."

Lieutenant Cross frowned at her. "And?"

"I don't know. The girl's family asked for leniency, and the guy still got five years?"

"He broke the law," Lieutenant Cross stated simply. "He did his time."

"Well, yeah, only now he gets to do it again because he didn't fill out his change-of-address form? I mean, it's not like he's a real rapist or anything."

"Right." Cross chewed on the inside of his cheek, breathing very steadily. "Well, the law's the law. If he failed to register, he goes back in." He gave her a stern look, then turned back to Rourke.

A sudden memory came to her—her dad ranting about "by-the-book" Dave. She couldn't remember if it was before or after her mother died, or if he had been ranting to her mother or to her, or just ranting. But she could clearly remember his disdain, his contempt over his brother's concern for the letter of the law more than its intent. For rules, rather than what was right.

Now, listening to Cross flatly reciting the law instead of considering its implications, she could feel that same anger inside her.

"Don't you think that's a bit harsh?" Madison gave an indignant laugh, like she thought it was ridiculous. Her voice was growing louder. "I mean, sounds like the guy already got the shaft once, you know?"

He seemed taken aback. "For God's sake, Madison, that girl was somebody's daughter."

"That's right, and the people whose daughter it was asked for leniency."

The quiet that followed made it apparent how loud their voices had been.

The lieutenant's eyes had narrowed. "We don't write the laws, Ms. Cross. We enforce them," he said flatly. "And even that's not part of your job, so it really doesn't concern you."

Madison lowered her eyes and picked up her HR papers, wondering once again if she should bother. Her gaze drifted once more to the fax. The name and contact number of Everett Munroe's parole officer, George Gossette, was listed on the bottom.

Making sure no one was watching her, she wandered back to the DNA lab, picked up the phone, and punched in the number. Gossette answered.

"Hi, Mr. Gossette, my name is Madison Cross, with the Philadelphia Police Crime Scene Unit."

Gossette breathed heavily. "What can I do for you, Ms. Cross?" He sounded like a heavy man, as if answering the phone were an immense effort.

"I wanted to talk to you about one of your parolees, Everett Munroe."

Gossette sighed heavily. "Let me get his file. He in trouble?"

"No, I don't think so," Madison said, looking around to see if anyone was listening. "I just wanted some background. His daughter may have been a victim of a crime."

"What, you think he did it?"

"I just want some background."

"Because between you and me, that man shouldn't've been in jail in the first place. I know the law's the law, and he shouldn've done what he did, but that loser got a raw deal." He breathed heavily again, apparently from the effort of opening the file. "Okay, what do you want to know?"

"What happened to the little boy, Eddie?"

"That's a good example of what I mean. The girl's family asked for leniency, and when he didn't get it, they took in that little boy. The babysitter and her mom, they took care of the kid while Pop was in jail."

Madison grunted.

"Yeah, that's just what I mean," Gossette said. "They

was close, like family close. I guess he got *too* close, or at least too early, but . . . well, I dunno what it's like in Philly, but in Virginia, we got enough real bad guys, you know?"

"Right." Madison couldn't think of anything else she could ask that wouldn't get Munroe in trouble. "Okay, thanks for your help."

"That's all you want?" He sounded relieved.

"Do you know what happened to his daughter when he went to jail?"

"There's another thing. When the mom died, he got a settlement, put nearly all of it in education accounts for the boy and the daughter. She went off to boarding school, then Princeton or something. Some Ivy League school."

"Penn?"

"Yeah, that sounds right."

"Hmm." Madison paused, thinking.

"Is that it, then?"

"Actually, do you have an address for the babysitter's family? The Olivers?"

Gossette breathed loudly for few moments, then grunted. "I got an address, but it's a couple years old. They moved, actually not too far from you, I think. Let me see if I got the new one . . . Here it is. You know a place called Gloucester, in Jersey?"

MADISON HUNG up the phone and grabbed her notebook and handbag. Turning down the hallway, she announced to no one in particular that she was going to lunch. Happily, no one seemed to notice or care.

As she was fishing the unfamiliar car keys out of her bag, she walked straight into Aidan.

"Want some company?" Aidan asked with a smile.

"Oh . . . hi," she said, flustered. She hadn't seen him coming.

"Lunch?"

"Actually, maybe tomorrow." She smiled. "I have to run some errands today."

"It's okay," he said bravely. "I'm no stranger to rejection."

"Tomorrow, okay?" she said, stepping around him and backing down the hallway.

As she started to turn away, he said, "Okay, it's a—"

She turned back around and held up a finger. "Don't."

He laughed. "Enjoy your errands."

THE DARK blue Crown Victoria was parked right where Cross had said it would be. The body had a slightly rumpled, not-so-new look, but there were no major dents, and it was clean. It took her a second to get the door open. Inside it smelled a little too much of fake new car. As if it had something to hide, she thought.

It started on the first try, though, and in the few minutes it took her to get to I-95, she had already bonded with the vehicle. By the time she had crossed the Walt Whitman Bridge into Jersey, she had the buttons set on the radio. She even found a song she liked on her first run-through.

MARILYN OLIVER lived on a dusty cul de sac in Gloucester City, New Jersey, just across the bridge from South Philly. She was just sitting down on a plastic chair on the porch, with a big plate of potato salad on her lap and a tall glass of something bright red next to her. The chair across from her held a small TV, blaring a soap opera along with a lot of static.

She eyed the car suspiciously as it pulled up. As Madison got out, she seemed to hasten her efforts to get a forkful of potato salad into her mouth, as if she knew this stranger was about to interrupt her lunch. When Madison got out of the car and actually started walking toward her house, Oliver redoubled her efforts.

"Hi," Madison said, smiling casually.

The woman tilted her head warily, chewing intently on her mouthful. Her faded sleeveless T-shirt was sweaty and clingy, accentuating the fact that her massive bra was clearly outmatched and outflanked on every side.

Mrs. Oliver took a long drink from her glass, swishing it around her mouth before swallowing. "What do you want?" she asked.

"I'm trying to reach Everett Munroe."

She shook her head in disgust and disbelief. "When are you people going to leave that poor man alone? Don't you think he's been through enough?"

"Actually, yes, I do. I just want to talk to him."

"Well, he ain't here."

"When was the last time you saw him?"

"I don't know."

"Have you seen him since he got out of jail?"

Mrs. Oliver bit her lip, eyeing the potato salad, perhaps thinking another forkful would give her time to think.

"Is Eddie here?" Madison asked quietly.

"You leave that boy out of it! Jesus, what is wrong with you people?"

"Is Eddie here?" she pressed, quietly.

"No. No, he ain't," Mrs. Oliver said defiantly. "He's at a friend's house."

Madison looked around and saw none of the mess that inevitably accompanied seven-year-old boys: no balls, no bikes, no headless action figures. Eddie was not living in that house.

She made a conscious decision not to ask about Sara. "Okay," she said. "Well, thank you for your time."

Marilyn Oliver stuffed a forkful of potato salad into her mouth, chewing angrily as Madison turned to leave.

THE DNA analysis was finished by the time Madison got back to the lab—a splash of goo miraculously transformed into a partial but vivid map of another human being's genetic material. Madison still couldn't help but be awed, not only by the fact that it was possible but that she was the one doing it.

As she carried the results to the scanner to upload them into the national database, she noticed some cell phone logs on Tommy Parker's desk: calls made by Ashley Munroe and Beth Mowry.

Beth Mowry's log barely filled two pages. Ashley Munroe's, on the other hand, was almost a quarter-inch thick. The list was a blur of phone numbers and girl's names, but one immediately stood out from the rest: Sara Oliver.

CHAPTER 11

SARA OLIVER lived in a modest home not far from her mother in a town called Oaklyn. It wasn't a large house, but it was a lot bigger than a single girl would need, and the toys that littered the front yard added to the impression that the place was a family dwelling.

Madison sat in her car, staring out the window, wondering, as she seemed to be doing more and more lately, what the hell she was doing.

A school bus turned the corner at the end of the block. Almost simultaneously, the front door opened and out stepped a woman who looked a lot like Marilyn Oliver, only twenty years younger and forty pounds lighter.

Sara came down from the porch, reaching the bottom step just as a blond-haired second-grader jumped off the bus, waving behind him to a chorus of "Bye, Eddie!"

He ran up the front path and jumped into Sara's arms. Madison felt herself smiling at the intensity of the hug. Sara put him down and looked at her watch, then crouched down and whispered in his ear. The little boy nodded, looking excited. Then they both sat down on the steps.

For ten minutes, Madison watched as they talked, tickling and playing tic-tac-toe with a big piece of sidewalk chalk.

The little boy stood up and pointed down the street.

Madison looked in the rearview mirror to see what he was pointing at, and to her surprise, saw tears coursing down her cheeks.

Her mother had been killed before Madison had ever ridden a school bus.

The little boy yelled, "Daddy!" and in the mirror, Madison saw Everett Munroe walking up the block. Her heart ached as the boy ran to greet him. Munroe picked up his little boy and squeezed him hard, squeezed him like only a parent who has already lost a child can. Or been lost himself.

After kissing Sara Oliver the way people do when they're still in love, he crouched down and listened with convincing interest as Eddie explained to him what some bug was doing on the ground.

Madison felt the salt contracting on her skin as the tears dried on her face. The raw, jagged pain that had erupted within her had been replaced once again by the cold, dull ache she'd been living with since she was six.

Madison took out her phone and punched in Marilyn Oliver's number. The poor guy was going to find out soon, anyway, she reasoned. If she was going to let him go, she had to be sure he was innocent.

"Hello?"

"Hello, Mrs. Oliver, this is Madison Cross, I spoke to you earlier about Everett Munroe."

"What do you want?" she huffed.

"First I have to ask you, why isn't Everett Munroe at his registered address?"

Mrs. Oliver sighed. "Well, if he ain't there, I would imagine it was so he wouldn't get harassed by people like you."

"Mrs. Oliver, I'm trying to help. Everett could end up back in prison if the police find out he's not at his registered address. If he moved without telling them."

She sighed again. "I know. I told them as much. But they're just living in fantasyland."

And Madison was going to destroy it.

"Mrs. Oliver, I'm afraid I have some bad news, but as bad as it is, it could get a lot worse if Mr. Munroe doesn't act quickly."

"What are you talking about?"

"The police are looking for Mr. Munroe right now."

"I thought you were with the police."

"I am, and I've already found him. I know he's with your daughter, but I don't want to send him back to jail. The thing is, his daughter Ashley . . . she's dead."

Madison continued on despite the gasp on the other end. "We think it was a drug overdose, but we're not sure. The police are trying to notify Everett, and if he's not at his registered address, they're going to send him back to prison.

"Mrs. Oliver, you need to call Everett Munroe right now, this instant, as soon as you get off the phone with me, and tell him about Ashley. And you need to tell him he has to call the registry, now, today, this minute, and give them his new address, before they send him back to Coffee-wood."

The only sound coming through the phone was a high-pitched weeping.

"Mrs. Oliver? Can you call him right now?"

Mrs. Oliver blew her nose. "Yes," she said, and hung up. Madison sank slightly lower in her seat and waited.

Her muscles were tense and she felt nauseous as she watched the trio outside. One minute ticked by, then two.

When the phone rang inside the house, Madison's fingernails dug into the steering wheel.

Sara Oliver came back out to the porch holding a cordless phone up to her ear. Her face brightened as she said, "Hi, Mom!" But her happiness was soon replaced by concern and confusion. Silently, she handed the phone to Everett.

He asked Sara a question before taking it, but she just shrugged and shook her head. As he started talking, he paced a couple of steps across the yard. Then he stopped and put his finger in his ear, listening intently.

The next thing Madison knew, he was on his knees, heaving with sobs, his anguish palpable. Sara and Eddie flew to his side, asking him what was wrong, embracing him.

Madison forced herself to drive away, telling herself she had done what she had to do to prove he hadn't killed his daughter. Perhaps, if he registered, he could salvage what would be left of his life.

SEEING EVERETT Munroe had left Madison shaken and drained. She took her time driving back to the crime lab, through Queen Village, past South Street, and into Old City. She picked up a cappuccino on the way back to the crime lab and sat for a while in her car in the parking lot, sipping it until she was sure she had regained her composure. When she was confident her eyes were no longer puffy and red, she went inside.

Aidan was waiting for the elevator as she stepped off it. "What's the matter?" he asked as soon as he saw her. "Are you okay?"

As her eyes welled up, she laughed at the transparency of her façade of composure.

"What is it?" he said.

She sniffed and laughed again, wiping a tear with the base of her thumb.

Parker's voice boomed from down the hall. Aidan gently steered her back onto the elevator and pushed the door-close button.

She looked up at him, confused. "What . . .?"

He shrugged. "You really feel like dealing with Parker?"

"Ever?"

He laughed. "Let me buy you a coffee."

"I just had one."

"Then make it a decaf. Come on. Something's bothering you."

"No, it's just . . ." The elevator door opened again, letting in Parker's overly loud laughter.

Aidan raised his eyebrows.

"Point taken," Madison conceded. "I'll tell you what, let me just check on the database search I'm running, and then we'll go."

ROURKE, SANCHEZ, and Parker were sitting at their desks. Sanchez was rolling her eyes at whatever Parker was laughing about. Rourke was ignoring them both.

Madison walked through the room, eyes focused on the computer, not looking at any of them. She felt strangely self-conscious, as if she'd forgotten how to move without thinking about it. Her plan was to click her mouse, make sure the sample hadn't hit anything, and get out of there without making a sound.

When the screen switched on, though, she couldn't help saying "Hmm" loud enough that all three of them heard it.

She'd gotten a hit on the database.

Sanchez wandered over to see what was going on. Madison concentrated on what she was doing, and a few keystrokes later, she was looking at a name.

"Holy shit," she said under her breath.

The name on the screen was Gary Swinson.

CHAPTER 12

"WHO THE hell is Gary Swinson?" asked Parker, now standing behind her, looking over her shoulder.

Madison ignored him, turning to where Rourke now stood. "That's the kid I was telling you about, the kid the Munroe girl had the restraining order against."

Parker grunted.

Rourke slowly nodded. "All right," she said grudgingly. "That could be something."

She picked up a phone and said, "Get me the University of Pennsylvania, please. Campus Security."

AIDAN WAS still waiting when Madison and Rourke came rushing up to the elevators. He didn't say anything, but he had a questioning look on his face.

"We might have found something," Madison said vaguely in explanation. "Sorry."

She smiled awkwardly as the elevator doors opened and she and Rourke stepped in.

A Campus Security vehicle was waiting for them in front of Gary Swinson's dormitory. The two campus police officers seemed conflicted, trying to maintain the same cool, bored demeanor for the benefit of the students, but at the same time clearly excited to be working with the Philly PD in what could turn out to be a real criminal investigation.

Madison and Rourke followed them up the stairs and down the hallway to Gary Swinson's dorm room. They knocked on the door and waited, then knocked again. When they knocked a third time, the next door down opened up. A massive nimbus cloud of pot smoke issued forth before a skinny white kid with ratty-looking dreadlocks stepped out and said, "Dude . . ."

He froze when he saw the campus police, unable to move except for a short, sharp cough that escaped his lips despite his obvious efforts to restrain it. He started to dart back inside but Madison barked, "Stop!"

The kid froze again, this time his eyes open wide.

Rourke stifled a laugh.

"Do you know Gary Swinson?" Madison asked.

The kid shook his head.

"Yes, you do," she said flatly. "Your room is next door to his. Where is he?"

The kid coughed again and a slight wisp of smoke escaped his lips. He shook his head and opened his mouth but Madison cut him off, craning her neck to look over his shoulder and into the smoke-filled room behind him. She turned her head so she was speaking to Rourke but her eyes stayed on the kid's dorm room. "If that cloud of smoke isn't probable cause, I don't know what is."

"He split," the kid blurted out in a hurry. He pulled the door closed behind him. "I think he went home."

"When did he leave?" Madison asked.

The kid shrugged, and Madison made a show of sniffing the air.

"Okay, okay. I don't know, okay? I think he left last night. He was pretty broken up about Ashley. He said he needed to get off campus."

"Where did he go?" Madison demanded.

The kid shrugged. "I don't know. Home, I guess."

"Where's that?"

"I don't know. Gladwyne, I think."

Madison turned and looked at Rourke, silently asking, *Are we done here?*

Rourke shrugged and nodded.

"Okay, we'll be back in about fifteen minutes. There better not be anything illegal in this room when we get back."

As Madison turned to leave, Rourke murmured to her, "Who pissed in your cornflakes this morning?"

THEY GOT Gary Swinson's parents' address from the admissions office. Now they were on the Schuylkill Expressway, headed west toward Gladwyne, one of the older towns on the Main Line.

Rourke seemed to loosen up a bit after Madison's performance at Gary Swinson's dorm, ribbing her as they got in the car. "So what, you been watching *Dragnet* at night?" She laughed. "Hell, I was ready to tell you everything *I* knew."

Madison shook her head. "I mean, come on. Do I look like that much of a fucking idiot? And do I look like I have that much time to waste?"

Rourke put up her hands and shook her head. "Hey, I hear you. You don't have to tell me. I just expected to you be more . . . genteel."

As she was about to say something else, her cell phone rang. "It's Kenny," she said, looking at the display.

"Hey, Ken . . . ," she said into the phone. "Yeah, you nailed it. Found him, talked to him, rattled him . . . No, but he did give us another name . . . Yeah, a guy named Ivan . . . Why? . . . Yeah, no good reason, that's for god-damn sure . . . No, they have us chasing down fucking everything, so we're looking into where the stuff came from . . . Yeah, I know . . . You don't think so, huh?"

She looked over at Madison and shook her head, but she seemed perturbed.

"Well, do you think you can poke around, see if anybody else knows him?" Rourke asked. ". . . Yeah, I don't know, first they wanted this thing finished up but quick. I think the mayor put out the word, then it got in the papers, now the commissioner is playing CYA, wants to make sure nothing is left out there in case something more's going on."

Rourke laughed. "Spoons is scared shitless. He won't even call a cause of death . . . No, he won't. We all know it was an OD, but until we have it official, we have to chase it down . . . Yeah, I don't know, maybe if we can bust the source, it might calm things down a bit . . . Yeah, all right, thanks, buddy."

As she put down the phone, she looked concerned.

"What's the matter?" Madison asked.

"He said he doesn't know of a guy named Ivan. Said it doesn't sound familiar."

"What else?"

"I don't know. He just sounded kind of weird, that's all."

"How do you mean, weird?"

"I don't know. Nervous. It was probably just my imagination. But he seemed to be holding something back."

Madison frowned. "Hmm."

Rourke turned to her and snapped, "Don't be trying to read stuff into it. He probably just had gas or something. Jesus, it's nothing, okay?"

THEY EXITED the expressway onto Hollow Road, then took Conshohocken State Road into Gladwyne.

As they drove through the town, Rourke turned to her and said, "Look, I know this case has some kind of a special meaning for you now. I know you're taking some heat, and I know you really want to crack it, if there is anything to crack. But there's a big difference between spooking some stoner into diming out his next-door neighbor and getting some rich Main Line matron to give up anything if there's the slightest inkling of any trouble."

Madison evenly met her gaze. "Okay, but if I think you're blowing this off, I'm going to jump in."

THE SWINSONS lived in a large stone house on a street with no sidewalks and very skinny trees. An Audi station wagon was parked under the carport.

Mrs. Swinson answered the door almost before the ponderous bell had finished reverberating. She was a slim woman in her late forties with excellent posture, jet-black hair, and high cheekbones. She had the demeanor of a former homecoming queen who had successfully gotten over her glory days, without forgetting them completely.

"Can I help you?" she asked, guarded without being unfriendly.

Rourke smiled sweetly. "Hello, Mrs. Swinson. My name is Melissa Rourke and this is Madison Cross. We're with the Philadelphia Police." She held up her ID just long enough for Swinson to see the police insignia. "We were hoping we could have a word with you."

Mrs. Swinson's demeanor faltered. "What's this about?" she asked through the remains of her smile.

"Actually, we're looking for Gary. He's not in any trouble; we just want to talk to him."

"Well . . . Gary's at school," she said, like she was stating the obvious.

"Actually, ma'am, he's not. That's why we're here."

"Okay, what's going on?" she asked, her voice and her face growing steely.

"Mrs. Swinson, perhaps we could come in and discuss it with you."

Swinson studied them for a couple seconds. She looked around to see if anyone was watching, and then let them in.

The interior of the house was like the exterior: neat and clean, well kept and expensive but not luxurious. The entrance opened out to a family room on the right, and the adjoining wall held a diamond-shaped arrangement of a dozen or so family photos.

The photo closest to Madison was a recent-looking one of Mrs. Swinson with her husband. He had thick black hair and a broad face, heavyset but solid-looking. His expression suggested a confidence bordering on arrogance, and Madison wondered if he had been the football star at her high school.

The next photo was of Gary, probably early in high school, painfully thin and smiling shyly. He had his mother's features and a shock of hair that was darker and thicker than either of theirs. There was a picture of a girl, probably a sister, also in high school. She had an open face, an outgoing smile, and a sweatshirt that said "Tracy."

Several pictures of Gary and his sister suggested she was a year or two older. In a few of them, she wore a

Villanova Wildcats T-shirt next to Gary wearing a shirt with the University of Pennsylvania crest. In one, they stood with their arms around each other's shoulders in front of the twin spires of the church at Villanova. The two were obviously very close.

Mrs. Swinson sat down in the armchair opposite the sofa. "Okay, so what's this about?"

Rourke took the lead. "It's about Gary's ex-girlfriend. Something has happened."

Mrs. Swinson put a hand to her mouth. "Something happened to Donna!? Oh, that's terrible! Is she okay?"

"Donna's fine. Actually, it was a girl named Ashley Munroe."

The hand fell away from her face, as did her expression of concern. "Oh," she said, flatly. "Well, I can't say as I'm all that surprised. I didn't know the girl, but from the little bit Gary has said about her, it seems she was no stranger to trouble."

"What did he say about her?"

She shrugged and opened her mouth to speak, then thought better of it. "Why are you looking for Gary?"

"Mrs. Swinson, were you aware that Ashley Munroe had a restraining order against Gary?"

"She had a . . . ?" She laughed bitterly. "That's ridiculous. See? That girl just creates trouble."

"She said in the restraining order that he had been stalking her."

"Stalking her? That's absurd. They were on the same campus together. Of course he'd run into her. What's this all about? You said Gary wasn't in any trouble, but it sounds to me like you're trying to pin some on him."

"Ashley Munroe is dead."

Mrs. Swinson sank back in her chair.

"It looks like an accidental overdose," Rourke continued. "But we're not ruling anything in or out. We found

DNA evidence on Ashley that suggests she had sex with Gary the day she died."

Swinson's eyes narrowed to slits.

"Gary is not a suspect in anything at this point, but we do want to talk to him. We went to his dorm room, but he wasn't there. One of his friends told us he had come home. He was apparently very distraught. We're concerned for his safety."

Swinson eyed them for another moment, taking in what Rourke had said. A moment later, she abruptly stood. "Get out."

Rourke and Madison looked at each other.

"I beg your pardon?" Rourke asked.

"Get out. Get out of my house." Her voice had started off unemotionally, but now she was starting to get worked up. "You come in here, telling me Gary is not in trouble, asking me questions without telling me what's going on. You try to get me to say something to falsely incriminate my own son, then you pretend you're concerned about his well-being? Get the hell out of my house," she yelled. "Now!"

They got up to leave.

Madison stopped at the door. "Thank you for your time, Mrs. Swinson."

"Get out!"

CHAPTER 13

"WELL, THAT was enlightening," Rourke said sarcastically as they got in the car.

Madison shrugged.

As she drove back through downtown Gladwyne, she took out her phone and dialed information.

Rourke glanced over at her, uninterested. "You're going the wrong way," Rourke said smugly when Madison turned left onto Conshohocken State Road.

Madison ignored her, and Rourke's expression changed when Madison said into the phone, "Villanova, Pennsylvania . . . Villanova University, Campus Security, please."

"Where the hell are you going?"

Madison held up a finger and spoke into the phone. "Hi, this is Madison Cross, from the Philadelphia Police Crime Scene Unit. I need to know if you have a Tracy Swinson living on campus there. Sure, I'll hold."

Madison turned to Rourke. "Gary and his sister seemed close in those pictures. I'm thinking, you've got major girl trouble with a girl your mom doesn't approve of—where are you going to go when shit hits the fan, home to Mom, or to your sister at another campus?"

Before Rourke could respond, Madison was back on the phone. "Great. Thank you. And do you have an address for her? Beautiful. Thanks again." As she put her phone away, she continued. "The sister had on a Villanova sweatshirt in some of the pictures, and one was taken at that chapel-cathedral thing. I figure, we're here, why not check it out, right?"

Rourke nodded grudgingly.

FEDIGAN HALL was a utilitarian three-story stone building with just enough fancy touches to achieve that university campus look. Tracy Swinson's room was on the second floor, guarded by a plain wooden door with a peephole and a number.

As Rourke was about to knock, Madison stopped her and suggested she stand to the side of the door.

"No offense," she said quietly, "but I might still be able to pass for a student."

Rourke gave her a look, but nodded and stepped back out of the way.

Looking down so that her face was mostly obscured by her long hair, Madison gave the door a timid knock.

The peephole darkened and a male voice asked, "Who is it?"

"It's Madison."

The door opened.

Gary Swinson's face was pale, red-eyed, and gaunt under his thick black hair, but he managed a smile when he saw Madison. "Hi," he said smoothly. "Are you one of Tracy's friends?"

Madison shook her head. "No." She felt a twinge of

guilt when Rourke stepped out and showed him her ID.

"Philadelphia Police," Rourke said. "We need to talk."

Swinson's shoulders slumped and his head sagged as he turned and walked into the room without saying a word.

The room was cluttered with books, CDs, and sports equipment. A basketball sat on one of the desks and a lacrosse stick was leaning in the corner.

Gary Swinson sat on a red futon sofa with his head between his knees.

"Do you know why we're here?" Madison asked.

He looked up at them, eyes even redder than before, but he didn't respond.

"Did you see Ashley Munroe this past Sunday?"

He stared at them, thinking, then shook his head. "No."

Madison and Rourke looked at each other.

"When was the last time you saw Ashley Munroe?"

He shrugged. "A while ago."

"Why did Ashley Munroe have a restraining order against you?" Madison asked quietly.

He shrugged again, his face growing blotchy.

"Did she break up with you?"

Swinson's lip started quivering.

Madison sat down next to him. "She hurt you, didn't she?" she murmured sympathetically, practically whispering.

Swinson broke down into long, loud sobs and a torrent of tears. Madison put her arm on his back, gently patting him until his crying quieted and slowed. Rourke shifted her weight impatiently from one foot to the other, but Madison sat and waited for the words to come.

"I was happy with Donna," Swinson said between the receding sobs. "We were going to get married when we got out of school. But Ashley . . . she was like a, like a goddess." He shook his head in disbelief at the thought of her. "I couldn't believe it. All of a sudden, I was with this goddess. Me."

He shook his head again. "When I found out how she was sleeping around, I couldn't deal. She was a whore. I freaked out, and she dropped me right there. But I still loved her."

"The restraining order said you were stalking her," Madison said quietly. "Were you?"

He looked up at her without lifting his head. "I'd run into her on campus sometimes. That's all."

"You said you hadn't seen her on Sunday, right?" Rourke interjected. "We found your pubic hair mixed with her pubic hair. How do you explain that?"

He looked up as his face began to crumble.

"I had to see her . . . just one more time . . ."

Madison looked up at Rourke. Was this turning into a confession?

". . . It cost me eight hundred bucks . . . ," Swinson continued, sobbing into his knees. "But still, she usually charged twelve," he explained with a momentary brightness. ". . . She . . . she gave me a discount."

"Wait," Rourke broke in. "What are you saying?"

"I paid her." The tears were falling freely down his face now, his nose running profusely.

"Did other guys pay her?" Rourke asked.

Swinson nodded through his tears. "I asked her to stop, but she dumped me instead."

Madison scooted a few inches away on the sofa, then stood up.

"Are we done here?" she asked quietly.

Rourke nodded. "That's all we're getting out of him today."

They both looked over as Tracy Swinson walked in.

"Excuse me," she said, "who are you?"

She quickly spotted Gary on the sofa. "Jesus, what did you do to him?"

Rourke ducked out, motioning for Madison to follow. "We were just leaving."

THEY PICKED up a couple of hoagies and ate in the car as they drove back to the city.

Rourke paused when she finished her first half, washing it down with a long swig of root beer. "I'll admit, I'm pleasantly surprised," she said, wiping her mouth. "You did a good job with the mother and with the kid. You have good instincts, but here's the thing: Sometimes instincts are just instincts. You know this is still probably going to turn out to be an accidental overdose, right?"

Madison looked over and smiled, accepting the compliment but conceding nothing.

"Anyway," Rourke continued. "I liked your style back there. Especially with that stoner. That was hilarious. Reminded me of your dad."

Madison's hands twitched involuntarily on the wheel. "You knew my dad?"

"In the old days, sure. Pretty much everybody did. Haven't seen him in a million years, though."

"What was he like?"

Rourke looked over hesitantly. Probably thinking about which part of her father she could talk about, Madison thought bitterly.

"Kevin Cross was a pistol," Rourke finally said. "One of the funniest guys on the force. Bit of a temper, you know, but a really good cop. One of the best. And he hated losing a case. A case went unsolved, it would drive him right up the wall. He hated it." She went quiet after that. "I guess you'd know about that part, though, huh?"

"That's about all there was left of him."

CHAPTER 14

LT. DAVID Cross was not completely happy that a new lead had turned up in the Munroe/Mowry case.

He listened intently as they had explained how Spoons had found the pubic hair, how Madison had done the DNA analysis, and how Swinson had said he paid Munroe for sex. Rourke let Madison do most of the talking.

"The girl who I . . . the girl who approached me at the crime scene, she used the word 'whore' to describe Munroe," Madison had explained. "I assumed she was bad-mouthing the girl. Same thing when the Swinson kid said it first, but he meant he actually paid her for sex. He meant it literally."

"Ah, yes." Lieutenant Cross nodded ponderously. "The anonymous source who started all the rumors that got into the newspaper and made my life miserable. The source who helped turn a simple but unfortunate overdose into a political shit storm. What else did this source tell us?"

"She told us about the restraining order against

Swinson, about Munroe's history of breaking up couples," Madison said defensively. "She said how she wasn't surprised Munroe was using drugs, even gave us a name of a dealer."

Cross gave her an infuriatingly indulgent smile. "Madison," he said. "That would all be very helpful information if there was an actual murder to investigate, instead of an accidental overdose."

He looked up at Rourke, but she averted her eyes.

"Okay." He sighed. "Since we're supposed to investigate every lead, I guess we'll investigate every lead . . . It's just as well we have a new DNA analyst."

IN THIS case, investigating every lead meant returning to room six at the Alpha Alpha Gamma house and searching it one more time. Cross led Madison into the corner of the room, where the laundry hamper overflowed onto the floor, and gazed at her expectantly.

Madison folded her arms across her chest. "What?"

"Every lead," he said. "You need to bag all this, take it to the lab, and search it for DNA evidence." He smiled grimly. "Use gloves, and pay special attention to the underwear, okay?"

ASHLEY MUNROE'S dirty laundry was piled high on a table in the crime lab. The multicolored mound had the earthy, sweaty smell of worn clothes with a faint mixture of other more floral fragrances.

Before she set about sorting through the entire load, Madison decided she should get the first batch started in the thermocycler—she could sort through the rest while it was running.

The thermocycler could handle four samples at a time,

but the first sample would be the control, a sample Madison had already prepared from a swab taken from inside Ashley Munroe's mouth.

Since the clothes were all mixed together, Madison had to assume the evidence might be, too, and that meant separating each hair into a distinct sample. Unless she was absolutely positive that more than one hair was from the same person—which she couldn't be—she would have to treat each hair individually.

Madison pulled three pairs of undergarments from the top of the pile and carefully spread them out on the examination table. She tagged and labeled each one.

Under the bright exam light, it was easy to see the hairs against the fabric. Using a pair of tweezers, she selected one complete hair from each garment. She set out a rack with four tubes, and put one hair each into the first three tubes. Using a glass pipette, she injected liquid medium into each of them. Into the last one, she injected the control sample she had prepared earlier.

Once the first batch was in the thermocycler, where the DNA from each sample would replicate, Madison stripped off her gloves and plopped down at her desk. It had been a long day, and she knew she had a long night ahead of her. She looked at her watch and calculated that she had just enough time to run out for a cup of coffee before it would be time to get the first batch onto the gels and start the second.

She was summoning the energy to make the caffeine run when she heard Lieutenant Cross's voice behind her.

"Well, now we're both in the doghouse," he said, leaning around the doorway. "You were supposed to come over for dinner an hour ago."

Madison looked at her watch. "Shit! I totally—"

Cross raised his hand in front of him. "Calm down," he said. "It's okay. I was supposed to be home two hours

ago to help prepare it. I called your aunt Ellen this afternoon and told her we'd stepped into an unexpected pile
of work."

"I totally forgot," Madison confessed.

"Occupational hazard," he said bleakly. "I'm afraid
Ellie's gotten used to it." He patted the doorjamb. "Well,
don't work too late."

"I won't. Good night."

Madison glanced again at her watch and recalculated.
The window of opportunity for getting coffee had closed.
Maybe after the next batch.

With the thermocycler humming in the background,
Madison plopped the entire pile of laundry on to the table
and started sorting.

Socks, jeans, shirts, and a couple of towels went back
into the evidence bag; they didn't seem particularly prom-
ising, but if worse came to worst, they might be worth a
look.

A couple of bras went into a separate pile. More prom-
ising than socks, but not quite panties.

When the first sort was finished, she was left with a
vividly colored pile of thongs, briefs, and hipsters, plus a
couple of lacy garments Madison couldn't even begin to
categorize.

Once they were all tagged and numbered, she laid them
out in a grid on the table, put on her magnifying goggles,
and bent to the task of searching each one. It wasn't difficult to locate hairs in the assortment of undergarments—
and there were plenty to find.

By the time she finished searching three items, she
had the four samples she needed for the second batch.
She took off the goggles, put each sample in a tube in a
rack, added the enzyme agent that would prepare them,
and placed them in the thermocycler.

After succumbing to an expansive yawn and a stretch,

she once more donned her goggles and pulled on her gloves. Deep in concentration as she pored over a pair of bright green satin hipsters, she didn't hear the footsteps behind her.

"You're not going to put those in with the whites, are you?"

She looked up to see Aidan holding two extra-large coffees.

"Oh, my God. Tell me that's not decaf."

"Just this one . . . Or was it this one? No, it was this one." He smiled. "Just kidding. No, it didn't seem like a decaf kind of night." He handed her one of the coffees.

Madison bowed her head. "I am forever in your debt."

They both paused to sip.

"So what are you doing here?" she asked.

"I stopped by Alpha Alpha Gamma, but they were wrapping up. Heard you had a heavy load."

Madison groaned.

"Okay, bad pun, but I thought maybe you could use a hand sorting this dead girl's laundry."

"The coffee's great, but you didn't have to . . ."

"I don't mind." He grabbed a pair of goggles and pulled on his gloves, pausing as he looked down at the skimpy scraps of brightly colored, satiny fabric. "Actually, I'm surprised Parker didn't volunteer for this."

They shared a guilty laugh, then Aidan clapped his gloved hands together. "Okay, so how are we doing this?"

Madison detailed the procedure for him: She would sort the samples and collect the hairs with tweezers; he would bag and tag them.

"For now, we're just concentrating on complete hairs, ones with the roots intact," Madison explained. "Those are the ones we'll prepare for analysis."

"What will we do with the others?" he asked.

"Probably nothing. We can do mitochondrial DNA

testing on them, but not a full analysis. It isn't anywhere near as helpful—it can kind of tell what family the sample is from, but not which family member. We'll save them anyway, just in case."

Aidan nodded and they got to work. It was an odd activity to be sharing, and at first they exchanged awkward small talk, but soon they settled into a quiet routine.

When the second batch was finished in the thermocycler, Madison immediately put in the third.

Aidan stopped for a moment and watched. "It's amazing this has become as routine as it has."

Madison smiled as she laid out a row of four-inch-square gel-covered pieces of white cardboard.

"That thermocycler makes it a lot easier than it would have been not long ago," she said, gesturing back at it.

"It basically just amplifies the sample, right? So you can use less material?"

"Well, yeah, but think about it: We don't have that much material to start with. I've got a single hair in each of those samples. Without the thermocycler, that wouldn't have been enough to do anything with."

"So what are you doing now?"

Using a glass pipette, she injected a portion of each sample into a groove in the middle of each of the cards.

"Getting them ready for electrophoresis. The thermocycler doesn't just amplify the sample—with the help of the enzymes I add in the liquid medium, it also digests it, cuts it into little manageable pieces. Otherwise, each strand of DNA would be over six feet long. It also kind of ignores the ninety-nine-point-nine percent that's all the same with everybody, and just leaves the bit that's unique."

"Really?"

"Really."

"Six feet long but really skinny. Sounds like someone I know . . ."

"You don't need me to explain all this, do you?"

"I do. Just some of it. Please, educate me."

She gave him a look.

"No, seriously," he said with a smile. "I'd like to learn how to use the equipment."

"All right." She carried the samples across the room and placed them on another machine. "This is the FMBio, the electrophoresis instrument. Once they've been amplified, you run electrical current through the samples. The electricity makes the snippets of DNA move across the gel, the smallest ones fastest and the largest ones slowest. You apply a set current for a set amount of time, and it gives you a pattern of bars or stripes. That's the DNA profile. You compare it to others to see if they match."

She made sure the gels were lined up correctly before turning a knob to apply the current. "Now it's running. Usually, we'd just wait."

"Usually?"

She smiled. "We've still got laundry to do."

CHAPTER 15

TWO HOURS later, they had two dozen hair samples labeled and sitting in enzyme solution. The first two batches had been analyzed and run through the database without a match. The third batch was still in the electrophoresis instrument, and the rest were lined up, ready to go.

When Madison capped the last tube, Aidan straightened and stretched. "Now what?" he asked with a yawn.

Madison yawned back at him. "I've got to wait for the next batch. I'm probably going to hang out and do at least a couple more tonight. I really appreciate your help, but it's mostly waiting now. You should go home."

He nodded. "You hungry?" he asked, looking up at her.

She smiled. Food was the last thing on her mind. "Aidan, that's sweet, but you don't have to."

"How about Chinese? When was the last time you had really good lo mein?"

Her stomach responded before she could, growling loudly as she opened her mouth to decline.

"Well, that's one vote in favor. Anybody else?"

Madison could only laugh.

"Nobody?" Aidan added quickly. "Good. Then it's settled." He took out his phone and held it up to his ear.

"Aidan." He held up his finger to quiet her.

"Aidan!" she said, louder.

He started talking into the phone.

"Aidan!" she barked loudly.

He turned to her reluctantly, his disappointment obvious on his face.

"Ask if they have moo-shu pork."

He raised the phone again and grinned. "And one order of moo-shu pork."

THE MOO-SHU was delicious, and so was the lo mein. Madison ate most of both of them. She was picking with her chopsticks at the last noodles in the corner of the container when the timer informed them that the third batch was finished and scanned.

The computer screen displayed the numerical values that it had attributed to the DNA in the gels. As Madison began uploading the data into the national database, Aidan got on the floor and started doing sit-ups and push-ups.

Madison looked down at him quizzically. "Does lo mein always make you do that?"

He paused mid-sit, his elbows on his knees. "Just trying to get the blood moving. Helps clear the head."

Madison reached down and gave him a hand up. He rose to his feet just inches away from her. For a moment, they stood in silence, looking at each other.

A single, loud ding rang out, letting them know that the database search had scored a hit.

Madison smiled, ruefully. "Ding," she said, quoting the computer.

Aidan straightened up and sighed. "Ding."

She turned and walked to the computer. "Let's see what we have here . . ."

She punched a few keys. "Know anybody named James Mulroney?" she asked, half jokingly.

When he didn't answer, she looked over her shoulder. Aidan's shoulders were slumped, his eyes rolled halfway up into his head.

"Oh, shit," he whispered.

"JIMMY MULRONEY is the quintessential Philadelphia gangster turned 'respectable' businessman," Aidan told her once he was able to speak again. "And I hope you picked up on the quote marks around the word 're-spectable.' He's got a shady past and a big future and a lot of powerful friends. He's everything you wouldn't want involved in a quick and quiet investigation."

She gave him a sharp look, having heard too much of that phrase over the last couple of days.

"Sorry," he said in response. "But this is going to make some very irate people a lot irater."

"Is that even a word?"

"It is now. Look it up and you'll find a picture of the mayor next to it."

The next batch dinged in readiness just as the clock clicked 11:00. Aidan dutifully helped Madison scan each gel card, but by that time they were both slowing down. The caffeine had worn off, and Aidan's forecast of an-other morning shit storm wasn't helping.

He seemed relieved when Madison announced that once the next batch of scans were loaded into the data-base, she was calling it a night.

"What about Mr. Mulroney?" he asked.

"I don't know. I think I'll leave that for the morning."

Madison opened her mouth to speak again, but it turned into a yawn.

"Pretty much sums it up," Aidan said, as Madison tried to stifle another one.

"Sorry," she said, embarrassed. "Thanks for sticking it out tonight. I really appreciate the help."

"My pleasure."

There was a pause. "Well," Aidan said. "We should probably get going."

"Yeah," Madison agreed. "We should."

DRIVING OUT of the parking lot, Madison decided she would wait until morning to update her uncle. She was too tired to make any decisions, and it wasn't like he would be able to do anything until morning, anyway.

It was late, and she was tired, and she realized as she drove that she had momentarily forgotten where she lived and how to get there. Barreling along down Race Street, she was regaining her bearings when she realized with a start that she was following the traffic toward the Ben Franklin Bridge, toward New Jersey. *Perfect,* she thought as she swerved back onto Race. *I'm trying to drive eight blocks home and instead I'm about to cross into another state.*

As she straightened out, she noticed a black SUV cutting across two lines of determined, New Jersey–bound traffic to get back onto Race Street behind her. Apparently she wasn't the only idiot not paying attention to where they were headed. Annoyed at herself and anxious to get home, she sped up a bit, leaving the SUV behind. She turned onto York, but found that her way north was blocked by the base of the bridge. She made a left, then a right, going up one small street and then down another,

all of them one way, and all of them somehow going opposite the way she wanted to go.

After eight or nine frustrating turns, she glanced in her
rearview mirror and noticed a black SUV half a block
behind her. A street lamp momentarily illuminated the
driver: a white guy with longish hair, a beard, and big
shades.

Coincidence, she told herself as she checked her door
locks. God knows there were enough SUVs on the road.

At that point, she was a couple blocks away from
home, but just to be sure, she drove past her street, making a right a few blocks after it. Her stomach flipped as
she looked in her rearview mirror and saw a black SUV
turning the corner behind her. She couldn't see the driver.

Coincidence, she told herself again, but her heart was
pounding. She sped up, turning first one way, then another. Every time she looked back, the SUV was half a
block behind her.

The first twinges of fear were becoming a palpable
panic as Madison suddenly found herself barreling down
a narrow, one-way street that had turned into an alleyway.
She could see the road narrowing farther up ahead and
she realized with a sinking feeling that someone had
double-parked, effectively blocking the road.

Just before the double-parked car, the sidewalk widened
next to an old garage. She managed to turn around before
the SUV caught up with her, but she left the car on the
sidewalk, lights off but engine on, waiting for her pursuers
to pass her.

She slid down in her seat, her heart pounding. In an effort to keep panic at bay, she took out her cell phone and
dialed Lieutenant Cross.

It seemed to take forever for the phone to connect, and
by the time it actually started ringing, Madison realized
the black SUV didn't seem to be coming. Was it possible

she'd imagined the whole thing? There were plenty of SUVs on the road, after all, and it was entirely possible that each time she had looked back, it had been a different SUV.

Feeling increasingly embarrassed and foolish, Madison was about to disconnect the phone when Uncle Dave answered.

"Hello?" He sounded more wary than surprised, and definitely not sleepy.

Madison felt suddenly flustered. "Oh, hi, Uncle Dave. Sorry to be calling so late."

"Maddy? Are you okay?"

"Yeah, I'm fine. I just . . ." Suddenly, it seemed like a terrible idea to tell him about the SUV. She didn't want him worried there was an actual threat, or for that matter, about the possibility that she had imagined the episode. "Actually, I just finished running some of those samples . . ."

"You're at the lab?"

"No. No." She put the car in gear. "I'm actually on my way home."

"Jesus, Maddy, it's after eleven . . . You can't . . . you shouldn't be . . ."

His voice trailed off. It sounded like Detective Cross was reminding Uncle Dave that they actually needed those samples done ASAP.

Madison pulled out into the narrow street and slowly drove up the block. "We got a hit on the database. I thought I should let you know right away."

"Okay, Maddy. That's good. I appreciate you working so late to run down all those samples, especially on a bogus case. We can talk about the results in the morning."

"Well, I didn't run them all down," she said as she reached the end of the block. No sign of the SUV. She made a left, cautiously looking around her. "There's still some more. But the hit I got was a guy named Jimmy Mulroney." She turned onto Third Street, and with no sign of any other vehicle, headed home. "Do you know him?"

A long silence was followed by a long sigh. "Yeah, I know him. I know him too well . . . So does the commissioner. And the mayor. Ah, shit. We've stepped in it this time."

"I'm sorry."

"No, no. That's good police work you're doing, Madison. A lot of the time it ends up being ugly." He laughed grimly. "Almost always, come to think of it."

She was quiet, listening to him think in the silence.

"So it was a hair?" he asked.

"Complete one. Stuck to her panties."

"Right." He took a deep breath. "Well, you go get some sleep. Tomorrow could prove to be an interesting day." He paused. "Oh, and Maddy? Let's keep this under our hats for the moment, okay?"

CHAPTER 16

THE NEXT day started out gray and wet—not incredibly hot, but so humid that the air conditioners just couldn't keep up. The air might get chilly, but it was not going to feel dry.

The incident from the night before had put Madison in a strange mood, like the feeling she got when she awoke after an especially vivid dream. She had pretty much convinced herself that it had been a string of coincidences tied together by nothing more than her imagination. But there was still some room for doubt, and room for doubt meant room for speculation; in particular, if she had been followed, who was doing the following?

But as she showered and caffeinated herself, the eerie feeling receded, and she became more convinced she had just overreacted. Driving to work, she kept telling herself that today was starting out better than the day before. At least she wasn't in the papers. Although she did check the papers to be sure. She stopped for more coffee and picked up some doughnuts to say thank-you to Aidan.

When she walked into the crime lab, she noticed the door to the lieutenant's office was closed. A tense quiet seemed to be hanging over the lab, but Madison considered the possibility that she was imagining the tension, too.

Rourke looked up from her newspaper and nodded.

"Hey," Madison murmured.

Parker gave her a smile. "Morning, Newbie."

Cross opened his door and poked his head out. He looked around the room, gave Madison a thin, forced smile and ducked back into the office.

Aidan wasn't in yet, so Madison put the bag of doughnuts on his desk and wrote "Thanks!" across the front with a ballpoint pen. As she sank into her chair, she noticed Rourke looking at her with eyebrows raised.

"What?" she asked defensively.

Her eyebrows rose higher as Rourke looked over at the bag of doughnuts and then back at Madison.

"Oh, stop it," Madison whispered. "He helped me with the samples last night."

"Damn nice of him."

"Yeah, it was."

"He's a good man," she said, standing. "Generous like that. With his time . . ." She sidled over to his desk and reached into the bag. ". . . With his breakfast."

"Okay," Madison scolded. "But just one."

"Don't worry," Rourke said, dropping sugar on Madison's desk as she passed. "I don't think these are the goodies he's after."

Madison's jaw dropped, but as she was about to fire a retort, Cross stepped out of his office, straightening his jacket and looking very serious. "Madison. Melissa. Could you both step into my office, please?"

It felt strange to Madison, knowing something Rourke didn't.

Cross wasn't sitting, and he didn't invite them to, either. "Did you tell her what you found?" he asked Madison.

Rourke looked over at her. "What?"

"We ran a bunch of samples last night. One of them scored on the database."

"Jimmy Mulroney," Cross interjected.

Rourke was unfazed. "The girl was a hooker, right? Mulroney was doing the nasty with a hooker? That's hardly news."

"Well," Cross explained, "it wouldn't be if the hooker hadn't turned up dead. But we're going to make sure it doesn't become news, okay?" He checked his watch. "You two are coming with me. We've got a meeting."

Rourke held up a hand. "Actually, boss, I'm pretty booked up today. I have to testify in the Rodriguez case this afternoon," she reminded him.

"That's okay," Cross replied. "We're going right now, and I don't think it's going to last very long."

"Okay," Rourke said reluctantly. "Who are we meeting?"

"Jimmy Mulroney."

MULRONEY'S OFFICE was at Seventeenth and Market, in one of the upper floors of Liberty Place.

The building was close to twenty years old, but Madison remembered when it was built—the first building taller than City Hall. She still thought of it as new, and in the back of her mind, part of her was still impressed.

On the way over, Cross told them that he had spoken to the commissioner earlier that morning. It was the commissioner who had arranged the meeting.

The ground rules were: Mulroney's office, no visible police identification, and absolutely no press whatsoever.

They got off the elevator on the forty-ninth floor and stepped into a waiting area overlooking the Benjamin Franklin Parkway and the Philadelphia Museum of Art. To the left was a glimpse of the Schuylkill River, and beyond that the greenery seemed to spread out for miles.

Elegantly lit cutouts in the walls held scale models of the various buildings Mulroney's company had built or financed.

"Mr. Mulroney is waiting for you," said a receptionist in an eight-hundred-dollar suit. "This way."

She led them down a wide hallway, past a glass-enclosed conference room to a smaller room with no windows.

Mulroney sat at the head of a conference table, next to a guy who looked like a lawyer, except more violent. He stood when he saw them and smiled silkily, as if he were welcoming them to poker night rather than a police meeting. Madison instantly disliked him.

"Dave, how you doing?" he asked warmly, stepping forward. He put out his hand and when Cross shook it, he pulled him close and slapped his back. Cross looked confused and uncomfortable with the familiarity.

"My goodness," Mulroney said, turning to Madison. "And this must be Maddy."

"Madison," she corrected him.

"Madison, okay. You must be very proud, Dave. A beautiful, beautiful woman. And brilliant, too, right? I think it's great that you two are working together. Just great."

He stepped back toward the table, motioning them to sit down. "Can I get you anything? Coffee? Water?"

"Coffee, please," Rourke said quickly. "Black."

Madison and Lieutenant Cross declined.

"Jeanine, can you bring us one coffee, please? Black. Are you sure you won't have anything? No?"

Almost before Mulroney's finger had slipped off the intercom button, Rourke's coffee was at her elbow.

Mulroney folded his hands on the conference table. "So, what can I do for you?" he asked.

Cross cleared his throat. "Well, a couple of days ago, two girls over at Penn were found dead in their sorority room. Looks like it might be an overdose, but we can't say for sure, so we're trying to be thorough. Turns out one of the girls might have been turning tricks. When we looked into that possibility, a sample of DNA evidence run through the database came up as matching yours." He smiled painfully. "We just want to ask you a few questions about it."

Mulroney's pleasant façade drew a little bit tighter. "This is all about whether I had sex with some college girl?"

"A dead college girl," said Rourke.

He cast his imposing gaze on Rourke, but she didn't flinch. He looked back at Cross, clearly starting to get annoyed. "Do I need to have my lawyer here? Joey here is a lawyer, but he's not my *lawyer* lawyer. Do I need to get my real lawyer here over a prostitution charge?"

"I assure you, Mr. Mulroney, we are not investigating any solicitation charges or anything of that nature."

Mulroney glanced at Joey, who stared back at him blankly.

Mulroney shrugged. "Okay, let's try this. What do you want to know?"

Cross opened his notepad. "Have you ever had sex with Ashley Munroe?"

He shook his head. "Never heard of her."

Cross took out a photo of Ashley Munroe. "Do you know this woman?"

Mulroney paused, considering his answer. "Yeah, sure I do. Her name is Brandy. I don't know her last name."

"Have you ever had sex with this woman named Brandy?"

"Why, yes. I have."

"When was the last time you had sex with Brandy?"

Mulroney thought long and hard on that one. "I guess, four or five days ago. I think it was Thursday."

"How would you characterize your relationship with Brandy?"

"Strictly professional."

"Do you know if Brandy was taking any drugs?"

He snorted. "Probably."

"Did you pay Brandy for sex?"

He looked a little annoyed. "I think I just answered that."

"Okay. How did you arrange to meet with Brandy?"

"Same way as always. I called her voice mail, she called me back."

"So you had done this before?"

He nodded slowly.

"Was it always with Brandy?"

He smiled. "Brandy was the best, but there was another girl as well. Sherry, something like that. I think it was just the two of them." He smiled again, remembering. "Sometimes we'd all hang out together."

"What does Sherry look like?"

"Sherry? Short blond hair, usually. A little thinner than Brandy. Blue eyes. Nose was a little pointy but cute. Full lips. She had great tits and a sweet little ass." He started grinning as he spoke about it.

"Anything else? Height? Weight?"

"I don't know. She got a couple of pierced things, maybe her navel or something. She's got a tattoo on her back, with a blue heart in the middle. She's about five-five, something like that. Her weight . . . I dunno, whatever is just right at five-five."

Madison leaned close to Parker and whispered, "Sounds like Beth Mowry."

Cross gave her a look, then turned back to Mulroney. "Was there anybody else?"

"What, with them?"

"Yes."

"No. It was just the two of them."

"How do you know?"

Mulroney grinned. "I asked."

"Can you think of anyone who would have wanted Brandy dead?"

"I'd say my wife would, but I'm not married anymore." He laughed. "I heard about those girls at the University of Pennsylvania, although I didn't know it was Brandy and Sherry. I also heard that the mayor wanted it to be settled quickly and with as little embarrassment as possible to the university and to the city. So I'm thinking, why are you here? Why are you in my office asking me these unpleasant questions?"

Cross looked down for a second before answering. "The commissioner has asked for a thorough investigation."

Mulroney smiled sympathetically. "Look at us. Doesn't seem like that long ago that you were walking a beat, giving me a hard time for running numbers down on Front Street. Now, here we are. Me, a successful businessman, with lots of powerful friends. You, a big-shot lieutenant, head of the crime lab with a bright future . . ." His face flashed hard. ". . . Or not."

He smiled again. "So the commissioner wants a thorough investigation, huh?" He leaned forward conspiratorially. "Commissioner wants to be mayor, too, but you know what?" He lowered his voice. "It's not going to happen." He sat back again. "At this rate, he might not even be commissioner much longer."

CHAPTER 17

IT WAS just starting to rain as they left Mulroney's building. Rourke held a newspaper over her head and Cross had his head down and his shoulders hunched, but Madison raised her face to the rain, enjoying the sensation. Cross and Rourke picked up the pace as the storm gathered momentum, but Madison covered the distance to the car with long, steady strides.

The drive back to the crime lab was quiet. Cross sat in the back, buried under the political ramifications of the situation. Neither Rourke nor Madison wanted to intrude.

"So, do you think that was worthwhile?" Rourke asked Madison through the side of her mouth.

"I think we learned some things," Madison replied quietly, trying to stay upbeat. "We know she was working—that helps Gary Swinson. We know she had a partner. That could be something, too."

Madison could feel Rourke's eyes on the side of her face. She knew that wasn't what Rourke was asking. And looking in the rearview mirror, at the deep creases on

Lieutenant Cross's forehead as he stared distantly out the window, she was wondering the same thing.

FOR A moment when they got back to the lab, Madison's optimism seemed to have been justified: The fourth batch turned up a few names. She called Rourke in and read them off: Calvert G. Thornton, Frederick H. Smith, and Wallace T. Jones.

"Do you recognize any of them?" she asked.

Hope faded as Rourke shook her head. "Nope." She looked at her watch. "Anyway, I got to get going. I'm in court today, so I'll be gone most of the afternoon." She started to leave but turned back. "Go ahead and run the rest through the database. I'll check in before I go home."

Madison had just started scanning the fifth batch into the system when Parker rushed into the lab and turned on the television.

As he flicked through the channels, he stepped sideways toward Cross's door, banging on it with the palm of his hand. "Boss! You should be watching this!"

Cross stepped out of his office as Parker cranked up the volume.

Sanchez came in from down the hallway. "What's going on?"

On the television screen, behind the anchorman's head, was a garish graphic with the words COVER-UP and MURDER stenciled over a bloodred fingerprint.

"New developments in a story we first told you about just yesterday," the anchor intoned with one eyebrow raised ominously, "involving the mysterious deaths of two students at the University of Pennsylvania. On Monday the two girls were found in their sorority room, dead from unknown causes."

As the anchor continued, the screen switched to

footage of Cross, Rourke, and Madison leaving Mulroney's office. Heads down, dodging the raindrops, almost skulking, they looked like they could be guilty of anything. With Rourke's newspaper obscuring her face, it looked like some kind of self-guided perp walk. The only face plainly visible was Madison's, inexplicably raised up to meet the rain.

"Rumors of a cover-up have swirled around the case, and police and university officials have refused to comment," he continued. "Today, the team supposedly investigating the deaths questioned prominent businessman James Mulroney, prompting increased speculation. It is unclear what involvement, if any, Mr. Mulroney has in the case."

The anchor announced that the weather was next and as they faded to a commercial, Cross slowly turned to look at Madison. So did everybody else in the room.

She put up her hands and took a step back, shaking her head. "Hey, not me. Not this time, no way."

The phone in Cross's office started to ring. He slowly walked inside and closed the door behind him. Over the next minute or so, one by one, every phone in the lab started ringing.

Madison was grateful she didn't have a phone on her desk. Her momentary relief disappeared, however, when her cell phone started ringing. The number on the display wasn't immediately recognizable.

"Madison Cross," she answered warily.

"Okay, so if we can't have dinner, how about lunch?"

"Aunt Ellie!" Madison cried with delight. "Aunt Ellie, I'm so sorry about last night, I just got buried and I wasn't expecting it and—"

"Madison," she cut her off. "It's okay. I'm married to one of them. One of you, now. I know what it's like."

"Okay."

"So, how about lunch?"

"Oh, Aunt Ellie, I don't know. This place is crazy right now, and, I . . ."

"Madison, you're allowed to have lunch. Especially at lunchtime. What are you doing right now?"

"What am I . . . ? Right now? I'm . . . Actually, right now I'm not doing anything. Everybody else is insanely busy, but I'm just sitting here."

"Well, there you go. Let's get some lunch then."

Madison laughed bitterly. "I don't know if you saw the news at noon. The problem is, they're all insane because of me."

"Actually, I did see the news. So how about lunch with a glass of wine?"

Madison looked around at the frenzy of activity around her and realized that she wouldn't be missed.

"You know what? Let's do it. Where should we meet? What time?"

"Sweetie, I'm double-parked in the lot outside. I've got the engine running."

FIVE MINUTES later, Madison was in the passenger seat of Aunt Ellie's LeBaron, hurtling down Race Street the way police lieutenants' wives do when they're in a hurry.

"Any preferences about where we go?" Ellie asked.

"Absolutely none," Madison replied.

"Great," said Ellie. "I made reservations at this Italian place on Delaware Avenue. We're actually already late." She turned to give Madison a reproachful look. "I wasn't expecting you to put up such a fight."

"Sorry, Aunt Ellie, I just—"

Ellie put up her hand. "Relax. I'm kidding."

She pulled over and handed her keys to a valet outside Ristorante La Veranda, an upscale Italian place overlooking the river. They had covered the ten blocks from the Roundhouse to the restaurant in less time than it took Madison to get downstairs to the parking lot. As they walked up the steps, it took Madison a minute or two to get her land legs back under her.

Their table had a nice view of the Delaware River and a marina. Sailboats and pleasure boats crisscrossed the paths of the tankers and tugs just outside.

The waiter approached as they sat, and Ellie asked Madison if she wanted a glass of wine.

"I'd love one," she replied, "But I don't think that would be smart."

Aunt Ellie looked disappointed. "All right. But next time let's do dinner instead of lunch. Iced tea?"

Madison nodded.

"Two iced teas," Ellie told the waiter.

Once they finally got settled, Ellie stared at her appraisingly for a moment. "You look great," she said.

"I look like shit," Madison replied.

Ellie laughed. "David's been telling me what's been going on the last couple of days. Considering that, you look great."

"So what all did he tell you?"

"Not much in the way of details; we stopped doing that a long time ago. Except for how they relate to you."

"And?"

Ellie shrugged. "Well, he told me how you've attached yourself to some case that the brass wishes would just go away. He said you're being very stubborn about it and it's causing a bit of a stir. But I know he can be pretty stubborn at times, and he knows it himself, too. He also knows you've got good instincts, you're clever, and that you're right a lot more often than you're wrong."

"Is he mad at me?"

"Is he mad at you . . . ?" She reached over and patted Madison's cheek. "Good heavens, of course not. Well, maybe just a little bit, yes." Aunt Ellie was a terrible liar. "But he knows he shouldn't be," she added quickly. "And he feels terrible about it."

The waiter came and they both ordered the chicken Caesars.

When he left, Ellie leaned forward over the table. "So, we haven't had a chance for a really good chat since you decided to move back to Philly."

Madison felt a bit like a gazelle who suddenly realized it had wandered a little too far from the rest of the pack. She knew it was coming, she knew it had to come at some point. She knew she was about to have a conversation she had been avoiding for more than a month.

"So tell me," Ellie said, pouring a splash of olive oil onto her plate. "What the hell is going on with you?"

Madison was about to reply, "What do you mean?" But she thought better of it.

"That's right, you better not ask me what I mean. You know what I mean. Now spill. What's going on?"

Madison shook her head, laughing at her aunt's forthrightness. "Honestly, Ellie, I have no idea."

She dipped a piece of bread into the olive oil on her plate and popped it into her mouth.

Madison cringed. "Oh, Ellie, I'm so sick of talking about it."

Ellie tore off an even bigger hunk of bread and dipped it in the olive oil as she swallowed the first piece. "Not to me," she said. She made a production of shoving it into her mouth, making it plain that she intended to be listening, not speaking, for the next several minutes.

"I don't know," she began. "I really don't. The thing with Doug was going nowhere. And the same thing was true with medicine. I enjoyed the lab work, but I didn't want to be stuck in a lab for the rest of my life. And as it turns out, I don't have anything close to the patience it takes to be a doctor. Even a surgeon with terrible bedside manner. I just couldn't do it. It's terrible to say it, but I just find sick people to be really depressing."

Ellie started laughing.

"No, I mean it," Madison said, starting to laugh, too.

"No," Ellie said. "It's not that. It's just that I've met your coworkers . . ." She started laughing again. "And you think *sick* people are depressing."

"Yes, they are a bunch, aren't they," Madison said, looking away.

"What?" Ellie said sharply.

Madison's head snapped back. "What do you mean, 'what?' "

"That look. I know that look. Who is it? Is it someone at work? That would explain it."

"What are you talking about?"

"Oh, my God, it's not Tommy Parker, is it?" She looked stricken. "Sweet Jesus, did nobody tell you about Tommy Parker? Not even David?"

"No, it's not Tommy Parker. And nobody would have to tell me about Tommy Parker. He makes it quite plain himself."

A knowing smile spread across Aunt Ellie's face. "Aidan Veste," she said slowly. Leeringly. "I get it."

"No!" Madison said sharply, realizing immediately that she was protesting a bit too much.

"Now that makes sense. Is that why you came here?" She leaned forward again. "Is that why you dropped Doug?"

"Ellie! No," Madison scolded. "Stop it right now."

"Maddy, Maddy, Maddy," she chided. "You know you

can't hide these things from me. Now why don't you come clean, and then I'll stop figuring out all the things you don't want me to know about."

"Okay, okay. It has absolutely nothing to do with Doug, or coming here, or anything. But yes, there is a little . . . flirt thing going on with Aidan. That's it. And that's all it's going to be. My personal life is a mess, my professional life is a mess; the last thing I need right now is to mess them both up even more by dating someone at work."

Ellie listened with a bemused smile on her face.

"Okay, I told you," Madison said. "Now stop it."

"Stop what?"

"The smile thing. The knowing everything thing. Stop it."

The waiter brought their salads, and stealing a page from Ellie's book, Madison shoveled a big forkful of lettuce and chicken into her mouth before her aunt could ask another question.

Ellie dug in almost as enthusiastically, and it occurred to Madison that she might have just been hungry.

"So how's the apartment?" Ellie asked after a few minutes of wordless salad eating.

Madison was relieved to change the subject, but she had been maintaining her "big bite" strategy of conversation avoidance, and she had too much food in her mouth to speak.

"She's an odd bird, that cousin Phyllis," Ellie continued. "Bit of a cold fish."

"The place is fine," Madison finally replied. "It's nice. A bit small, a bit impersonal, but it's nice. Great view of the bridge."

The rest of the meal was occupied by small talk and extended family news. Ellie always kept Madison up-to-date on the latest news about distant aunts, uncles, and cousins whom she had never met and did not care about. It seemed to mean a lot to her, so Madison always sat through it. She should be grateful, she thought, because without this nexus of information, she wouldn't have gotten the great deal she did on her sublet.

After the salads, they both ordered coffee but declined dessert.

The waiter took their plates and Ellie continued her exhaustive list of distant relative updates. Eventually, she trailed off.

"Have any of them seen my father?"

Ellie was completely taken aback by the question. She seemed almost as surprised as Madison, who sat back after asking it with a dazed expression on her face.

They were both silent for a second, until Madison snapped out of her daze and sat up. "I'm sorry, I didn't mean that. I don't know where that came from, Aunt Ellie."

Ellie reached over and cupped her cheek. "Sweetie, that's okay. That's a perfectly normal and, well . . . just a fine and normal question for you to ask. I was just surprised because you normally don't, that's all."

"I'm sorry."

"It's okay. Don't be sorry. I wish I had more to tell you, but I don't. There was one, actually—it was one of your cousins, Brian, I think. He's with a department down in Chester. About six months ago, he said, he was in on a bust at some roofer bar down there. Said your dad was there, but he disappeared. Brian went back after the bust, but your dad was gone."

Madison could feel her eyes welling up. There was nothing she could do to stop it, nothing she could do to stop the tears from rolling down her face.

Ellie handed her a tissue and put her hand over Madison's. "I'm sorry."

"How was he? Did he say?"

"Not good. He'd been drinking, obviously. He caused some trouble with one of the other officers down there, that's how come Brian noticed him. He said he didn't look good."

Madison nodded.

"If it helps any, I think it's really healthy that you even asked."

CHAPTER 18

WHEN MADISON got back to the crime lab, everyone was just where they'd been when she'd left, all on the phone. Apart from the take-out containers on the desks, the lab was exactly as she'd left it. No one even seemed to have noticed she had been gone.

She was starting to wonder if she should try to find something to do when her cell phone rang, for the second time that day. She probably wouldn't have recognized the ring tone if she hadn't just heard it an hour earlier.

The number on the display was unfamiliar, but she answered it anyway. "Hello?" she said, unable to keep the wariness out of her voice.

"Well, I don't know who your publicist is, but you're not paying him enough."

"Who is this?"

"Oh, I get it, now that you're famous you don't remember the little people?"

"Is this Spoons?"

He cackled thickly. "Yeah, it's me. How you holding up, kid?"

"It's all very strange."

"Yeah, I know. Us cellar dwellers don't usually see anywhere near this kind of daylight." He laughed, but he sounded a little nervous. "Speaking of strange things, there's a couple of things I've come across, thought you might want to hear about."

"Like what?"

"Well, speaking of daylight, let's meet someplace where there isn't any."

"What?"

"How about Toad's? Do you know Toad's?"

"On Eighth?"

"Meet me there in a half hour."

TOAD'S WAS a hole a couple blocks away. She remembered her dad once mentioning it to her. There were two things every cop needed to know, he told her: the places where cops liked to hang out and the places where they didn't. Sometimes, he said, you needed a place where they didn't. A place like Toad's.

Madison was surprised to find Spoons sitting on a stool near the middle of the bar—from the unease in his voice on the phone, she had expected him to be hiding in a corner booth. He grunted when she took the stool next to his, and slid a bowl of peanuts her way. A half-full bottle of beer sat in front of him, next to an empty one. He ordered two more.

"What's on your mind, Frank?"

He ate a handful of peanuts and washed them down with beer, stocking up for the exertions ahead. "We got a problem."

"Who's 'we'?"

The bartender put two more beers in front of them.

Frank took a drink before speaking. "Who's 'we'?" He laughed. "Well, *I* got a problem with *my* report. My report on *your* case."

"You mean the report you haven't finished yet? The one Cross is waiting for?"

"Yeah, that's the one." He sucked a quarter of the beer out of his new bottle. "I got no time of death."

"Kind of basic information there, but I don't think they need it to be too exact." Madison took a sip of her beer. "Everybody seems to think it was an accidental overdose, right? What does it matter exactly what time?"

He gave her a look. "Do you mean *everybody* thinks it was an accidental overdose, or everybody *else* thinks it was?"

"What do you mean?"

"I mean, you're the one who stirred up this mess. Do you still think there's something there, or should I let it go?"

"Come on, Frank, what have you got?"

He looked around nervously. "I got like six different times of death. None of it adds up."

"Go on."

"I take the body temperatures and the ambient temperature. I figure it musta took a while for the bodies to get that cool, calculate body weight, little clothing, ambient temperature, puts the time of death at around two A.M., okay?

"I check for rigor mortis, a hot room speeds it up, so I figure they musta been dead no more than an hour or two. Then I check the eyes. They're a little red, just starting to get really cloudy. They're telling me four to five hours, putting time of death at three or four A.M."

He looked down at his beer, fidgeting with it. "A lot of times, with a case like this, you just split the difference.

But this is a big difference. There's got to be a reason for it, you know? And I can't quite figure it out."

"Anything else?"

"Well . . ."

Madison looked around the bar; Frank's paranoia was rubbing off on her.

"What is it?"

"The fly eggs."

"What?"

"Fly eggs. The bodies had a decent amount on them. Especially in the big wound." He gave her a sideways look. "I thought you found her in her room."

"Window was open."

He looked dubious. "Nice night for it. Jesus. Shame they didn't have an air conditioner."

"They did, but it wasn't on."

"In this heat? Damn, they *musta* been on drugs." He thought for a moment. "But that's not all with the fly eggs."

Spoons finished his beer and ordered another one. "I'm no forensic entomologist, okay? But you do this kind of work around here, you end up doing some of that anyway. I found eleven batches of fly eggs on those two bodies. I removed them and incubated them."

Madison shot him a questioning look.

He shook his head. "Nothing elaborate. A row of jars, some medium, which I got from the back of the staff refrigerator, by the way. Anyway, in those conditions, the eggs should hatch between eight and twenty hours after they were laid. A pretty wide range, but pretty dependable."

"And?"

"And . . . none of them hatched less than seven hours after the call came in. The last ones didn't hatch until nineteen hours after the call came in."

"Which means?"

"Which means? Well, nothing means anything, absolutely, you know? But what it suggests is that the eggs
had only been laid for an hour or so when the call came
in, putting the time of death at about eight A.M."

Madison says "Unless . . ."

"Unless what?"

"Unless they *did* have the air conditioner on, but someone came in and turned it off. Would that make sense?"

"Not if it was an accidental overdose."

They sipped in silence for a moment.

"Well," Madison said as she slid off her stool. "You
tell me if you find anything else unusual, okay?"

"No sweat."

"Good."

"No, I mean it. No sweat. I swabbed the bodies and I
didn't find any sweat. I mean, a teeny tiny little bit. I know
ladies like to think they don't sweat, but it didn't get below
eighty-six degrees that night, and they were doing enough
speed that some people, myself not among them, would
argue could have killed them. But still, no sweat."

"Which means . . . ?"

He smiled impishly. "Nothing means anything, remember?"

Madison rolled her eyes. "Okay, which suggests . . . ?
Someone tampered with the scene?"

Frank put a few bills on the bar. "I said all I'm gonna
say. But that's one way of interpreting it."

CHAPTER 19

WITH EVERYTHING that was going on, Madison didn't particularly want to go back to the crime lab. She also didn't want to have to ask anybody in the unit if what she was doing was a good idea. She knew they'd say no.

That's why she was standing on the porch of Alpha Alpha Gamma, alone, taking a deep breath and ringing the bell.

Through the gauzy curtain hanging in the window, Madison could see someone moving. She heard rustling and scratching, then a click. The door opened a few inches.

The girl standing behind it looked vaguely familiar. She had a blond ponytail and a small diamond stud in her nose, and the expression on her drawn face showed vague recognition as well. Madison figured she had been one of the girls gathered in front of the house the day they had found the bodies.

"Can I help you?" the girl asked quietly. Her eyes were red rimmed with dark circles. Madison could sympathize with her—she knew what it was like being forced to deal with tragedies you weren't prepared for.

"Hi," Madison replied, her voice taking on the same volume and tone of the girl's. She held up her ID briefly. "I'm with the police. I'm looking for Donna LaMott."

The girl nodded slowly. "Right . . . You were here the day that . . ." Her voice trailed off and her eyes seemed to moisten. "Come on in."

"Thanks," Madison said, following her inside. "Were you close with them?"

The girl sniffed and looked around the house with a shrug. "Like sisters, I guess. You know?"

"How are the other girls doing?"

"It's just so sad. Everybody's sad about it. Some of the girls are taking it better than you'd think, and some worse, but we're all pretty devastated."

Another girl came down the stairs and brushed past them. She had short, very pale blond hair, cut kind of spiky, and big, dark rings under red-rimmed eyes. She gave Madison and the other girl a glare as she pushed past them and went out the front door.

"That's Valerie, Valerie Chirelli," the girl said quietly when she was gone. "She's taking it pretty hard. It's strange. I mean, she was friends with Ashley Munroe, but she seemed to be such a cold fish, I just didn't think she'd be that upset by anything. Her room is next to Ashley and Beth's room. I don't know. We're all hurting."

Madison nodded again with a sympathetic smile.

The girl swallowed. "Hold on. I'll get Donna for you."

Just inside the vestibule was a small table with a lamp, a phone, and a notebook computer on it. Beyond that was a sectional sofa arranged around an entertainment center. A large potted ivy sat in the fireplace. Even with no one occupying it, the room seemed hushed. Madison felt herself trying not to disturb the silence.

Donna LaMott's approach was announced by the soft shush of socks shuffling on a bare wood floor. She was a couple of inches shorter than Madison, with neatly cut shoulder-length blond hair held back by a black band.

She pushed a stray strand behind her ear as she walked up. "I'm Donna LaMott," she said guardedly.

Madison identified herself as being with the Philadelphia Police Crime Scene Unit. Donna's shoulders sagged when Madison said she wanted to ask her a few questions.

"You know, I've already told the police what happened, many times." She smiled regretfully. "It was kind of unpleasant, you know? So I'd really rather not go over it again."

"I know," Madison said gently. "And if it wasn't important, I wouldn't be here."

Donna closed her eyes and sighed. "All right. We can talk in my room."

She led the way up to the second floor and down a long hallway, toward the back of the house. It occurred to Madison that the house was much larger than it looked on the outside. Finally, Donna opened the door to a small, dormlike room. A computer was on with a page of text on the screen. A reading lamp cast a bright circle of light over the stack of books next to it.

"Studying for finals?" Madison asked.

"They said I don't have to, but I'd rather just do it, you know? Get it over with."

Donna sat on the edge of the bed, letting Madison have the desk chair. "What would you like to know?" she asked.

Madison took out her notepad as she sat.

The room was tidy, but an overabundance of knick-knacks gave it a vaguely claustrophobic feel. A photo on the desk caught her eye, a familiar-looking face looking out from under a head of dark hair.

"Tell me what happened," Madison said, her pen hovering over the pad.

Donna flinched, but all she said out loud was, "Okay."

She told Madison about how Beth hadn't shown up for her final painting crit, and how their professor—mistakenly thinking she and Beth were still friends—had sent Donna to go get her.

"Why did your professor think you two were friends?" Madison asked.

"We used to be."

"What happened?"

"I didn't like her new friends, or the person she was turning into . . . People change. I think it happens a lot in college, you know?"

Madison smiled. "So then what happened?"

"I walked into the room . . ."

"You just walked in?"

"Oh, no," she said quickly. "Actually, I knocked a bunch of times first. You can ask Valerie, the girl in the room next door. She finally came out and told me to go in. She basically said if I knocked one more time she was going to punch my lights out."

"Nice. Is that Valerie Shirley?"

"Chirelli. Yeah, she's a real sweetheart. Anyway, I went inside, and . . . well, that's when I saw them." She tensed up visibly. "It was . . . really bad. Do I have to go through this part again? I swear, what I told the other officers was everything I remembered about it."

"Maybe we'll skip it for now, and if we need to, we can come back to it, how's that?"

"Thanks."

"Just one question, though: Were the windows open?"

She thought for a second. "Yes. Yes, they were definitely open, because I watched a fly come in, through the holes in the screen."

"Okay, so what did you do after you found the girls?"

She smiled sheepishly. "I think I screamed for a while. Then I ran downstairs to Debra's room, and we called campus security. The security guys got there in like two minutes. I think the PR guy was there before that."

"Who's that?"

"Oh, you know, the university's PR guy, Harold or something. He gave me his card, it's somewhere." She laughed grimly. "I just found two dead bodies and I'm supposed to be worried about the university's PR problems?" Donna said sarcastically. "Right."

Madison laughed. "Oh yeah, I think I know who you mean." She was about to ask another question, but the familiar face in the photo on the desk caught her eye again. She lost her train of thought.

Stalling until she could remember what she was going to ask, she flipped to a new page in her notebook and wrote "Donna LaMott" across the top. She stared at the name for a second, her forgotten question receding further as she started to remember something else. Donna LaMott.

She looked back at the photo on the desk. "Is that Gary Swinson in that photo?"

Donna was taken off guard by the question, turning to look behind her at the photo on the desk. "Gary? Why, yes, it is. Do you know . . . ?" Her voice trailed off and her face hardened. "Is that what this is about? Gary?"

"No, that's not it at all," Madison said calmly.

"What, first you think Gary did it, now you think I killed that slut because of Gary?" She laughed bitterly. "If that's what makes me a suspect, you're going to have a lot of suspects on your hands."

"Donna . . ."

"You want suspects? You should look in that damn book of hers, get the names of all her ex-boyfriends and all their ex-girlfriends. You'll get hundreds of suspects."

"Her book?"

"Yeah, her diary, date book, phone book, whatever. Big, ugly pink thing with a big gold lock on it, like a damn twelve-year-old's. It was sitting right there on her desk, with barf all over it."

AS SHE headed up the stairs to room six, Madison came to the unpleasant realization that she needed a crime scene investigator to come with her.

Things got worse when she remembered that Rourke was testifying in another case that day. She took a deep breath and punched another number into her phone.

As the phone rang on the other end, she was half hoping he wouldn't answer and half wondering what she would do if he didn't.

But he did.

"Parker here."

"Hey, Parker. It's Madison Cross."

"Newbie? Where the hell are you? You're missing all the fun."

"I need your help."

She could almost hear the smile spreading across his face. "Oh, you do, huh?"

"Can you meet me at Alpha Alpha Gamma?"

"Alpha . . . ? Aw, Jesus. What are you doing now?"

"Look, I just need you to meet me here. Can you come now?"

"Why?

She paused. "I'll explain it all when you get there. I think someone tampered with the scene."

"Oh, goddamn it, Newbie. Get over it. Jesus! In case you don't know it, there's still a major shit storm raging over here. You need to get over it."

"Sponholz thinks so, too."

He stopped with a grunt. "All right. I'll be there in about ten minutes."

PARKER WALKED up to room six and gave Madison a wordless look by way of a greeting. She had been waiting outside the room for him, patiently resisting the urge to enter alone.

Parker slit the crime scene tape with a penknife. "I can't believe I'm getting involved in this," he muttered.

Everything inside room six looked just as they'd left it, but with the windows closed to keep out the flies, the smell was substantially worse.

Madison walked in, but Parker waited at the door.

"First, I want to know what this is all about," he said, crossing his arms.

"Frank can't come up with a time of death," she explained. "He keeps getting different estimates, very different estimates, depending on which method he uses."

Parker cocked one eyebrow skeptically.

"Using body temperature, the time of death would have been early, because they had cooled down a lot, considering the room was hot, remember? The windows were open and the AC was off. But rigor mortis puts it hours later, again, because they were in a hot room, which speeds it up. And then ocular fluids put it right about in the middle. There was some other stuff, too, but basically, none of it fits together."

"So?"

"Well." She paused. "None of it fits together unless . . ."

He watched her face. "Unless . . . ?"

"Okay, well, unless the air conditioner was on, like you'd expect it to be on a hot night like that, and then sometime after death someone came in, turned it off, and opened the windows."

Parker sucked in his bottom lip.

"Then," Madison continued, sensing she was losing him, "I talked to Donna LaMott, the girl who found the bodies."

"You did what!? Who went with you?"

Madison held up her hand and pushed forward. "Turns out she was the girlfriend of Gary Swinson, who we talked to earlier. The kid with the restraining order. She denied anything to do with it and I didn't push it, but she did say Munroe had a diary or a date book or something, big pink one with a lock on it, that she said was right on the desk when she found the bodies. Said it was sitting there with vomit all over it."

Madison slowly turned to look at the desk, which did not have a big pink diary on it.

Parker reluctantly walked in.

The vomit had dried on the desk. There was a mound of it where Munroe's mouth had been, and a smudge where it had seeped under her face. The rest of the desk was covered with papers, and the papers were spattered with mess.

Parker stood, staring at the desk for more than a minute. Madison waited patiently, impressed with the intensity of his gaze.

Parker's head tilted one way, then another. Then he grunted and raised his eyebrows.

"What?" Madison asked.

Parker thought for a moment before answering. He seemed reluctant to speak. "Well," he said finally. "This might be something." He waved his hand over a piece of paper that, to Madison's eyes, looked exactly like the rest of the ones scattered across the desk.

She turned her head the way he had, but still didn't notice anything. "What?"

Parker was frowning. "No, that's definitely not right. Look, see the other pieces of paper around this one? They're spattered more heavily, and the spatters on the other papers all seem to radiate from a spot near where her head was. This one paper, the spatters seem to be coming from a different angle, almost sideways."

Once he pointed it out, it was obvious.

Parker grunted again.

"What?" Madison asked, squinting at the desktop, trying to see what Parker was seeing now.

Again, Parker held his head at a variety of angles, studying the desk further before saying anything.

"Well . . . Look here." He drew an imaginary rectangle at a skew angle from the suspicious paper. "There's spattering under this piece of paper. You can see where it soaked through from underneath. Look, see these little spots? Where the paper is wrinkled but there's nothing on it?"

He looked at her and she nodded.

"That probably means something soaked up from underneath. And look, there's a pattern, a rectangular outline, see? Like a stencil. Inside that rectangle, there's no spattering; outside, there is, and it matches the pattern of the surrounding area."

He stared for another second. "Goddamn."

"What? What now?"

He walked around to the other side of the desk. "Right here, there's no spattering at all. Around it there's light spattering, but right here, nothing."

He walked back around to the front of the desk and shook his head. "Looks like something could have been right here, something smaller than this piece of paper. Sometime after death, or at least after the vomit, someone removed whatever was there, and replaced it with this piece of paper, which was probably over there, where there's no spattering."

He looked over at Madison. "Good job, kid."

Parker took a half dozen more photos of the desktop before he moved anything. When he was done, he dusted the top of the piece of paper, gently peeled it off the desk, and dusted the other side.

"Find anything?" Madison asked quietly.

Parker looked up. "Nope." He shook his head with a grim smile. "But that don't mean there ain't nothing there."

CHAPTER 20

BACK AT the lab, Aidan and Sanchez were both on the phone. Parker slid the evidence bag under his arm and motioned for Madison to follow his lead, walking past them quickly and quietly.

He knocked on Lieutenant Cross's door and opened it enough to poke his head in. Cross was on the phone. He looked over at Parker and Madison and slowly shook his head.

Parker immediately retreated, looking vaguely relieved. He closed the door behind them. "We'll tell him later."

He darted over to one of the auxiliary rooms and pulled Madison inside.

"Here," he said as he closed the door. "Hold this."

He handed her the evidence bag and started crisscrossing the room, opening cabinets, and pulling out trays and bottles and tools.

"We used to use something called ninhydrin to get prints from paper," he explained absently. "Stuff was a pain in the ass. Took a day or two, had to be just the right temperature, right humidity. Sucked."

With a practiced efficiency, he opened a bottle and quickly poured enough liquid to cover the bottom of the tray. "This stuff's a lot better. DFO. Quick and easy."

He pulled on a pair of exam gloves and held out a hand to Madison, motioning for her to give him the bag. He gently slid the paper out of the bag and submerged it in the fluid.

Madison watched him intently as he held it down with his fingertips for a moment, then lifted it out with tongs and clipped it onto a drying rack.

"What now?" she asked.

He shrugged. "Now?" He laughed. "Now we wait until it dries."

"And how long does that take?"

He shrugged again.

MADISON SAT impatiently in the chair next to Parker for five minutes. Ten minutes later, she retrieved a portable hair dryer from Sanchez's desk and started gently blow-drying the paper.

"What happens after this?" she asked loudly over the roar of the hair dryer.

Parker was reading a newspaper he had found somewhere. He now folded it down to reply. "Well," he shouted back, "normally, we would put it in the oven, but if you're in a hurry, I know a trick."

Madison looked at him dubiously as she waved the hair dryer back and forth. She looked back at the paper even more dubiously: Not only were there no fingerprints miraculously visible, but the traces of vomit were gone as well.

"Are you sure we're doing this right?"

"I'm always sure," he said with a wink. "Even when I'm wrong."

When the paper was dry, Parker gently slid it into a clean evidence bag.

"What now?" she asked.

"Come on," he said, tucking the bag back under his arm and leading Madison back through the crime lab and toward the elevators. Once again he kept his head down, slipping unnoticed past the desks. Madison followed his lead, unable to resist a sideways glance.

Aidan appeared to be on hold, and he caught sight of her out of the corner of his eye. He looked over, questioningly. Madison stared back blankly, not knowing how to respond. Then Aidan abruptly looked away, as if whoever had put him on hold was back. With his attention diverted, she hurried after Parker.

"Where are we going?" she asked as they left the building.

"Guy I know in Chinatown. He's helped me out before in similar situations."

"How?"

"You'll see."

They walked briskly through the parking lot and across Eighth Street to Cherry.

Cherry Street was almost the geographic center of Chinatown, but this far east, it was little more than an alleyway, consisting mainly of back entrances to the buildings that faced out onto Arch and Race.

A few of the buildings had Dumpsters on the sidewalk, and countless trickles of liquid joined to form a thin, cloudy stream into the gutter. Powered by the hot midday sun, it was more than enough to fill the street with the stench of garbage.

Madison thought it odd that Parker had been walking in silence, but she realized that for the second half of the block, he had been holding his breath.

At the end of the block, they turned right onto Ninth. Suddenly, it seemed a lot more like the Chinatown Madison remembered.

The street bustled around them: Bikes, cars, and buses all pressed against each other, moving up and down the street. The pedestrians were going at an even more frenzied pace—local residents, office workers, tourists from the nearby convention center, all moving seemingly at random, bouncing around like molecules in a hot gas. Occasionally, one would be absorbed into a storefront, replaced by another one stepping out a doorway down the street or turning the corner.

Parker joined the maelstrom without pause, crossing the street diagonally, timing his pace and gauging his angle so he could cross the street without breaking stride.

Madison felt momentarily overwhelmed and a touch claustrophobic, as everything whirled so closely around her. But her feet remembered the dance and she crossed the street just as Parker had, through the next gap in the traffic.

Her heart sank and she slowed her pace for a moment as Parker appeared to be headed for a fortune-teller's shop, but as he stepped onto the curb he adjusted his angle and darted between two old Chinese men and into a dry-cleaner's shop.

The guy behind the counter looked up as they walked in, but he didn't get out of his chair. He looked to be about sixty years old, slightly built but with a weathered toughness to his face.

"Sorry, Tommy Boy," he said when he saw Parker. "You know I can't clean your cheap clothes. You get some decent clothes, won't fall apart, you come back."

"Ha, ha," Parker replied sarcastically. "No need to get up, you lazy dog. I just need a quick press."

He waved Parker through, seeming not to notice Madison. "Maybe someday, you actually get some clothes pressed," he yelled after him. "Stop running around looking like you just get out of bed."

Parker weaved his way through the tables and machines to the back of the place, where the clothespresses were.

For the first time since they left the Roundhouse, he looked over at Madison, then did a double take, reading her expression.

"What?" he asked as he opened the evidence bag.

"What?" she said back to him.

He laughed. "Yeah, okay. Here's the thing." He slid the paper out of the envelope and placed it onto the press, then closed it. "Takes almost an hour to do this in the oven . . . but putting it in this baby," he said, opening the press, "takes ten seconds."

He pulled the paper out and held it under the light.

Looking over his shoulder, she could see two pinkish purple oval smudges. "Is that it?"

Parker flipped the paper, revealing a third mark.

"Yup. And that's a thumbprint."

"Is that usable?"

He nodded as he slid the paper back into the envelope. "Oh, yeah. Under the right light, these babies'll light up like neon."

THE LAB was still bustling when they got back. Parker wordlessly led the way to one of the auxiliary rooms.

In this case, the right light happened to be a small, handheld fluorescent wand. With a grin, he turned off the overhead lights, and the prints suddenly seemed illuminated from within.

Parker snickered at Madison's gasp.

"Yup," he said. "They came out pretty good, didn't they?"

He hooked the wand onto a stand and set up the digital camera on another. Between the two devices was a small platform, onto which he placed the prints. "Gotta try to do this pretty quick," he explained. "The longer it's been away from the heat, the dimmer the prints get. But these should come out fine."

He took a couple of shots of one side, then a couple of shots of the other. The images came up on a computer screen. He tapped a few keys, isolated the prints, and enlarged them. One by one, he clicked on each print, waiting as the computer plotted a series of points on each image.

"The system quantifies the identifiers on the print, giving them a digital value. If it comes up with a match on the database, we do a visual comparison to confirm."

By the time the last print was digitized and uploaded, the first one had found a match.

"Is it right?" Madison asked. She had to restrain herself from hopping up and down.

Parker didn't say anything. By the time he had made a visual comparison of the first match, the other two had hit, too.

"Do they match?" she demanded, poking him in the shoulder. "Who is it? Is there a name?"

Parker stopped what he was doing and turned to look at her. "Do you mind, woman?"

"Well?"

He turned back around and tapped a couple more keys on the keyboard. The printer clicked and whirred, then started printing.

"Index finger and middle finger on one side of the page," he told her, "and a partial thumb directly opposite."

He handed her the printout. "Belonging to a Frederick H. Smith."

"Frederick Smith?" Madison said, grabbing the printout.

He corrected her. "Frederick *H*. Smith."

She looked up at him. "That was one of the names that hit on the DNA search. I haven't had a chance to do anything with them."

"Let's see what we have on him," Parker said as he tapped on the keyboard. "Caucasian, fifty-three years old, last known address was . . . on Elmwood Avenue, in Narberth." He turned to Madison. "Can you get the phone book, see if there's a Frederick Smith listed on Elmwood Avenue, in Narberth?"

Madison fought the impulse to bristle at being told what to do, though she couldn't help grumbling as she searched the lab for the Narberth white pages.

"Got it," she called. "He's here. Ten-fifty-one Elmwood."

Parker thought for a second, then yelled, "Boss!"

CHAPTER 21

LIEUTENANT CROSS was still on the phone. He had his mouth open, as if he were waiting for the chance to speak. Apparently the person on the other end wasn't letting him get a word in edgewise.

Cross looked at Parker and shook his head more emphatically than before. But this time, Parker countered with an equally emphatic nod.

Cross held up one finger. He had the body language of someone about to jump into a double-Dutch jump rope. "I . . . I . . . I . . ." Finally he blurted out, "I appreciate your concern but I have to go now."

He slammed the phone down and took a breath before looking up at them. "What?" He said it in a flat tone that reserved the right to get annoyed.

"I'm pretty sure we got someone tampering with the scene at Alpha Alpha Gamma."

Cross kept his face blank. "Go on."

"Madison picked it up," Parker said.

For a second, he looked like he might smile, but he controlled himself.

"She spoke to the girl who found the bodies," Parker continued, "and the girl made reference to a date book or a diary or something. Said it had been on the Munroe girl's desk when she found them. But it was gone when we got there."

Parker explained the anomalies in the spatter marks and the fingerprints they had found. "They matched one of the DNA samples Madison got from the hamper. One 'Frederick Harold Smith.' "

Madison gasped.

"Did you say Frederick *Harold* Smith?" she asked breathlessly.

"Yeah," Parker replied. "Why?"

Madison dashed from the office and grabbed her handbag, frantically rummaging through it until she came up with the business card she had been given by the university's PR representative, the guy who Donna LaMott had said arrived almost before campus security. He had introduced himself as Harold Smith, but his business card said differently.

Madison ran back into the room and shoved the card into Parker's hand. Her eyes gleamed as he read the name aloud. "Director of External Affairs, F. Harold Smith."

BOUNCING ACROSS the uneven streets of West Philadelphia, Madison felt a twinge of excitement every time the interior of their car was splashed with red or blue light from the squad car speeding along behind them. But it paled in comparison to the excitement, the giddy pride she'd been feeling ever since Cross had smiled, clapped her on the shoulder, and said, "Excellent work, Madison."

Many times growing up, she had felt the glow of his praise; he was always generous with his support for every milestone or academic achievement. But this was different. This time he was proud of her for doing what he did. Police work.

And even more meaningful was the relief on his face when he realized they had finally caught a break. They finally had something concrete to take some of the pressure off. Even Parker seemed to have found a new respect for her. Madison's only regret was that Rourke wouldn't be there with them when they spoke to their first real suspect.

F. HAROLD Smith's office was on the sixth floor of Nichols House, a sixteen-story jumble of plain concrete blocks at the corner of Thirty-sixth and Chestnut Streets. They parked on Chestnut and marched up the concrete steps that led to the inconspicuous front entrance, Lieutenant Cross in front, followed by the two uniforms, then Madison and Parker.

The pizza place next door had an outdoor seating area. A table full of students watched lazily and chewed their pizza like cud.

The receptionist on the sixth floor seemed mildly surprised when they all stepped out of the elevator.

"We're here to see F. Harold Smith," Lieutenant Cross told her, emphasizing the first initial.

"Okay," the receptionist said slowly. "I'll tell him you're here."

She spoke quietly on the phone for a second or two, then hung up and smiled brightly. "He'll be right with you."

The two uniforms hung back, close to the wall. Smith didn't seem to notice them at first. He walked down the hallway toward Lieutenant Cross with an arrogant sneer on his face.

"This had better be important, Cross," he said impatiently. "I'm up to my ears in it trying to clean up the mess your . . . people . . . made for me." But when he saw the uniforms, he slowed down.

"Well, it's important to us, Mr. Smith," Lieutenant Cross said calmly.

The receptionist was diligently trying not to look like she was listening as Smith attempted to regain his air of superiority.

"Well," Smith said cheerfully. "Perhaps we should talk in my office."

"I was thinking perhaps we could talk in *my* office," Cross replied without moving. "If that's okay with you. We can take my car."

The receptionist was making no effort to hide the fact that she was watching them now.

Smith mustered a feeble smile. "Of course . . . Anything I can do to help."

LIEUTENANT CROSS'S face was impassive as they got on the elevator, but when they stepped off on the ground floor, his jaw tightened. Through the glass door, a local TV news crew was visible across the street, waiting for them to leave the building.

One of the uniforms said, "Oh, fuck."

Smith had regained his composure on the elevator down, but when he saw the news crew, he blanched. He hesitated for a moment, hanging back in the elevator, but then he squared his shoulders, held his head up high, and plunged forward.

As they approached the glass door, he adopted an abnormally long stride and started swinging his arms. It took Madison a moment to figure out that he was walking that way so that no one could possibly think his hands or feet were shackled. He'd probably seen the news footage of them leaving Mulroney's.

A reporter stuck a microphone in Lieutenant Cross's face, asking if the police suspected foul play in the deaths of Ashley Munroe and Beth Mowry. Cross ignored him, gently pushing the microphone out of his way.

Smith put up his hand as well, shielding himself from the camera. But then he had an even better idea. As the reporter swung the microphone toward Madison, Smith reached out and pulled it back to himself.

"Look, we're just trying to be thorough here," Smith explained, holding out his arms to include the whole group. "The university and the police department are committed to doing whatever we can to find out how this terrible accident happened, so we can prevent anything like this from happening again. Thank you."

Smith picked up his pace after he made his statement, so that he reached the car at the same moment Cross did. He put his hand on the door handle, to ensure that no police officer would be opening his door for him.

BACK AT the Roundhouse, they parked Smith in an interview room and left him alone for ten minutes to give him a chance to think about things.

Lieutenant Cross made it clear before they entered the room that even though Madison and Parker would be there with him, he would be the one asking the questions. "If you have something that needs to be said or needs to be asked, you will look at your watch and say, 'Excuse me, Lieutenant Cross, but can I have a word outside?' Are we straight on that? Not a word in front of Smith."

He said it to both of them, but Madison knew it was primarily for her benefit.

"And whatever it is you have to tell me had better be earth-shattering." He stared at them for a moment, and then pushed open the door.

Smith looked like the ten minutes had taken its toll.

"Okay," he said when they walked in. "I'm happy to help and everything, but I am very busy with everything that's going on. Can somebody please tell me what this is all about?" He'd worked up a good sweat in his time alone.

Lieutenant Cross smiled, but didn't answer. "How did you find out Ashley Munroe and Beth Mowry were dead?" he asked.

"One of the students called it in to campus security. They notified me on their way over."

"And what did you do when you heard?"

"I got over there as soon as I could."

"And what did you do when you got there?"

Smith paused with a nervous laugh. "I don't know. I waited for the security guys, I guess."

"You waited for the security guys."

"Yes, that's right."

"You didn't maybe go into the room alone?"

He shrugged. "No. I don't know. Why?"

"What did you do with Ashley Munroe's diary?"

"I have no idea what you're talking about." The sweating got worse.

"The diary. Big, ugly pink one. You know. It's got a big lock on it."

F. Harold Smith stumbled, his mouth starting several words before his brain overruled each of them one at a time.

Lieutenant Cross gave him a couple of extra seconds to stammer, then he pushed on. "We know you took the diary. Your fingerprints were on the piece of paper you put in its place."

Smith's mouth went slack as his head swiveled over to look at the wall. Just as quickly, it snapped shut, opening only briefly to say, "I want to talk to a lawyer."

Lieutenant Cross smiled. "Sure, you can talk to a lawyer, if you like. Of course, we're just talking to you about tampering with evidence. It would be a bit of a waste to bring a lawyer out just to talk about that. Maybe we could find some other things to talk to your lawyer about as well. That part's up to you. Of course, your lawyer is probably going to say something like, 'If you're not going to charge my client with anything, then you have to let him go.' "

Cross smiled again. "You know what happens then, right? I don't think the university is going to like it when their head of PR is charged with felony obstruction of justice."

Smith actually squirmed. To be fair, Madison thought, the chair he was sitting in did look uncomfortable, but she was impressed with the way Lieutenant Cross was toying with him.

Cross leaned close and lowered his voice. "Look, if you took something, now would be the time to give it back, before things get totally out of hand."

Smith slumped in his chair. "All right, I took it."

"What?"

"The diary." His head hung back. When he spoke, nothing moved except his mouth.

"Where is it?"

"In my house. I can get it for you."

"Why did you take it?"

Smith sat up a bit. "My job is to protect the image of the university. That diary could be very embarrassing."

"Embarrassing to the university."

"That's right."

Cross nodded his head, considering. "Is your name in that book?"

Smith stared at him. "No," he said without conviction.

"When did you have sex with Ashley Munroe?"

"When . . . ?"

"We found some evidence of that, too."

"But I, I used a . . ."

"Semen's not the only thing you can leave behind, you know."

"Oh, fuck," Smith moaned.

This time when he slumped, he went forward instead of back, and his head banged loudly on the table. He didn't seem to notice.

"Why don't you tell us what happened," Cross suggested, now sounding more like a priest or a counselor. "Start from the beginning."

When Smith lifted his head, his eyes were wet and his nose was running. Cross slid a box of tissues to him. He wiped his eyes and blew his nose loudly.

"Oh, fuck," he said again, shaking his head in disbelief. "I met Ashley at a school event. I was there in a professional capacity."

He laughed bitterly. "I guess she was, too. She approached me. She was smiling at me, looking in my eyes, laughing at all my jokes. Then she was putting her hand on my arm, standing right up against me. God, she was beautiful. I'll admit it, for a little while there, I thought she had somehow fallen in love with me."

He shook his head again, like he still couldn't believe what was going on. "I offered to drive her home, and as soon as we got in my car, she was all over me. I couldn't believe it. I mean, I do okay, you know? But she was . . . she was . . . I mean, have you seen her?"

He shook his head again, looking in Cross's eyes for sympathy, then finding it in Parker's. He didn't bother looking at Madison. "Then she told me it was going to cost me. And I . . . I paid her. I stopped at an ATM and then we went back to my place."

He sighed deeply. "I was disgusted with myself, but then a few days later I saw her again on campus . . . I called her that night. I've been with her maybe half a dozen times since then. I mean, I don't make a whole lot of money, you know? It's not like I can afford it, but . . ."

He fell silent.

"Harold," Cross said, waiting for Smith to make eye contact before continuing. "Why did you kill Ashley Munroe and Beth Mowry?"

Smith sat bolt upright, looking legitimately surprised and confused. "Kill? I . . . I didn't kill them . . . Wait a second, you mean you guys really do think she was murdered?" he asked, sounding shocked. "Jesus . . . I thought she OD'd."

The room was quiet except for Smith's heavy breathing. "So what happens now?" he asked.

A single vein throbbed in Cross's forehead.

"You are going to give us that diary and write a statement detailing exactly what you did in that room and with that diary, and why. You will be released on your own recognizance, and we will let you know if charges are going to be filed against you."

Smith nodded and wiped his nose.

When Cross turned to go, he looked up. "Lieutenant?" he called quietly.

Cross stopped but didn't turn around.

"Do you have any . . . political aspirations?"

Madison could see her uncle's eyes narrow.

Smith smiled grimly. "The reason I ask is, well . . . there are a lot of names in that book. You could make yourself a lot of friends . . . or a lot of enemies."

CHAPTER 22

THEY LEFT in silence. Madison felt physically ill. Although no one was saying it, they all knew that Harold Smith had nothing to do with the two girls' murders. He was just hiding evidence of the fact that he'd been paying one of the university's students for sex.

Something inside had convinced Madison it was a murder, but more and more it was looking like an unfortunate mess that just wouldn't go away. And it was all her fault.

Lieutenant Cross and the uniforms accompanied Smith to his house to get the diary. "It's still a good lead," the lieutenant said as the two groups split off.

As she got in the car with Parker, Madison stared out the window and sighed.

He looked over at her and laughed. "Don't feel too bad, Newbie. Hell, you had me believing." He shrugged. "Vaguely suspicious death . . . improper sexual contact beforehand . . . tampering with the evidence afterward . . . Who could blame you for suspecting something was up?

And hey, there *was* something going on; just not the crime we were looking for."

Madison gave him a brave, appreciative smile, but didn't say anything.

LIEUTENANT CROSS arrived back at the lab just a few minutes after they did. He walked in holding a folded white evidence bag in two hands and went straight into his office, without saying a word.

Madison and Parker sat at their desks and watched him pass by. They didn't say anything, either. The vindication Madison had felt barely an hour earlier seemed laughable now.

After a few minutes, Parker looked at his watch. It was a few minutes before noon. "Let's get this over with," he said, turning on the TV.

There had been a spectacular warehouse fire in another jurisdiction, otherwise, they might have been the lead story. As it was, they were second.

"The investigation into the mysterious deaths of two University of Pennsylvania students took another strange turn today," said the breathless reporter, standing in a picturesque campus courtyard nowhere near anything having to do with the case. "Members of the Philadelphia Police Crime Scene Unit arrived on campus and left with the university's director of communications, F. Harold Smith."

Aidan walked into the room as the television cut to the footage of them leaving the building earlier that day, with Smith in tow.

"The controversy started on Monday," the reporter's voice continued, "when University of Pennsylvania juniors Ashley Munroe and Beth Mowry were found dead in their sorority house. A cause of death has yet to be determined, but the case has been dogged by rumors that the two girls were involved in a campus prostitution ring. There have also been accusations of a cover-up." They replayed the footage from outside, this time including Smith's performance.

"It is unclear if today's development is related to the prostitution or the alleged cover-up. Stay tuned for the latest developments."

The TV cut to a commercial just as Rourke walked in from her afternoon in court. "Okay, what'd I miss?"

As Parker filled her in, Madison slowly shrank into her seat. Aidan stepped up to listen.

At least Parker was charitable, playing up the parts Madison had gotten right and casting the mistakes in an understandable light.

"She did good, though. She did," he said, as if Madison wasn't there. "Stubborn as a mule and tenacious as a pit bull. She's got a good eye."

"So where's Cross?" Rourke asked.

Parker tilted his head toward the door to Cross's office. "In there. Curled up with a good book."

Rourke raised an eyebrow.

"The girl's diary," Parker clarified. "He came in with it maybe a half hour ago, went straight in there and closed the door."

"Bet that's some good reading."

They laughed at that, then Parker went off to do some actual work.

Rourke walked by Madison. As she passed, she whispered, "Meet me in the ladies' room."

Madison glanced around, and then followed.

Rourke was examining herself in the mirror and touching up her sparse makeup. Her eyes shifted to the door when Madison walked in, but her head stayed forward until she finished with the task.

"Okay," she said, turning around. "I know it seems like I'm always saying this, but I think I need to with you, and so far as I can tell, I've been right every time. So here goes: This probably means nothing, so don't read anything into it, okay?"

"Okay," Madison said slowly. "What?"

Rourke took a deep breath. "I did some asking around at the courthouse, and I did some digging. Everyone I talked to said they'd never heard of Ivan. But some of them got really weird about it, like Kenny did."

Madison nodded.

"The other thing? I did some digging around, and I did get a name, Demetrius Ivins. That's Ivan's real name."

"Well, that's something."

"Yeah, but here's the thing. When I search his file, I'm locked out."

"What do you mean?"

"I mean, if I search for his file, it's supposed to be there. But it's not."

"Huh. And what does that mean?"

"Probably nothing, but it could mean someone is protecting him and his information."

"Why would that be?"

Rourke shook her head, noncommittally. "I don't know. Could just be a computer glitch, or an administrative error. Like I said, it's probably nothing, but I thought you should know about it."

Rourke clapped a hand on her shoulder as she left the bathroom.

MADISON RETURNED to her desk, still a little shaken by what Rourke had told her.

Aidan plopped down next to her. "Sounds like a hell of a day. Sorry I missed it."

"What?" Madison replied. "Oh. Don't be. You're lucky you weren't there."

Aidan shrugged. "It sounds like everything you did made sense; your assumptions were all valid . . . You might catch some heat for questioning LaMott on your own without telling anybody, but the rest of it is hard to argue with."

Madison thought for a moment, a furrow deepening between her eyebrows. "Wait a second. There's something else." She looked at Aidan, suddenly frantic. "Someone else was at the scene, too."

"What do you mean?"

Madison started to speak, but she was interrupted by Rourke's sarcastic voice. "Good Lord, it's the dark angel himself. What are you doing aboveground?"

Frank Sponholz stood in the entrance to the hallway.

He held up a manila envelope. "Hand delivery," he said. "Toxicology."

"No shit," said Rourke. "What'd you finally come up with?"

"MEK. Methyl ethyl ketone."

Madison screwed up her face. "The solvent? You mean they were huffing?"

"Yes, the solvent." Sponholz shrugged. "And if you mean, 'Were they squirting it into a paper bag and breathing the fumes to get high?' I don't know. I don't know what they were doing, I just know they tested positive for MEK. Maybe not enough to kill them on its own, but enough to interact with the methylphenedrine in their systems. Fatal interaction. I found a few citations in the literature, a couple with Ritalin and even a couple with this new stuff, which is surprising since it hasn't been around that long. There's already been a couple lawsuits as well." He held up the envelope again and closed his eyes, reciting, "Cause of death: heart failure due to a fatal interaction of large doses of methylphenedrine and methyl ethyl ketone."

"Finally," said Parker. "Thank God."

Rourke looked relieved, too. As Frank went to Cross's office, she looked at Madison and said, "Forget about what I told you in there. It's all academic now."

Madison shook her head. "Huffing? I didn't see any sign of that at all."

Rourke shrugged. "You don't always find everything you're looking for," she said, in a slightly patronizing tone. "There were art supplies all over that room. That stuff can be nasty."

"Don't worry about it, Newbie," Parker called out. "You found just about everything you need for a good murder investigation, except a murder."

Spoons came out of Cross's office. "Ta-ta, surface-dwellers."

Cross was right on his heels. He looked old and tired.

"Okay, everyone," he said in a quiet voice that carried. "The ME has listed a cause of death in the Munroe and Mowry investigation. A fatal interaction of high doses of the drug methylphenedrine and the solvent methyl ethyl ketone, or MEK. We're ruling the deaths accidental over-dose. The case is closed."

Madison stood up. "But, Lieutenant . . ."

Cross silenced her with his hand and went back into his office.

With a muffled curse, Madison took off after Sponholz.

"Let it go, Newbie," Parker shouted after her.

She caught up with him just as he was getting on an elevator. He let out a deep sigh when he saw her.

"Frank, what the hell was that?"

"What?"

"Those girls didn't show any sign of inhalant abuse: no

unusual redness around the eyes or mouth, no spray cans or bags lying around."

"Well, there was one thing," he said as the elevator doors opened.

"What was that?"

He smiled as the doors started to close. "They were dead."

"YOU DON'T look happy," Aidan said when Madison returned to her desk.

"I just don't believe it," she said softly.

"The MEK?"

"The whole thing."

"Overdoses do happen."

"Not like that."

Aidan didn't say anything.

"I'm serious," she went on. "It's bullshit. I've seen deaths from inhalant abuse. There's two ways it can happen. One way is over the course of a long time, as a result of chronic abuse. You know what they call the other way?"

"What's that?" Aidan said, wearily indulging her tirade.

"Sudden inhalant death syndrome. And you know why they call it that? Because it's fucking sudden, that's why. Kids who die like that are found with a bag in one hand and a tube on the ground next to them. You do it, you get high, boom; if it's going to kill you, it does it quick. You don't usually have the time to clean up afterward. Or the inclination. And maybe I didn't see it because I wasn't looking for it, but there was no sign of any paraphernalia there."

Aidan shrugged and looked away. She put her hand on his arm to bring him back.

"Look, Aidan, the reason I talked to Donna LaMott

was because Frank had said there were inconsistencies in the markers for time of death—body temp, rigor mortis, ocular indicators, fly eggs—they all pointed to different times of death."

"It's not an exact science, you know. And besides," he said slowly, choosing his words carefully, "Frank's not exactly renowned for the accuracy of his work."

She shook her head, resisting the impulse to remind him she knew more about it than he did. "What are you getting at?"

"Let's just say that for some people, pathology can be very . . . thirsty work."

She thought back to lunch, to the bottles in front of Frank at the bar.

"Look, I don't care about any of that. What Frank said makes sense. The only scenario we could come up with to reconcile the different times was if the air conditioner was on when the girls died, but then someone came in later and turned it off.

"LaMott said the windows were already open when she was there," she continued, "but she also said the diary was still on the desk."

"So?"

"So Smith took the diary *after* LaMott was there, but the windows were opened *before* she was. Someone else was in there, before Donna LaMott. Someone opened the windows, at least, and turned off the air conditioner. Maybe they cleaned up the huffing mess, too, I don't know." She looked him in the eye. "Someone other than Harold Smith tampered with that crime scene."

"Madison. Why would someone come in and open the windows?"

"Who knows? It smelled pretty awful in there."

He looked dubious.

"Seriously," she continued. "Maybe they were trying

to get rid of the smell. Or maybe . . . maybe they were trying to get rid of the MEK fumes."

He sighed heavily, looking decidedly unconvinced. "Even if someone did go in there, it's not tampering with a crime scene if there's no crime."

"Ignoring the fact that illegal drug use is a crime, what do you think happened, someone came in to borrow a cup of sugar? Didn't want to be a bother? Bullshit! If they saw what I saw, they're either screaming and calling the police, or they killed those fucking girls!"

"So what do you plan to do?" Aidan asked, keeping his voice level and low.

"I have to get back into that room before they release the crime scene." She looked him in the eye again, this time lingering. "And I'm going to need you to come with me."

CHAPTER 23

MADISON FELT a twinge of guilt as they entered room six at Alpha Alpha Gamma. She hadn't exactly batted her eyelashes to convince Aidan to come, but she hadn't been far from it, either.

He had smiled knowingly, letting her know that he knew what she trying to do, and that he wasn't falling for it.

"Well, if it means that much to you," he had said wryly.

Now he was pulling on a pair of exam gloves and looking around the room. "So what exactly are we looking for?" he asked.

"I don't exactly know." She walked over to the easel on the floor and picked up one of the tubes of yellow and orange paint sitting on the floor next to it.

"These are acrylic," she said, half to herself.

"What's that?" Aidan asked.

"The paints. They're acrylic." She turned to look at him. "That's not something you can inhale, is it? I don't

think these are the kind with lots of chemicals in them."
She unscrewed the cap and sniffed. "Barely any scent at
all . . . but you know what? When we first got here that
first day, I could definitely smell the paint."

Aidan shrugged. "Just because it's not some horren-
dous toxic oil paint, doesn't mean its not going to have
some kind of smell. Take a sample of it. Scrape some off
the canvas, too."

Madison squirted a small amount of paint from each
of the tubes into a small vial. She noticed Aidan examining the window. "Got something over there?" she asked.

"This is weird," he said.

"What's that?"

"I'm not sure. There are holes drilled into the wood
windows."

"Some kind of lock, maybe?"

"Yeah, I guess. You said you figured the air conditioner had been on, right?"

"That's what Sponholz's measurements suggested."
She started scratching at the canvas with tweezers, col-
lecting the flecks of paint in another vial. "Why?"

Aidan walked up to the air conditioner and pulled off
the front cover. "If there was MEK in the air and the air
conditioner was on, it should show up in the filter."

"Good thinking."

Aidan pulled the filter out and gently slid it into a large
evidence bag. "It looks pretty clean."

"Yeah, I think the unit's pretty new," Madison said as
she scratched more dried paint from the palette.

Aidan was quiet for a second, then he grunted audibly.

"What?" Madison asked.

"Look at this."

She came across the room and looked over his shoulder.
Aidan pulled the lever to open the air conditioner's

vent. It seemed to be disconnected from the inside of the unit. The vent didn't budge.

"It's broken," he said. "And the piece that connects the switch to the vent is missing."

"Could an air conditioner break like that?" Madison asked.

"I guess it could happen," he murmured. But he didn't sound so sure.

THE SUN angled close to the horizon as they drove between Thirtieth Street Station and the post office. The two buildings looked like Greek temples, bathed in the radiant red of the setting sun.

The Market Street Bridge took them over the Schuylkill River from West Philly to Center City. Skyscrapers loomed ahead of them, ablaze with that same fleeting light. As they drew closer, they were absorbed into the shadows, evening already filling in the spaces between the buildings.

The crime lab was empty by the time they got back, everyone else apparently gone for the evening.

Aidan set Madison up dissolving the paint samples in distilled water while he started gently rinsing the filter in a ceramic-coated bowl. He moved with a determined efficiency that suggested he didn't want to be doing this all night.

She finished quickly, and as soon as she did, she walked up and watched over his shoulder as he mixed and measured chemicals.

After less than a minute, he looked over at her with a blank expression on his face.

"Are you hungry?"

She shook her head. "No."

"Well, I am. Why don't you go buy me some dinner? That moo-shu was good the other night."

Madison didn't want to leave, and she suspected he was just trying to get her out of the way, but the guy was working late on account of her hunch. Buying some Chinese was the least she could do.

She called in their order as she walked outside, surprised to see that it was already dark out. A cool breeze came off Eighth Street, kicking up some trash, but also making the city feel fresh and alive. Madison knew the order wouldn't be ready by the time she got there, so instead of cutting up Cherry Street, she walked around to Arch.

The streets had a totally different feel compared to earlier, when she'd been with Parker. The feeling of intensity remained, but the intent behind it had changed from business to pleasure. The lights and colors were dazzling in the dark, and the summer breeze seemed to invigorate everything.

Instead of the garbage smells emanating from the Dumpsters behind the restaurants, Arch Street was awash in the smells of the Chinese food itself. Every restaurant she walked past issued forth a slightly different aroma, but they were all variations on a theme, and they all smelled delicious.

The restaurant where she had placed her order was small and not particularly clean, but the aroma from the kitchen was by far the most delectable. Madison had said she wasn't hungry, but as she waited, the smell of the food inspired an immediate grumble from her stomach.

The grumbling increased, and by the time she returned to the lab with the food ten minutes later, the rest of her insides were nervously backing away from her stomach.

Aidan had cleared a space on his desk for them to eat. He had laid out chopsticks and paper plates, and lit a Bunsen burner in the middle.

"Nice touch," Madison said as she put the food on the desk. "So, are you finished with the . . ."

He shook his head and put a finger to his lips. "Let's eat."

He opened the bag and lifted out the food, placing one spring roll and a mound of moo-shu on each of their plates.

"Eat," he said, biting his spring roll in half.

Madison took a small bite of hers and chewed. "Those are good," she said as she swallowed. "Now talk."

Aidan smiled, brushing his hands against each other. "Well, it was nice while it lasted."

She smiled back. "Yeah, we'll do it again some time, I'm sure."

"I'm going to hold you to that, you know," he said, wiping his mouth. "Okay, as with everything regarding this . . . well, not case, because the case is closed. As with everything regarding this thing, the results don't make much sense."

She folded her arms and sat upright, waiting.

"I tested the wet paint, the dry paint, and the filter. The filter was clean. The wet paint tested negative, too. The dry paint tested positive, which is weird. A fair amount of MEK—not a ridiculous amount, but I don't know how much would turn up in dry paint anyway."

Madison screwed up her face. "How could there be some in the dry paint, but not in the wet paint? Shouldn't it be the other way around?"

"You'd think. Maybe she used a fixative, or something, and it came from that. I don't know. But the thing about the filter—"

"A fixative? What's that?"

"Artists use it sometimes. It's something like a shellac, a clear coat you spray on to keep paint or charcoal or whatever in place."

Madison's eyes went wide. "A fixative. Maybe she did

use a fixative. If someone was in there afterward, they might have taken it."

"Yeah, they could have. But there's one other thing about the filter . . ."

"Why would they come and take the fixative, unless they had something to hide? Unless they had put it there in the first place." Madison's voice was growing excited.

"Well, I don't know about that," Aidan said. "But—"

They were interrupted when Lieutenant Cross walked into the lab. He seemed decidedly distracted and the white evidence bag was once again folded under his arm.

"What are you guys still doing here?" he asked, in a tone that said he expected a short answer.

Aidan caught Madison's eye, shaking his head and silently mouthing the word, "No."

"Well," Madison plunged ahead, "there's still a few things that don't add up with the sorority case, sir."

Aidan slapped his forehead.

"The sorority . . . ?" Cross let out a small, exasperated laugh. Madison know that sound—it was his "I'm out of patience" laugh. She hadn't heard it since she was a high school senior, when she got caught sneaking out of her bedroom at night. "I thought I said that case was closed."

"Yes, sir, I know. But you see, the questions that Harold Smith cleared up for us weren't really the big questions."

Cross smiled tightly. Madison remembered that look, too. It didn't bode well.

"I know you're new at this job," he said patiently, "so maybe you didn't understand. When I say the case is closed, that means we've decided we know what happened and we are not investigating anymore. So I don't want you anywhere near Alpha Alpha Gamma, okay? Do you understand now?"

Madison thought she might have caught a whiff of Scotch.

Aidan was frantically signaling her to stop.

"But—"

"See?" Cross cut her off. "There's another mistake. There are no buts."

"Except—"

"And no exceptions, either." His expression grew angrier. "Madison . . . it's been a hell of a week . . . You've been working too hard and I don't want you burning out in your first week. You're taking tomorrow off to get some rest."

She started to protest, but he put up a hand to stop her. "You're taking tomorrow off to get some rest," he said, his voice stern. "Now go home, Madison, and get some rest. Now."

He waited and watched until she gathered her things and left.

Madison stomped across the parking lot in anger. When she reached her car, she threw her handbag onto the passenger seat, where it promptly fell over and emptied onto the floor.

She let out a growl. "Perfect," she said as she slammed the door. The thought of going back to her tiny condo suddenly seemed very depressing.

For the first time since she had returned to Philadelphia, she thought about her home in Seattle. She thought about the hammock on her balcony, how she would lie in it, gently swaying, listening to the rain. She thought about Doug, about how stable and secure life had seemed with him.

"Yeah," she muttered to herself. "You fucked that up pretty well, didn't you." She slammed her hand on the wheel in disgust. She cursed again, violently, when she realized she was going the wrong way on Market Street.

She signaled and pulled into the right lane, so she could turn off and turn around.

In her rearview mirror, she saw a black SUV change lanes a half a block behind her. "Oh, great, not this again."

This time, she was more annoyed than scared. She made a right onto Tenth Street, then a left onto Arch. She circled around, going south on Eleventh. She zigged, and zagged, and looped around, all very deliberately. All the while the black SUV stayed a half a block behind her.

Whoever was following her knew what he was doing.

It occurred to her that maybe the guy was a cop. Maybe he was keeping an eye on her to make sure nothing happened. Maybe as a favor to Cross. Or even out of respect for her dad.

A chill went up her spine as she considered the possibility that maybe it was the guy who was protecting Ivan's file. Someone who was in business with him. A dirty cop.

She needed to get another look at him. She turned up the alleyway behind Jefferson Hospital and immediately pulled over and killed the lights. Let's start with the license plate, she thought.

But as the minutes passed, Madison realized the black SUV was gone.

Her mood darkened even more. "You just can't get anything right, can you?" Making a sound of disgust, she slammed the car into gear and pulled back onto the road. On the way home, she stopped at the liquor store and picked up two bottles of merlot.

Back in her apartment, Madison pulled an armchair in front of the window, next to the half-dead ficus. She drank the first bottle, watching the lights on the bridge. There had to be something she was missing. Some connection she was failing to make. Every instinct she had was telling her the two girls had been murdered. It was just a matter of pitting the pieces of evidence together.

Madison sat for hours, constructing, revising, and then discarding one idea after another. One thought in particular kept lingering in her mind.

Halfway through the second bottle, the details effortlessly falling into place, she fell asleep in her chair with a small, resolute smile on her face.

CHAPTER 24

THE CLOCK said 9:45. Madison was thirty miles west of Philadelphia on the Pennsylvania Turnpike, headed toward a town called Wardleyville. She'd decided the night before that she would spend part of her unexpected day off driving out and talking to Beth Mowry's family.

She eased off on the gas for a few miles as a few lingering second thoughts flickered in her head, but she quickly recovered. Too many things weren't adding up.

Maybe Ashley Munroe's folks didn't have any money or connections, but Beth Mowry's family was a different story. They would want to find out for sure what happened to their Beth, and that might provide just the kind of pressure Madison needed to get the investigation reopened.

Besides, she reasoned as she pressed the accelerator back down, she couldn't just do nothing.

Wardleyville was about twenty miles north of the turnpike, halfway between Philadelphia and Harrisburg. The town itself was only a few miles across, a scattering of modest ranchers and Cape Cods punctuated by the occasional small block of apartments. It all surrounded a quiet, two-block-long business district that consisted of a town hall/post office, a hardware store, a bar, and a diner with no sign out front. The town center had a distinct lack of vibrancy, suggesting that a Wal-Mart might be lurking nearby.

The whole place had the feeling of a Norman Rockwell painting, thirty years after Mr. Rockwell packed up his paints and went home.

Vincent Mowry's home address was on the outskirts of town, his business address closer to the center. Madison had planned to cruise by the house and get a clearer idea of whom she was dealing with, and then ring the bell. If he was home, she would talk to him there; if not, she would stop by the office. But by the time she pulled up at the stop sign outside the diner, her grumbling stomach had convinced her to make a detour.

The breakfast rush was over and the lunch rush was at least an hour away. The sprinkling of senior citizens lingering over their coffee seemed to be killing time more than anything else. In the back corner, a girl in her early twenties sat reading a book.

Madison obliged the sign that said SEAT YOURSELF.

She grabbed a menu and had been studying it in silence for a minute or so when she overheard an old man in a John Deere cap at the next booth say, "At least that's what he told me."

It was so out of the blue it startled her. She looked around her, but nobody else seemed the slightest bit perturbed.

Silence settled back over the diner, interrupted only by the grumbling noises from Madison's midsection. She turned her attention back to the menu, the size of her order increasing with each passing minute.

Two minutes had passed when one of the old men at the counter said, "Well, you know what he's like."

Madison's head spun around, and she saw the guy in the John Deere cap slowly nodding in response as he lifted his cup of coffee.

She realized she had walked into the middle of a very slow conversation. Or maybe the end of it, because no one spoke after that.

By the time the waitress, Marge, asked her what she'd like, Madison's order had grown to two eggs over easy, bacon, a side of scrapple, coffee, OJ, and wheat toast. Marge seemed to approve.

"I'll have that right out for you," she said with a slight country twang.

While Madison was waiting for her food, she tried to rehearse in her mind what she was going to say to Mowry, but the reality was she had no idea. In the end, she convinced herself it was best to be spontaneous. Happy to have an excuse to stop thinking, she studied the old photos hanging on the wall.

Most of the gallery was occupied by ribbon cuttings and whistle-stops and autographed headshots of helmet-haired local newscasters in plaid jackets. Mixed in were a few snapshots of the Pennsylvania Turnpike under construction, even older shots of railroad tunnels being dynamited, and photos of the area's industrial past.

One photo in particular caught Madison's eye. It looked like it was from the early seventies, a stout, robust-looking man with receding hair and glasses standing in front of a three-story, industrial-looking building. The man was smiling broadly, and across the top of the building was a sign that read MOWRY CHEMICALS in large block letters.

Marge returned with Madison's order, announcing each item proudly as she put it on the table.

"Thank you." As Marge turned to go, Madison called out, "Excuse me."

Marge turned and smiled. "Sure, what is it, hon?"

"Can you tell me who that is?" Madison asked, pointing to the man in front of Mowry Chemicals.

"That? Why, that's Mr. Mowry," she said, as if it were obvious. Which, in a way, it was.

The old guy in the John Deere hat turned around to look at her, his arm on the back of the seat between them. "That's the old boy. Roger. I was there that day, when they opened the factory."

"That was a big day in this town," Marge chimed in, nodding at the memory.

"Do you know the Mowrys?" John Deere asked, a tinge of reverence in his voice.

"Not really," Madison said. "I've met Vincent."

"So what brings you to Wardleyville?" Marge asked in a friendly tone. Everyone else in the place already had a cup of coffee, and Marge seemed appreciative of someone new to talk to. The other customers did, too, and a couple of them turned to look as they listened in.

"Actually, I'm here to see Vincent."

"Oh," Marge said brightly. "That's nice."

"Man saved this town, he did," John Deere said, nodding deliberately.

"How so?"

He adjusted his posture for a longer conversation. "Roger Mowry just about built this town. Not long after the turnpike went through. He owned a mine not too far from here. Where was that? Salisbury?"

"Strasburg," declared one of the men at the counter.

"Strasburg, that's it. Mowry just grew and grew and grew." He smiled and shook his head, thinking back, happy, then sad. "Then when Elaine died, his wife, he just kind of . . . let it go . . . The whole family took it hard, but Roger especially. Luckily, young Vincent was already working there. Within a few months, he pretty much took over the company, but the place was a mess by then. You were working there at that point, weren't you, Hank?"

"Yup." Hank got off his stool at the other end of the counter and ambled down to a closer one. "He saved the place. He did. And I don't know how he did it, either. He practically lived in that office. I know that much. He sold off some, but then he started building it back up, just like his old man."

John Deere frowned as he continued. "Roger didn't really snap out of it, either. At least not until he met Maureen a few years later."

Marge tutted her disapproval and walked away.

"What?" John Deere protested, laughing mischievously. "It's true."

"And I'll tell you," Hank confided, leaning toward Madison, "Vincent was spitting mad, too. Never forgave him, I don't think."

Madison leaned forward, raising her eyebrows questioningly.

John Deere picked the story back up. "Well, when he first came out of it, Roger regained control of the company. By that point, it was even bigger than when he left it. But he wasn't really paying attention. His heart wasn't in it and the company started suffering again."

"He was out gallivanting with that hussy," Marge said as she returned to refill Madison's coffee.

"I can't say I blame him," Hank said. "She was a fine-looking woman, and in the prime of her life and all."

"But Vincent took it hard," John Deere continued. "Part of it was watching his hard work going down the tubes, but all of the sudden he's got a new mom, not ten years older than him. A new sister to boot."

"Eventually, the old man cashed out," said Hank. "He

retired. Left the business to Vincent and traveled the globe with his bride. That man enjoyed his golden years."

Marge tutted again.

"And it was just as well he did, wasn't it?" Hank said after her, challenging her to disagree.

Marge walked away, but John Deere nodded solemnly.

"What happened?" Madison was surprised to hear herself whispering.

"Car crash. Both of them," John Deere said quietly. "He was practically dead by then anyway. Cancer," he added knowingly. "He was an old man, but she was, what, fifty-five?"

"Fifty-two," Hank said, looking down.

"That poor family," Marge chimed in, shaking her head.

Madison took a deep breath. Vincent Mowry had seemed a little uptight when she'd met him, but hearing about his past humanized him. Suddenly she empathized with all he had been through.

"Vincent was pretty broken up," John Deere said, slowly nodding.

"And some people were so mean to him," Marge added.

"Well, they loved Roger, too, you know," Hank said.

"Yeah, they've been through it," John Deere agreed.

They were quiet for a moment, until Marge smiled bravely. "But at least it's nice that the kids have patched it up."

Madison looked up at her. "The kids?"

"Vincent and his stepsister," John Deere confided. "They didn't get along so good at first."

"They hated each other," Hank added. "But they're a family now."

Madison felt terrible as she realized they still didn't know Beth was dead.

"When her mom died, I thought Elizabeth would

just . . . go away," Marge continued. "But she and Vincent have really grown close, over the last year especially."

"Yeah . . . It's true," John Deere agreed, with a hint of disbelief in his voice. "She even came home on the weekends a couple times a month, spend time with Vincent."

"They're close," Marge repeated.

"Maybe a little too close," Hank added with a snicker.

"Oh, stop," Marge scolded him. "Rich people are just different from the rest of us," she said matter-of-factly. "And besides, it's not like they were really brother and sister." She tutted to Madison. "Don't mind him, the old fool. Can I get you anything else right now?"

"No, I'm fine, thanks," Madison replied.

"Well, you make sure you come in and see us again sometime."

CHAPTER 25

VINCENT MOWRY'S house was twice the size of the next-largest house in Wardleyville. It was surrounded by a tall concrete wall, with a row of oak trees in front. The house was built of concrete and stone and couldn't seem to make up its mind whether it wanted to be modern or traditional.

The tennis courts along the side had an accumulation of leaves and other yard debris, and the garden in the western corner was a little overgrown. The place had the feel of money, but perhaps not as much money as before.

Madison stopped the car halfway up the cracked asphalt driveway, wondering if she would lose her nerve or if common sense would persuade her to turn around and go home. Neither happened.

She drove the rest of the way up the driveway, parking midway around the circle in front of the entrance, which was flanked by two large conifers in massive planters. They had a vaguely irregular, unnatural shape, almost like the house itself.

The doorbell sounded muffled and distant.

Madison was surprised when Vincent Mowry opened the door himself. She had expected a maid or a butler, or a servant of some kind.

He had on chinos and a yellow polo shirt. His arms were sinewy, but the reading glasses dangling from a chain around his neck made him look older. The effects of the past week were evident on his face, which was gaunt and deeply lined with stress and sorrow. He cocked his head slightly to one side, a faint glimmer of recognition fueling his confusion.

"Hello?"

"Hi, Mr. Mowry, my name is Madison Cross. We met at the coroner's office in Philadelphia."

Mowry took a step back. His eyes narrowed and his face grew hard. "And?"

She smiled. "I was hoping to speak to you for a moment."

"Okay," he said grimly. He opened his mouth, as if to speak, but instead sneezed explosively.

Madison tried to conceal her revulsion as she felt a cold, wet fleck of moisture land on her cheek. "Bless you," she said, wiping her cheek and trying to make it look like she was brushing back a hair.

"Thank you," Mowry said coldly, wiping his nose with a tissue. "About what?"

"Um," she stammered nervously, "about Beth?"

Mowry stared at her. "What about her?"

"The investigation has been closed," she told him. "It's been decided that Beth and Ashley's deaths will be declared accidental drug overdoses."

"Really?" He seemed taken aback.

"That's right, sir. I can't really go into detail about why, but I think there are a few too many unanswered questions to close it. I think the only reason they did was because there was so much pressure from the university."

She was hoping for some kind of response from Mowry, but all she got was a blank stare.

"I was hoping you could help, sir," she pushed on. "I believe that with a little pressure from one of the victims' families, we might be able keep it open, keep trying to find out what happened."

Mowry folded his arms and leaned back, a wry smile on his face. "I saw you on the news, didn't I?"

"You might have."

"Ms. Cross, why can't you just leave us alone? This family has been dragged through the mud. On television, people have been implying that my little sister was involved in . . . in all sorts of unseemly activities." He laughed bitterly. "I don't know what you're after, what publicity or promotion or . . . seeing yourself on TV, whatever your sick motivation is. But please, leave us alone so we can grieve in peace. Surely in a city as big as Philadelphia, you can find other tragedies to exploit. Leave ours alone."

He stood in the doorway for a moment, looking at her, waiting for a response. But she was speechless.

He nodded smugly to himself, as if his suspicions had been confirmed, and then slowly closed the door.

A HOLLOW feeling overwhelmed Madison as she drove back to Philadelphia on the turnpike. She didn't know exactly what she had expected from Mowry, but his sheer loathing and contempt took her by surprise.

Looking back, she could easily see things from his point of view, and she could understand exactly how he felt. Throughout most of her childhood, she could remember wishing her father would drop his obsession with justice, wishing he would stop spending his entire life looking

for the person who had taken her mother's life. Even as
a small child, she could vividly remember wishing he
would mourn and heal, so he could take care of her. But he
never did.

Glancing at the speedometer, she realized she'd lost
track of how fast she was going. She eased up and checked
the rearview mirror, surprised at the blotchy red face that
looked back at her, and at the fact that she'd been crying
again.

It occurred to her that she knew how Vincent Mowry
was feeling. Inside the uptight rich guy was a little boy
whose family had left him. A little boy who was alone.

The more she thought about it, the more she understood how fed up everyone felt, and the more she beat
herself up for pushing things so far.

She already knew police work was almost never neat—
there were always loose ends and leftover pieces, things
that didn't quite fit. But that was just the nature of the
game. She felt suddenly compelled to talk to her uncle, to
apologize for the way she'd been acting and promise it
wouldn't happen again. Maybe she'd even call him tonight.

Her instincts still told her something wasn't quite right,
but why she should care what her instincts told her? Her instincts had told her to throw away a perfectly nice boyfriend,
and a perfectly bright future, and where was she now?

A passing sign told her the answer: ELVERSON, PA.

THE EXPRESSWAY curved along the Schuylkill River
and into the city. On the opposite bank, Madison could
see people running, biking, rollerblading along Kelly
Drive. As Boat House Row slid by across the river, she
considered trying to enjoy the rest of her day off, maybe
go for a run. A black SUV was behind her, and she didn't
even care. She just slowed down and let it pass.

Boat House Row slipped behind her as the art museum
rose up on her left. Maybe that was what she needed—
quiet reflection in the museum's art-filled halls.

The Vine Street exit came up next, the exit that would
take her home. But before she could decide one way or
another what she wanted to do, a trio of police cars flew
off Vine Street and sped past her, their lights flashing.
"Not my problem," she said out loud. "I have the day off."
But as the expressway plunged into the semidarkness under Thirtieth Street Station, an anxious speculation about
what was going on at work took control.

The Schuylkill River and Center City were still visible
through an opening on the left, as were the old stone
bridges that spanned the river, connecting West Philly to
Center City: Market Street, Chestnut Street, Walnut
Street. Madison realized there were only a couple exits
left before the expressway would take her out of Center
City, past the airport and into New Jersey.

As she drove through the semidarkness, running out of
places to go, something in the sunlight caught her eye. On
the other side of the river, the Center City side, lights
from a cluster of police cars flashed blue and red at the
foot of the Market Street Bridge. A paramedic unit was
there, too, its lights blinking orange.

Brake lights lit up in front of her and Madison rolled
her eyes at the gapers needlessly starting a jam that could
slow traffic for half an hour or more. But then something
else caught her eye, and she tapped her brakes even harder.

Lt. David Cross.

He was standing there across the river, talking to a couple of uniforms by the freight tracks that ran along the east
bank of the Schuylkill. She quickly recognized Rourke and
Sanchez standing not far off.

The paramedic unit drove off, revealing a white sheet

draped over a figure lying partially on the train tracks. Probably some unfortunate homeless person, she thought with momentary sadness.

She stayed in the left lane, up the long ramp of the South Street exit. The traffic light at the top of the ramp turned red just as she reached it. When the light turned green, she turned left without thinking, across the river and into Center City.

"Shit," she whispered.

THE SOUTH Street Bridge took her across the river forty feet above the crime scene. After ten minutes of negotiating the maze of narrow streets and dead ends on the other side, she eventually found a little gate at the Twenty-fifth Street end of Locust Street that gave her access to the scene.

She parked a ways off, behind an ambulance and some bushes. The river was about twenty yards away, and the stone bridges arched dramatically overhead, casting thin swaths of shade. Outside of that shade, mosquitoes floated, illuminated in the hot sun. Dragonflies darted this way and that, their quickness out of place in the heat.

Lieutenant Cross was still talking to the uniforms. One of them was Rourke's friend, Eddie, whom she recognized from her first day. As she got out, she was careful to stay down low, inching closer and keeping a few people between her and her uncle.

When she was as close as she could comfortably get without revealing herself, she heard a southern drawl behind her. "How'd you find out?"

She practically jumped out of her skin, but tried to regain her dignity as she turned around.

Parker didn't seem to have noticed her reaction.

"Find out about what?" she asked nonchalantly.

He tipped his head toward the body on the tracks. "About the Chirelli girl."

Madison fought unsuccessfully to keep her eyes from bugging out. She pointed at the shrouded body. "That's Valerie Chirelli?"

Parker seemed confused. "You didn't know? Then what are you doing here?"

"What happened?"

"Shit," Parker muttered. "What are you doing here then?"

"I was driving by. I saw you guys. What happened?"

He shook his head. "She fell. Onto the tracks. Train clipped her a little, but she was already pretty dead by that point."

Madison looked up at the overpass, shielding her eyes from the sunlight. "She just fell?"

Parker shrugged. "I don't know . . . She smells like she drank a snootful of something before whatever happened happened. Could be she just pitched over."

Madison gave him a dubious look and opened her mouth to speak, but Parker silenced her with an upraised hand.

He turned to check where Lieutenant Cross was. "All right, you wanna take a peek?"

Madison stood on her toes, craning her neck to look first at Cross, then at the body, trying to calculate the likelihood that she'd be able to get over there without him noticing her.

"Yeah, but I don't want the lieutenant to see me."

Parker laughed. "Yeah, I wouldn't want him to see me if I was you, either." He straightened up and looked around.

"Lookit, you wait here, I got something up the tracks to show him anyway. See that gate up there?" He pointed to a spot about forty yards away.

She nodded.

"I'll bring him down there and make sure he stays a minute or two. When you see us up there, you go take a peek. I'll get you about a minute, maybe a minute and a half."

"You sure about this?"

Parker laughed. "Sure I'm sure. What's he gonna do, yell at me? Besides, there really is something there I want to show him."

"What is it?"

He winked at her. "I don't know, but I'll find something."

Madison ducked back as Parker walked over to where Cross was talking to Eddie and the other uniforms.

Crouching down behind a squad car, waiting for Parker to work his bullshit, she felt absolutely ridiculous. The sensation grew more intense when Eddie snuck up behind her and said, "Boo!"

He got a good laugh out of that, and as angry as she was, Madison couldn't help a begrudging snort of her own.

"Okay," she conceded, "you got me."

Eddie was still laughing. "Sorry. Parker sent me over to look out for you. It was just too easy."

"Yeah, yeah."

They took up their positions, Madison leaning against the body of the truck and Eddie watching over the hood. Luckily, the car was parked just inside the shade from the bridge, but even so, it was hot and buggy.

"So what is it about you and that fucking sorority case?" Eddie asked without looking down. "I've been hearing all sorts of shit."

"Yeah? Like what?"

"I dunno. That you won't let go of it, you're pissing people off, getting the news assholes involved, that sort of thing. What's up with that?"

"Jesus, I didn't think it would be such a big fucking deal. And I had nothing to do with the news stuff, at least not intentionally. It looked suspicious, so I thought maybe, since after all we're the *police* and everything, maybe we should look into it."

"Yeah?" He wiped his forehead with his wrist. "And how's that working out for you?"

"Well, I'm hiding from my boss because he told me to go home. I'd say that about sums it up."

Eddie laughed. "I hear you."

"So what's going on up there?"

"Parker's still making his case. The lieutenant seems reluctant to go along. Don't worry, Parker can be very persuasive."

"Let me ask you a question, then, while we're waiting. You know anything about a drug dealer named Ivan? Big, light-skinned black guy, bald, little goatee? Ring any bells?"

"Yeah, why?" His eyes narrowed as he looked down at her.

"I want to talk to him."

"What about?"

"About the case. I think he was the source of the drugs they took."

"I thought the case was closed."

"Well . . . yeah . . . it is. But now there's another body over there, right? You really think it's going to stay closed?"

Eddie laughed again. "Man, you are amazing. I know what it's like, to have the hots for a case like that, but man, you're something else."

He said it in a tone that was both impressed and derisive.

"Okay." He snapped back to attention. "They're going . . . They've stopped . . . Okay, go!"

Madison scrambled over to the body, drawing a couple

of confused looks from uniforms nearby. As she stepped across the tracks, she made sure to keep the truck between her and Cross.

She gave one last look around before kneeling down and pulling back the sheet that was covering the body.

Valerie Chirelli looked different without the scowl on her face, but it was definitely the same girl Madison had seen at Alpha Alpha Gamma.

Her mouth was slightly open, like she had just thought of something she wanted to say. Her head lay back a little bit further than it should have, as if it were resting in a slight depression. But the depression wasn't in the ground, it was in the back of her head, where her skull had been flattened by the impact. A small pool of blood had collected around her, and there were trickles of it coming out of her nose and ear.

A couple of flies tried to land on the body as soon as it was uncovered. Madison waved them away.

Parker walked up and knelt down next to her.

"Where's the lieutenant?"

"It's okay. He's over there by the gate. I sent Eddie over to keep him occupied. But I wouldn't hang out too long. Eddie don't have quite my flair."

"Well, who does?"

"Finally, you understand." He grinned.

Madison looked up at the bridge overhead. "What's that, about thirty feet?"

"Little more."

"Ouch."

"Psh." Parker stifled a chuckle. "You want to talk about ouch?" He lifted the sheet some more, revealing one of Chirelli's legs. It was crudely severed where it had crossed the track, about six inches above the ankle. There was surprisingly little blood, even though the wound was a jagged mass of shredded, bloody flesh and bone.

Madison suppressed a shudder, waving again at the flies.

"Yeah, I know," Parker said. "She didn't feel it, though; she was already dead by then."

Madison nodded. "By the looks of it, at least a couple hours."

"I doubt she felt any of it," Rourke said, suddenly standing over them. "And what are you doing here, anyway? Thought you were taking the day off."

Madison looked up at her, squinting in the light. "What do you mean you doubt she felt any of it?"

Rourke stuck her nose in the air and sniffed. "That ain't petunias you're smelling."

The air was thick with that unique mixture of metal, oil, dust, creosote, and ozone that was always present around the rails. To Madison, it had always been a nostalgic, old-fashioned smell. Even when she was a child, it had evoked the past.

She sniffed the air the way Rourke had pretended to, and suddenly she recognized another smell in the background—another smell that reminded her of the past. She bent closer to the body and the smell grew stronger. Vodka, and lots of it, filtered through the stomach, liver, and skin of Chirelli's body.

"Hey, girl," Sanchez said, now standing next to them as well. "I thought you would be down in Atlantic City, or something. Someone says you got a day off, you need to take it."

Madison started to respond, but Parker cut them all off. "Oh, fuck, here comes Cross!"

Rourke and Sanchez spun on the heels, walking in opposite directions. Parker headed straight for the lieutenant, deflecting him, diverting his attention, pointing left, right, up, down; every direction except where Madison was now crouching, back behind the front wheel of the squad car.

As Parker harangued the lieutenant, a pair of morgue attendants lifted Valerie Chirelli into a body bag. They looked over at Madison, then at each other, shrugging as they zipped the bag closed and loaded it onto a gurney. The wheels dropped down as they hoisted it, and they rolled the morbid package over the bumpy terrain toward the ambulance.

Parker seemed to have successfully coaxed Lieutenant Cross away from Madison's hiding place. As they headed off down the railroad track, he smiled furtively over his shoulder.

Madison realized with dismay that the shade from the bridge was slowly sliding upriver, away from her. Five minutes later, she had lost it entirely. She took a deep breath; she had to get out of the stifling heat. Over the hood of the cruiser, she could see her car, a long twenty yards away. An ambulance was parked midway between them. If she used that as cover, Madison figured she could make it.

She coiled her legs underneath her, balancing on the balls of her feet, but just as she sprang out of her crouch, the taillights of the ambulance lit up. She was almost halfway to it when it abruptly pulled away, leaving her exposed except for the gravel and dust it kicked up.

She froze. Parker and the lieutenant were returning, the lieutenant fortunately looking down. Parker, though, was staring right at her, his eyes showing white on all sides.

Before the small cloud of dust had settled, Madison was back behind the squad car, breathing heavily and cursing quietly but enthusiastically.

To her chagrin, as her breath quieted down, the sound of voices grew louder. Parker and the lieutenant were right on the other side of the squad car.

Cross was giving Parker hell for getting distracted on the job, showing him a bunch of stuff that had nothing to do with the body, which had obviously just fallen from the bridge.

Parker laughed nervously, responding with vague aphorisms about how you never know for sure. "Hot as a bitch, ain't it?"

"Yes, it is," Lieutenant Cross said dismissively. "Anyway, we're just about done here."

"Yup," Parker replied quickly. "You headed back to the lab, then?"

"No, you go ahead. I'm going to make sure they wrap up right, maybe have another walk around the perimeter, see if any of this bullshit you've been talking about starts to make sense."

Madison slumped to the ground, her back against the car. She was screwed. Cross was going to find her, directly disobeying orders, and to make matters worse, hiding behind a squad car like a high school kid.

She was so dejected, when her cell phone sounded, it took two rings before she managed to turn the ringer off. She cursed silently, hugging the phone to her chest and trying to curl herself into an even tighter ball.

"Is that your phone?" Lieutenant Cross asked Parker.

"Ah . . . um . . ." Parker stammered. "It might have been. I didn't hear anything."

"You sure you're okay?"

Parker laughed. "Hell, I've never been sure of that."

The lieutenant said something else after that, but thankfully they seemed to be walking away. Through the cruiser's window, she could see they were headed back to Parker's vehicle.

"Fuck," she cursed with a mixture of self-reproach and relief. She looked at her cell phone—Spoons had called. Peeking through the window again, she saw Parker and Cross were now fifty feet away, and hit reply.

"Sponholz," he answered.

"It's Madison. Did you call me?"

"Where are you?"

"Why?"

"You got sent home, huh?"

"Yes, I'm in the doghouse. What's going on?"

"You know they brought this girl in?"

"Are you talking about Valerie Chirelli? Yeah, I know."

"Bit of a coincidence, don't you think?"

"What's that?"

"I don't know. Girl lived in the room next to Mowry and Munroe, now she turns up dead. Accidentally, of course, but still."

"What are you saying?"

"Well, I heard you had the day off, unexpectedly. I'm a little shorthanded here today. I figured if you wanted to come down and help me with the autopsy, maybe we could move Ms. Chirelli to the front of the line."

Madison sighed, exasperated. "You know I would, Spoons, but I'm kind of in the middle of something."

"Hey, no problem," he said, sounding defensive. "I just figured, since you got such a hard-on about this case, you know . . ."

"I would, Frank, really, it's just . . ." Her voice trailed off when she noticed the pair of black oxfords on the ground in front of her. She looked up to see Eddie grinning down at her. "Hold on." She put her hand over the phone. "Can't you see I'm on the phone?" she said facetiously.

Eddie laughed. "You got to get the fuck out of here. And I need to take your little hideout back on the road. Can I give you a lift?"

"Thank God, yes. My car's right there," she said, pointing.

Eddie opened the back door. "Get in. And keep your head down low."

Madison held the phone to her ear. "Okay, Spoons. I'll be there in ten minutes."

Eddie didn't stop snickering until they pulled up next to Madison's car twenty yards away.

"Okay," he said, turning halfway around to talk to her. "Your car is right there." He pointed out the passenger window. "The lieutenant is twenty yards over there." He hooked his thumb out the driver's side window. "I'll wait here until you pull away, but keep your head down until you get through that gate, okay?"

Madison released the door and pushed it open with her feet. "Thanks, Eddie."

"No problem." He laughed again. "But, Cross?"

"Yeah?"

"No more stupid shit, okay?"

CHAPTER 26

VALERIE CHIRELLI was lying naked on the metal table. The sheet covering her had been pulled down to her knees, and a plastic block had been placed under her back, thrusting her chest out for easier access to the organs inside.

Madison was struck by the paradoxical vulnerability and haughty indifference of the naked dead. Valerie Chirelli was helpless to conceal herself, lying there on the slab. But on the other hand, she certainly didn't seem to care.

Her hair was short and bleached a yellowy-white blond. Even though her face was vaguely misshapen, it was still obvious that she had been beautiful—not like Ashley Munroe, but close. She had a very straight nose, a faintly pointy chin, and just enough of an overbite that it might have made her even more attractive.

Her fingers were bare except for the marks where her rings had been, but a diamond stud was still in her nose and a silver hoop was still in her navel. Valerie Chirelli's last ties to the physical world, Madison thought as she removed them. Or just cheap jewelry on a cadaver.

Spoons was still lining up his instruments. She thought she caught a whiff of stale beer coming off him, but he didn't seem impaired in any way. She decided just to let it go.

"So what does it look like?" she asked.

Spoons pulled the sheet back the rest of the way, revealing the oddly bloodless wound that tore through Chirelli's shin. The bottom portion of her leg was lying there in place, but it had rolled to the side, at an angle that would have been impossible had it still been attached.

Her skin was mottled with small bruises, but there were also a couple of big ones: one across the abdomen, one under the ribs. In fact, her back looked like one big bruise. Madison knew that was mostly the effect of the blood settling after she had died, but could that account for all of it?

"What does it look like?" he parroted back to her.

Spoons cupped his chin in his hand for a moment, deciding whether or not to play along. "Well . . . she fell," he stated simply.

Madison shot him a look.

"Okay, okay. The fall killed her," he elaborated. "Looks like she landed on the tracks. Train came and took the foot off, but that was a while after she died. The train engineer's the one that found her. He was a mess."

"This bruise under the ribs here," she said, indicating with her hand. "It's just about the same height as the railing on the bridge, where she would have hit if she was pushed, right? If there's bruising on the other side, they can't both be from impact, can they? Unless she totally flipped over? Think she was pushed?"

He shrugged. "Coulda been. Who knows how she tumbled on the way down, or when she hit. Plus, the smell of the vodka coming off her is so strong, it's starting to make me feel fucking wobbly. Who knows what bruises she picked up before she even fell?"

Madison nodded, bending down for a closer look, getting a stronger whiff in the bargain. Maybe Chirelli was the source of the stale beer smell, as well.

She had a large bruise on the side of her head, spreading out from under her hairline. The hair on the back of her collapsed head was caked with blood, and a small amount had trickled out of her left ear. Her dark pubic hair was trimmed to a small, neat triangle.

Madison spotted something on Chirelli's thigh and leaned in to examine it. "Huh. Look at that."

Spoons came closer. "What?"

Madison moved the left leg over and pulled the flesh of the right thigh up, so it was more visible.

"That's the same tattoo Munroe had. Same place." She looked up at Spoons.

"You think that means something?" he asked with an indulgent smile.

"It could."

His smile turned sympathetic. "I know you're a lot closer to her age than I am, but I think you forget how fads spread and die out on campus. Just cause these two got the same Smurf on them don't mean a fucking thing. There's probably two hundred other girls on campus with the same tat, and in a month they'll have forgotten what it was about."

"Yeah, but it's a permanent tattoo."

Spoons laughed. "Showing the same sound judgment as when they decided to take enough of some seventh grader's prescription to make them barf and die. You'll go crazy trying to find good reasons for any of this."

Madison wasn't satisfied.

"Look, you ever seen one of those *Girls Gone Wild* videos?" he asked.

She snorted.

"Okay, the commercials, you know what I mean. Those girls aren't stupid, not really, they're just acting stupid. They're just of an age when they do stupid things. Hell, you look at what happens to some girls"—he gestured toward the body of Valerie Chirelli—"makes them girls gone wild look downright smart."

He rested his hands on his hips. "Come on. Let's get to work."

Madison nodded and put on her cap. As she was tying on her smock, a buzzer on the wall sounded.

Sponholz huffed and pressed a button with his elbow. "What?"

A staticky female voice announced that the Chirelli family was here to identify their daughter.

"Now?" Sponholz said, exasperated. "Okay, give us a minute." He turned to Madison. "You can help me with this." He wet a paper towel under the faucet and handed it to her. "See if you can get rid of some of the blood on her face."

While Madison dabbed at the blood, Sponholz tightly twisted a towel and curled it around her head, hiding the deformity where her skull had shattered.

He leaned back and appraised their efforts. "Okay," he said, "now take off your hat and smock and help me get these tools out of the way."

VALERIE CHIRELLI'S parents didn't look much like Valerie Chirelli. Her father was dark and hairy, with an enormous stomach that stretched his stained Phillies

T-shirt and caused the waistband of his sweatpants to fold over at least twice.

Mrs. Chirelli was even heavier, but her weight was concentrated in pockets under her chin and above her elbows. The rest of her was hidden under a flowing, tentlike flowered shirt.

Both of them had extremely large noses: hers hooked upward, his curved down. Apparently they were genetically different enough to have canceled each other out.

They seemed sad, but also angry in a dull sort of way.

Spoons looked duly somber as he greeted them. "Hello, Mr. and Mrs. Chirelli," he murmured. "Thank you for coming down today."

Madison smiled sympathetically.

The Chirellis nodded, their eyes nervously darting about.

"This way," Spoons said, leading them to the table where Valerie lay covered.

"All right," he said, "you just have to tell me if this is Valerie, okay?"

They both nodded again.

He drew back the sheet and folded it over Valerie's collarbone.

They both looked slightly confused. Mrs. Chirelli tsked and Mr. Chirelli let out a long, loud sigh. They looked at each other solemnly before either spoke. "She looks different, don't she?" Mrs. Chirelli said.

Mr. Chirelli's face hardened. "Well, she is different, ain't she?"

"Is this your daughter?" Spoons asked.

They looked at each other again, shrugging and nodding at the same time.

"I think so, yeah," Mr. Chirelli said. "But she looks different, you know?"

"People do often look different after . . ." Spoons's voice trailed off.

"How does she look different?" Madison prodded.

"Well, I'm not used to seeing her blond," her mother said. "And she's so skinny, isn't she? Her face looks different." Her husband nodded. "And her eyebrows look different."

"She changed," he said hoarsely. He put his hand on the back of his head and then slid it down to his neck. "All that stuff they was saying on TV . . ."

"When was the last time you saw her?" Madison asked.

"It's been a while," Mrs. Chirelli whispered.

Mr. Chirelli looked down. "I think it was right before Thanksgiving . . . She came home for one day."

"Are you sure this is Valerie Chirelli?" Sponholz asked.

They nodded. "Yes," said Mr. Chirelli. "She's changed, but it's her."

CHAPTER 27

WHEN SPOONS returned from seeing the Chirellis out, he gave Madison a look.

"What?" she asked as she pulled on her gloves.

"I think I'm more upset about this kid than her folks," he replied. "And I don't really even give a shit."

"They didn't seem the touchy-feely type, did they? But they're hurting."

"I guess." He shook his head and exhaled loudly, rubbing his hands together. "Oh, well. Back to business. Now, this one came in as an accidental death. But I thought, you know, since you're all invested and everything, you might want to check her out. You can collect anything you find before we start slicing and dicing."

"Right. Thanks," she said, suddenly feeling extremely self-conscious as Spoons stepped back and waited for her to get started.

In medical school and her internships, she had performed dozens of autopsies, but this was the first time she was specifically looking for a suspicious cause of death.

She had to resist the urge to start cutting in search of a pulmonary embolism or some other common fatal body malfunction. Still, she had a lot more experience in autopsies than in criminal investigations. What did she have to lose?

She looked in Valerie Chirelli's cloudy eyes. The right pupil was blown, completely dilated, a thin ribbon of blue surrounding a large disc of black. When Madison shone her penlight into it, she could see the fluid in the eye was mixed with blood.

The hands didn't have jagged, broken fingernails, or any other signs of struggle, but they weren't clean, either, so Madison took cuttings, just in case. She turned to ask Spoons for a small specimen bag, but he was already holding one out for her.

"Thank you," she said as she placed the nail cuttings inside.

Spoons just smiled.

Madison was suddenly blank about what else to do before cutting. She stared at the body, but nothing came to mind. When she turned to admit to Spoons that she was stumped, she saw him holding the camera. Of course.

She smiled nonchalantly.

He smiled back, making it plain he knew she had forgotten.

Madison took pictures from as many angles as possible. Frank's expression went from blank, to approving, to confused, to bemused as he watched her take dozens and dozens of exposures.

When she had taken a shot from every angle she could think of, she stopped and took a step back.

"All done now?" Frank asked, a cherubic smile on his face.

Madison shot him an acid glare.

He pulled a six-inch ruler out of his shirt pocket and held it out to her.

"For the close-ups," he explained. "The bruises and the leg wound. Gotta know how big they are."

With a sigh, Madison resumed taking pictures. She lay the ruler down next to the amputated leg and took a few, then a few more with the ruler leaning up against the leg. Next, she removed the foot completely and took some shots of the stump, then some more of the foot alone with the ruler.

Frank started laughing. "Jesus, you got enough frames there to make a freakin' Gumby movie. You want, I can go get a movie camera, might make it easier."

Madison gave him a dirty look. "I'm just trying to be thorough. But I guess I'm done then."

"All right," Spoons said with a throaty laugh. "Do me a favor, though, before you put that thing away, get a close up of that nose thing, the belly button thing, and the tattoos on her thigh and on her back."

Madison put the ruler next to the nose ring and took a picture, then did the same with the navel ring and the tattoo on her thigh.

"Frank," she called. "Can you help me turn her a bit so I can get a picture of her back?"

Frank put a hand under one shoulder and lifted the body to one side.

Madison lifted the camera to her eye, then lowered it. "Oh, shit."

"Take the picture," Frank reminded her.

She quickly snapped a couple of shots, and Spoons lowered the body.

"Okay, now what's the matter?"

"That tattoo. When we questioned Mulroney about Ashley Munroe, he said there was another girl that sometimes worked with Ashley, called herself Sherry. Sometimes he was with the other girl instead of Ashley, or sometimes with the both of them."

"Wish I had his problems."

"The way he described her, it sounded like Beth Mowry, but he said she had a tattoo, a blue heart, right at the small of her back, just like that one."

"They do look alike."

She looked over at him. "Sherry, Chirelli. Chirelli was the other girl."

Spoons nodded, impressed. "No shit." He had two plastic face shields in his hand.

Madison started frantically untying her smock.

"What are you doing?" Spoons asked.

"This changes everything. I got to go talk to Parker and Rourke."

"Not now you don't."

She stopped and looked at him, confused. "What do you mean?"

"I mean, I said I needed help here, and that if you wanted to, you could participate in the autopsy. You came here to help me with the autopsy. That was the price of admission." The irritation in his voice was unmistakable. "And by the sounds of it, you got your ticket's worth."

"But . . ."

His glare cut her off. She eyed the door and considered trying to make a break for it. "Don't even think about it. I'm faster than I look."

"Oh, come on, Spoons."

He ignored her entreaty, instead wheeling over the tray of instruments he had assembled for the autopsy. He placed her face shield on the tray. When she looked back up at him, he was holding up a scalpel for her to use.

With a sigh, she took the knife and turned to Valerie Chirelli.

Judging from the blown pupil, she had been alive when she fell. The cause of death was the massive blunt force trauma to the back of the head. The instrument that caused the injury was the planet she'd been born on, gravity, and an unfortunately speedy transition from potential energy to actual energy.

But the autopsy was legally mandated, and Madison had said she would help. Besides, after all the fuss she had made about not closing the case on Mowry and Munroe, it would be a little hypocritical if she rushed it now.

She moved the tray back a bit from the body, adjusted the lights, and took a good, long look at Valerie Chirelli.

The first cut in any procedure always made Madison uneasy. It wasn't that she was squeamish—it just somehow seemed rude. Intellectually, she knew she was doing whatever she was doing to help the person in some way, whether trying to help them get healthy or trying to solve the mystery of what killed them.

But emotionally, in this case, she couldn't help feeling she was just desecrating the dead.

And, even though she and Valerie Chirelli had never even exchanged words, the fact that Madison felt like she kind of knew her made it even worse. She had never operated on anyone she knew, much less performed an autopsy on them.

But there she was . . . knife in hand . . . about to stab a naked, one-legged girl. And Spoons was getting impatient.

With a deep breath and a silent apology, Madison plunged the knife into Valerie Chirelli's chest just below the sternum. She nodded as she felt the scalpel cut through the skin, muscle, and connective tissues. She cut lower, toward the pelvis, detouring around the navel and stopping a few inches south of it.

There was virtually no blood.

She made two cuts across the chest, from the front of each shoulder to where the first incision started, below the sternum. She sliced in an arc so as to avoid the breasts.

She paused for a moment, confronted by those parts of

Valerie's anatomy. They were flawless and upright. Madison felt a twinge sadness over the waste of beauty and youth in front of her, in life as well as in death.

Shaking her head, she began cutting away the connections underneath the skin and muscle, creating flaps that she then pulled back, exposing the rib cage.

Madison stepped back for a moment, taking a breath and looking at the work she had done. It had been relatively easy going until that point, but now the hard labor was about to begin. It might have been easier on the psyche to work with something that no longer looked like a person; physically, it was even more demanding.

Spoons wordlessly handed her the rib cutters, a pair of stainless-steel shears. Madison widened her stance and started snapping ribs. She worked her way up one side of the rib cage and down the other. When she was three-quarters of the way done, she stopped and looked over at him.

He was eating an apple.

"I didn't have time for lunch," he said, his mouth full.

Madison made a face and returned to the task at hand. When she was finished cutting, she was left with a butterfly-shaped chest plate resting on top of Chirelli's lungs.

"Here, give me a hand with this," she said.

Luckily, Spoons had finished his apple. She didn't like the thought of him putting down his snack to help, and then picking it back up again.

Together, they raised the chest plate. Madison had to cut away some remaining soft tissue, but then they lifted it completely up and off, revealing the organs underneath.

Spoons placed it on the table behind him. "Okay," he said, turning back to her. "So, you know what you're doing here, right?"

"Why? Where are you going?"

He gave her a wink. "Paperwork, my sweet." He turned away and called over his shoulder, "I'll be back in a few. Don't start the head without me. That can get kind of dicey."

With a sigh, Madison got back to work. She sliced through the larynx and the esophagus, cutting away the connecting tissues as she pulled them away from the body.

Slicing through the diaphragm, she continued gently pulling the organs away from the body cavity, until she had one long tangle of insides, still connected to the rest of the body by a few ligaments, and the ends of the digestive tract, the rectum and bladder.

A few economical flicks of the scalpel disconnected the entire mass of organs from the shell that used to be Valerie Chirelli.

Madison carried the bundle over to the dissecting table. "If he thinks I'm dissecting all these, he's nuts," she muttered.

"Chatting away already, are you?" Spoons asked from another room. "Most times it takes a week or so before they start talking to the stiffs. You must have a natural affinity."

"I'll help you with the head," she told him, "but I'm not dissecting all the organs."

"Fair enough." He pulled the plastic block out from under the trunk. He gently eased it under the back of the head, then added a folded towel in order to achieve the right elevation. When the head was correctly positioned, he wheeled over another cart of instruments, including an electric vibrating saw.

Madison picked up the scalpel again and made a single deep incision across the top of the head from ear to ear. She grabbed a handful of hair from the front of the

head and pulled hard. The front part of the scalp slid forward an inch or two, but soon Madison realized she had
to readjust her grip. She slipped a couple of gloved fingers under the scalp in order to coax that portion of it
loose, so she could drape it forward over the face.

Underneath, the skull glistened under a sheen of blood.

"Now comes the fun part," Spoons said grimly.

Madison grabbed a chunk of hair from the opposite side
of the incision and pulled backward. The scalp pulled off
easily. Without the front half holding it in place, it basically fell off on its own.

A slurry of blood, brains, shards of skull, and cranial
fluid sloshed out and onto the table.

"Think maybe we found the cause of death?" Spoons
asked.

"That would definitely slow you down." Madison
picked up the electric saw, but Spoons put his hand out to
stop her.

"Better let me. It's going to be a mess, and I don't want
you getting all bent out of shape, thinking you fucked it
up."

He switched on the saw, which gave off a vaguely angry buzzing whine. The sound deepened in tone as he
touched it to the front of the skull. He started working
slowly around to the back, proceeding steadily until the
buzz increased in pitch and started wavering. As a few
small fragments of skull tumbled down onto the table,
Spoons pulled the saw away.

Returning to the middle, he started cutting around to the
other side, stopping once again when the tone changed.

He put the saw back on the table and looked over at
Madison. "Usually I'd cut all the way around, but this is a
mess back here. It's too compromised to cut through."

He wiggled his fingers like a safe cracker, placing his
hands on either side of the skull. But before he could touch

it, the shiny top shifted, sliding backward slightly. Spoons paused, then moved to readjust his angle.

Just as he was about to touch it again, the top of the skull slid off completely and did a half roll before toppling over, slowly spinning a couple inches away.

Spoons grinned. "Is this a great job or what?"

CHAPTER 28

MADISON HELPED remove what was left of the brain, and pitched in with the weighing of the organs, but she left the dissection of the organs to Spoons. She'd been at the ME's office a little over two hours. Now she hurried back to the crime lab.

"Jesus," Parker said when she walked in. "You don't know when to quit, do you?"

Aidan got up from his desk. "Madison, you keep this up and you're going to really piss him off."

She ignored both comments. "You remember when we were talking to Mulroney? He said there was another girl working with Ashley Munroe, remember?"

"Yeah," Parker replied warily.

"Well, I just helped Frank with the autopsy on Valerie Chirelli, and I'm pretty sure she's the second call girl, not Mowry. Valerie Chirelli was Munroe's partner in crime."

Parker rolled his eyes.

"Why?" Aidan asked.

"Well, she totally matches the description, moreso than

Mowry. She had that same little gnome tattoo, same place on her thigh, whatever that means, but she had another tattoo, as well, the one Mulroney described. A little blue heart, right in the small of her back, just like he said."

Aidan started to protest when he noticed Parker slowly nodding his head and rubbing his forehead thoughtfully.

"He's going to kill her if he sees her here," Aidan continued."

"Oh, I know that much." Parker laughed. "But you gotta admit, that's interesting information."

Aidan turned to Madison. "Then bring it up on Monday, okay? You're not going to talk him into anything today anyway. All your going to do is work your way up a few spaces on his shit list."

She turned to Parker. "It sounded like Mulroney was describing Mowry, but she doesn't have a tattoo on her back. I went back and looked. If this is the other girl, and now she's turned up dead just a few days later, it looks a hell of a lot more suspicious, doesn't it?"

"Madison, listen," Aidan pleaded. "Cross is up against it right now. He's getting it from all sides. There's incredible pressure to wrap this up, quickly and cleanly. It's too late for quick or clean, but the longer it drags on, the worse it's going to be for him."

Parker nodded thoughtfully. "He's right, you know. And it's not just the lieutenant's career you should be worrying about. There's some people in high places with very long memories. I don't know how long you plan on sticking around here, or if this is just a semester abroad for you or something, but shit like this could stick to you for a long, long time."

"So what? That means you let some John in that little pink book get away with murder? Because he's got powerful friends? *Three* murders, for Christ's sake? Jesus!"

"It's a shame the department's like that but he's right. It is," Aidan said, slightly cowed.

But Parker looked more amused than anything else. "Hell, in the long term, eating shit like this is an integral part of the job."

Madison put her hands on either side of her face. "I have a feeling that in the long term I'm not going to have this job."

"Madison," Lieutenant Cross's voice, weary and disappointed, rang from across the room. "I need to speak to you in my office."

As she walked in, she could see that he was already shaking his head. "What the hell are you doing here?"

"Sponholz called. He said he was short staffed. Needed some help."

"Yeah? Was that before or after you visited Munroe's brother?"

She hadn't counted on him finding out about that so quickly.

"Madison, I know this is all new to you, but did you really think lobbying the dead girl's family behind my back was an appropriate way to approach things?"

The way he said it made it hard to defend. "That girl they found today," she said quietly. "That was the other girl Mulroney talked about."

"I don't care."

"She matched the description exactly," she said a bit louder. "She even has the tattoo with a blue heart on her back."

He closed his eyes. "I don't care."

"Look," she continued, "I was ready to let it go, I was. A lot of things didn't add up, a lot of things didn't make sense. People tampered with the scene, people lied, the physical evidence contradicted itself, but okay, case closed, fine. I didn't like it at first."

Madison could feel her voice getting louder, but she couldn't seem to get it under control. "But now, another girl is dead, Ashley Munroe's prostitution partner. Come on, that's a lot of coincidences, don't you think?"

"I don't CARE!"

"Why, because you're afraid of some name in that book!?" She immediately wanted to take it back, but she knew she wasn't totally off the mark.

Cross looked wounded. "They're a bunch of college kids, doing drugs and sleeping around and dying," he said flatly. "It's a shame but it happens. You might not have seen it during your four days on the job, but in my thirty years on the force I've seen it plenty."

"So you won't reopen the case?"

He sighed wearily. "Just because it's political suicide, Madison, doesn't mean it's the right thing to do."

"HOW'D IT go in there?" Parker asked when she emerged.

She gave him a look as she grabbed a few things off her desk. "How can you work for someone so stubborn?"

"Worst part is he's usually right."

"Yeah, maybe, but usually isn't always."

"No." Parker laughed. "You're right. How 'bout, 'He's usually right, but he's always in charge.' "

Madison shook her head and growled in frustration. "Hey, Parker, I have a question for you."

"Shoot."

"Do you know of a guy named Ivan?"

"Ivan?"

"Yeah. Drug dealer. Black guy, big, shaved head, little goatee. Know anything about him?"

"Yeah, I know him. Not well, but I've encountered him several times over the years."

"Know where I could find him?"

"Is this about the case?"

"Do you know where I could find him?"

Parker shook his head. "He should be in the system somewhere. Last I heard, he'd been taken in. You should talk to Rourke, it was one of her friends who busted him. Guy named Kenny Jensen."

CHAPTER 29

HER UNCLE'S words about political suicide echoed in Madison's ears as she exited the turnpike on the way back to Wardleyville.

There was no way of knowing in what way this was going to come back to haunt her, although she was pretty sure it would. Nevertheless, she felt obliged to tell Vincent Mowry that no matter where things went from here, Beth had pretty much been cleared of involvement in the prostitution ring, if that's what it was. Mulroney had said there were only two girls involved, and Beth wasn't one of them. If she could relieve him of that part of his pain . . . well, she figured it was the least she could do.

Once more it occurred to her as she approached Wardleyville that it had been a while since she'd had anything to eat. At least this time, she knew where to go.

ALL THE same people seemed to be inside the Wardleyville Diner, including Hank and the guy in the John

Deere hat. They looked like they hadn't moved, except now they were all quietly reading the local paper.

Nobody looked up as Madison walked in and took the same seat she'd occupied that morning. She studied her menu, expecting someone to chime in on whatever conversation had been going on before she walked in. But the place remained quiet.

"Are you ready to order?" a subdued voice asked.

Madison looked up to see Marge standing in front of her. She looked like she'd aged ten years since that morning.

"Oh, hi there." She smiled weakly. "Well, it's a nice surprise to see you again so soon. What can I get for you?"

"How are you doing?" Madison asked.

Marge sniffed and curled a finger in front of her mouth. "I'm sorry," she said, holding back tears. "I guess you heard about Beth Mowry."

"Yes."

"I just read about it in the *Eagle,*" Marge said with a soft sob. She put a hand over her mouth. "Excuse me, I'll be right back," she said, as she hurried back into the kitchen.

Looking around, Madison saw that everyone was grimly reading the *Wardleyville Eagle.* The headline on the front page was "Drugs, Prostitution in Death of Local College Girl."

"Oh, shit," Madison muttered to herself.

A yellow newspaper box sat right outside the window, the words *Wardleyville Eagle* written across it in gothic script. Fishing two quarters out of her purse, she slid out of the booth and went outside.

As she dropped her quarters into the slot, a voice behind her said, "Are you with the police?"

She turned to see the skinny girl who had been reading

her book in the diner earlier. A copy of the *Eagle* was folded under her arm.

"I'm with the Crime Scene Unit in Philly. How could you tell?"

The girl smirked. "Have you ever looked at your car?"

Madison couldn't argue; even if it had lights and a siren, it could scarcely look more like a police car.

"You know you skew the age curve in there by about fifty years."

"Not that many places to sit in this town. The bar's a little too smoky for me."

"Did you know Beth?"

"I used to." The girl nodded and looked away. "I haven't seen her much since she went away to college. Not at all this year."

Madison nodded sympathetically.

"Hearing all those people talk about how close she was to her brother—it's really weird."

"They weren't close?"

"I don't know . . . They seemed to be, lately, I guess. I'd see them driving around together and all . . . Like I said, I haven't spoken to Beth in a while . . . But the weird thing is, she used to hate her brother, Vincent. Her stepbrother. He used to skeeve her out, totally."

Madison waited for the girl to continue, but she didn't. "How?" she prodded.

The girl looked around, then shrugged defiantly. "It was just . . . he wouldn't leave her alone, you know? I mean, she was, like, thirteen or something when their parents got married, and Vincent was in his thirties, still living at home.

"He was always showing up to give her a ride home from school, or taking us out for ice cream. And it bothered her how he was always pretending to be into stuff

224   D. H. Dublin

she was into. Like when Beth started listening to Dave
Matthews, all of a sudden Vincent did, too. And I don't
know . . . She starts doing yoga, he starts doing yoga.
Beth had terrible hay fever, and I guess Vincent did, too,
but she used to joke that he was even faking that. At first
she thought it was kind of cute in a weird way, but then it
got kind of creepy."

"Did he ever . . . ?"

"Oh, no. No, I don't think so . . . it was just that . . .
well, I mean . . . I mean, I know none of that stuff sounds
terrible or anything, and it wasn't really. It was just a
vibe, I guess. And Beth really didn't like it. She was
openly contemptuous of him, but he seemed oblivious."

"But they seemed to be getting along better lately,
right?"

"Yeah, that's how it seemed. I don't know what happened. Maybe she realized he was holding the purse
strings or something."

The girl looked off in the distance, silent for a moment. Then she continued. "Anyway, I just thought you
should know it wasn't all sweetness and light."

BACK INSIDE the diner, Marge was nowhere to be
found. A cup of coffee and a piece of lemon meringue pie
had appeared on Madison's table, along with guest check
with the word "Compliments!" scribbled across it.

The caffeine status of the coffee was unknown, but
Madison figured it was okay either way: She should have
decaf, but she wanted regular.

The newspaper reporter for the *Wardleyville Eagle*
seemed to have gone to all the trouble of watching the TV
news report, but little else. The only substantive difference between it and the report in the paper was the emphasis on Wardleyville native Beth Mowry.

It took Madison about three minutes to read the entire story. It told her nothing she didn't already know, except how much everyone else now knew.

As she was finishing her pie, Marge emerged from the kitchen with her composure regained. Her makeup had been reapplied, and when she walked up to the table, Madison could smell cigarettes.

Marge slipped her order pad under her arm and leaned forward, into almost a bow. "Sorry 'bout that," she said quietly.

"That's okay," Madison said reassuringly. "Thanks for the pie."

"I saw you were getting the paper . . ." she said, pointing. "It's just so sad. That poor, stupid girl. I mean, drugs and, and prostitution," she said in a whisper. "What in the world was she thinking?"

"Well, actually—"

"Can't say I'm totally surprised," John Deere butted in, putting down his paper and turning around in his booth. "She was a different girl after she went to college. It changed her."

"Well, isn't that the point of college?" asked Hank, a little sarcastically.

"Not like that, numbnut. She was a nice young lady when she lived in this town. I almost didn't recognize her when she came back."

Hank snickered. "Well, she did have that nose job."

Marge shook her head. "I couldn't even tell the difference with that nose thing . . . The rest of her sure did change, but that nose looked just like her old nose. Maybe even more so."

Hank nodded his agreement. "Except she was pointing it up in the air. Too good to talk to plain old townsfolk."

"Yeah, that's true," John Deere agreed. "Seemed that once they started getting along with each other, she wouldn't get within a hundred yards of any of us. But that's not what I'm talking about. She was different, a lot more grown-up, like she lost her innocence all of the sudden." He cupped his cheek in his hand.

"It's true," Marge agreed. "She seemed more like she was about to turn twenty-nine than twenty-one."

"It's amazing. After all she'd been through," John Deere continued, "all she'd gone through with her parents and whatnot, she was still that sweet girl. You would have thought she'd have kept some of that through college. But when she came back she'd drive down the street, she'd act like she didn't know you."

"George, she was a pros-ti-tute," Hank snickered, sounding out each syllable.

Madison was about to protest when Marge started up again.

"I guess we should have known something was wrong when she came home with that tattoo."

"Tattoo?" Madison said.

"Oh, I know all the kids are getting them these days," Marge went on, "but I never thought Beth would be one of them."

"A tattoo?" she repeated.

"Yeah. She got something in her nose, and then a big stupid-looking thing, down on her back," Hank said, looking far off. "What was it? It was a . . . a . . ."

"It was a heart," Marge answered. "A blue heart."

CHAPTER 30

MADISON'S HEAD swam as she drove back to Philadelphia, a swirl of scraps of information, nascent theories, and unfounded suspicions. What she needed was someone to talk to about it. Lieutenant Cross would be the ideal person, but that was obviously out of the question. Rourke or Parker would be helpful, too, but the whole thing had become too political, too charged to go to them. Besides, she thought, she didn't really need a police mind—just someone intelligent enough to listen while she thought out loud, maybe help her get her thoughts organized so she could figure out what she did think.

The sun was behind the trees behind her as she drove east, the sky orange and pink in her rearview mirror. Ahead of her it was deep blue, darkening to purple.

She dialed 411 and got Frank Sponholz's number at home.

"Yeah?" he answered, breathing heavily from the exertion of answering.

"Hi, Frank, it's Madison Cross."

"Calling me at home now, huh? You just can't get enough of me, can you?"

She smiled. "Can you blame me, Spoons?"

"Okay, what lame excuse are you hiding behind to call me now?"

"Am I that transparent? I'm wondering if you noticed if Beth Mowry had ever had a nose job."

"No, I'm pretty sure I would have noticed, and I definitely would have remembered. But I betcha I know what your next question is."

"Yeah?"

"Yup. And yes, Valerie Chirelli did have a nose job."

A honk from the car behind her reminded Madison to put her foot back on the accelerator.

"You still there?" Frank asked.

"Yeah, I'm here."

"What the hell is going on? What's up with Chirelli and Mowry now?"

Madison sucked in a breath. Frank was already aware of the inconsistencies of this case, and while he seemed to be absolutely cowed by internal politics of any kind, he seemed to have a well-honed ability to discuss the facets of a case, even if he knew that expedience would prevent him from doing anything about them. He would be an almost ideal candidate to hash things out with. But to talk on the phone with him for hours? Possibly all night? She just couldn't stomach the prospect.

"Do you have Veste's number at home?"

He gave her Aidan's cell phone number.

"Oh, and kid, as it turns out, those tattoos might mean something after all."

"What are you talking about?"

"Those tattoos, the ones the girls had on their thighs. You were wondering if they meant something."

"You mean the tattoos you insisted meant nothing? The ones that two hundred other girls on campus have?"

Spoons laughed. "Yeah, you got me. Well, if two hundred other girls on campus have those tattoos, I'm going back to college."

"What are you saying?"

"I did some research—went on the Internet, then talked to one of the Egyptologists at the university. Believe it or not, those tattoos are of the Egyptian god Bes. Well, not just Egyptian, but mostly Egyptian."

"Bes? Egyptian god? What are you talking about?"

He sighed. "It was such a strange tattoo, I felt like I had to look into it. And that's what I came up with—the Egyptian god Bes. Way I understand it, he's a god of a bunch of different things, but back in ancient Egypt, the prostitutes used to have tattoos of him on their thighs. He was supposed to protect them from the clap and getting knocked up, that sort of thing. Some people think it was just prostitutes, some think it was 'holy' prostitutes, like part prostitute, part priestess."

"What do you think it means?"

"Nothing means anything, like I told you. What do you get from it?"

"I don't know. I guess it helps confirm that they were working girls. Maybe they liked to think it was something more than that."

"I heard of some of these upper-middle-class suburban girls think it's a hoot to go out and sell some, get some pocket cash. Girls gone wild, remember?"

"Right . . . Hey, thanks for the homework, Spoons. I appreciate it."

"You got it, sweetheart. You call me if you need me, okay?"

"Thanks."

She left a message on Aidan's cell phone, figuring that if he wasn't answering by the time she got back to Philadelphia, she'd call Frank again.

Valerie Chirelli had a nose job and a tattoo, and Beth Mowry had neither. Chirelli had been spending weekends with Vincent Mowry, not his sister.

It just didn't make sense. What was their connection? If Valerie was Ashley's partner in prostitution, then the obvious answer was sex for money.

But if Valerie was visiting Vincent on weekends, and often enough that the locals thought it was Beth, it would seem to be more than sex. Maybe he had her on retainer. Maybe they were in love, she thought, laughing out loud at the prospect, but then giving it some serious thought.

Even if there was some kind of relationship between Vincent Mowry and Valerie Chirelli, what did that have to do with anything? And was Chirelli's growing resemblance to Beth Mowry intentional? Was she actually pretending to be Beth Mowry, or were the locals just jumping to conclusions, an honest mistake amplified via the rumor mill?

Madison dialed 411 again and got Aidan's number at home. She had just pressed "1" to dial automatically when another call came in on her cell phone.

It was from Aidan's cell phone.

"Did you just hang up on my home phone without leaving a message?" he asked impishly.

"That depends; do you have caller ID?"

"No."

"Then no."

"Actually, I lied. I do have caller ID."

"Well, I lied, too."

"I know. I have caller ID, remember?"

"Right."

"What's up?"

"What are you doing?"

"What do you have in mind?"

"Talking about a case."

"Somehow, I knew that, too."

AIDAN LIVED in a cavernous loft in Fairmount, a few miles north of the art museum. He met her at the door and led her upstairs.

An exposed brick wall ran along one side of the apartment, and the wall opposite was almost entirely glass. There was an open kitchen at one end. At the other, white partitions blocked off the sleeping quarters.

A clarinet in an open case sat on the sofa.

"Clarinet?" asked Madison, impressed.

"I dabble," he said modestly. He closed the case and set it aside, inviting her to sit. "Beer?"

"See? Already you're helping clarify my thinking. Absolutely."

He went into the kitchen area and returned with a couple of Yuengling lagers.

"Thanks," she said, tapping his bottle with hers.

"So what did you want to talk about?"

"I went back out to Wardleyville."

He laughed ruefully. "You keep annoying that guy, it's going to keep coming back on you, you know that, right?"

"I know, I know. I went out there to tell him Beth was no longer implicated in the whole prostitution thing, tell him her name had been cleared. I don't know, I thought it might make him feel better."

"So what did he say?"

"I never spoke to him. I stopped back at the same diner. The locals told me some things, and I've been trying to sort it out ever since."

"What did they tell you?"

"Okay." She took a deep breath. "I don't know where to begin. You already know most of this." She sipped her beer. "Okay, you remember what Mulroney said about the second girl, the one with the tattoo, right?"

"Yeah. And you think it was Chirelli?"

"Yeah, but first, we thought it was Beth Mowry."

"Yes."

"And why was that?"

He shrugged. "She fit the description."

"Right, only then we found Valerie Chirelli, who also fit the description. Plus, she has the tattoo."

"Okay."

"When I went out to Wardleyville the first time, before I spoke to Vincent Mowry, some of the locals gave me some background on the Mowry family. Vincent's father and Beth's mother married about seven or eight years ago.

"Apparently Vincent and Beth didn't get along too well at first, and it got even worse after the parents died. But over the last year or so, Vincent and Beth grew a lot closer. She would come home from school on weekends. They'd spend time together. She never had anything to do with her old friends anymore."

"I don't think it's that unusual for friends to drift apart once they go off to college. And Vincent and Beth were each the only family the other had left, right?" he asked. "Maybe they got over their differences as they got older."

Madison held up a hand. "Maybe, except just now when I was in Wardleyville, I learned some more. One of Beth's old friends said that Vincent always wanted to be a little too close to Beth. She said it was creepy, and that she was surprised they seemed so buddy-buddy all of the sudden. Suspicious, even."

Aidan's eyes narrowed.

"There's more," Madison continued. "The other locals were going on about how different Beth seemed this past year—not talking to any of them, that kind of thing. But they also said she looked different. Especially after the nose job, they said, which somehow didn't seem to make her nose look any different, but did make the rest of her look different."

The furrow on Aidan's brow deepened. "So did Beth . . . ?"

Madison held up her hand again. "Guess what else they said was different about Beth?"

He raised an eyebrow.

"A tattoo. A blue heart across the small of her back. And no, Beth Mowry didn't have a nose job. But you know who did?"

"Valerie Chirelli."

CHAPTER 31

AIDAN SAT back and let out a deep breath. "Whoa."

"Right?" Madison said triumphantly. "So something's up. But now comes the hard part. I know there's a connection between Vincent and Valerie, but so what? What does it mean?"

Aidan thought for a moment. "Well, what's the connection we're looking for? Are we saying Beth and Ashley were murdered? Are we saying Valerie was murdered? If so, we need to know how and why, right?"

"Okay. So lets start with Beth and Ashley. Yes, I think they were murdered. And . . . I don't know how. We know they were taking methylphenedrine, right? And now we know they were using inhalants, or at least that they had absorbed this MEK, somehow, and the MEK interacted with the methylphenedrine. So where does that leave us?"

"There was something else," Aidan said quietly.

"Something else. What's that?"

"I tried to tell you before," he explained defensively. "Remember we tested the paints and the filter from the air conditioner?"

"Oh right, that's another thing, the fact that the dried paint contained MEK and the wet paint didn't. That doesn't make sense."

"I told you before the filter from the air conditioner was clean, but I don't think you understood what I was saying. When I said the filter was clean, I mean, it was *totally* clean. Not just no MEK, no nothing. It was clean, like out of the box. No dust, no pollen, no nothing."

Madison shook her head. "That can't be. I mean, that girl I talked to the first day, she said girls used to hang out with Beth Mowry just to bask in the air-conditioning. They used that thing."

"Maybe they had just replaced the filter."

"Maybe. It would be a hell of a coincidence . . . Hey, wait a second, it seemed like someone had gone in there before the LaMott girl, remember? All that stuff Frank couldn't reconcile? Wait, wait, wait. That makes perfect sense. Frank said between the body temperature, the rigor mortis and the eyes, it seemed like the room had been cool when they died, meaning the air conditioner had been on . . . so there would have been something in the filter. Someone did go in there, and they didn't just turn the air conditioner off—they switched the filter, too. Holy shit, those girls really were murdered!"

Aidan was sitting forward now, elbows on his knees, his chin resting on his thumbs. "And the air conditioner was broken," he murmured.

"That's right! The vent switch was broken." When it hit her, Madison clapped a hand over her mouth. "Vincent Mowry bought her that air conditioner."

They sat in silence for several minutes.

"So where did the MEK come from?" Aidan asked, looking for holes.

Madison thought for a moment. "Maybe the killer came back and got it, whatever it was from. We only tested one tube of paint. Maybe it was in one of other tubes . . . Oh, shit, the paints!"

"What?"

"The paints! Vincent got them for her, too! He bought her a whole new set of paints."

"Hmph."

"We've been looking at Ashley, thinking Beth was just an innocent bystander. Maybe she was the target the whole time."

"You do realize this still isn't enough to bring to the lieutenant."

"Then I guess we need more."

They were quiet for a moment.

"I'll tell you what," Aidan said, putting down his beer and sliding imperceptibly closer. "Why don't we both get up early tomorrow morning, have some breakfast, see if we can dig something else up."

She looked at him, reading his face. Breakfast.

"Aidan . . . Even with all this going on?"

"It's not your first day anymore," he pointed out, hopefully.

"It's probably my last."

He inched closer. "They say you should live every day like it is your last."

"Aidan . . . Please. It's just not the right time."

He looked at her dubiously and drained his beer. There was a fair amount of it left, but finishing it gave him an excuse to stand up.

"Do you want another one?" he asked as he walked into the kitchen area.

"No. No, thanks," she replied. "I should probably get going."

He returned with a sad smile on his face. "You don't have to go just because . . . you know."

"Yeah, I know. Thanks, but I really should go."

He nodded, following her down the stairs. "Call me if you need anything," he said. "Or, if, you know . . . If you think it's time."

They both laughed.

"Thanks, Aidan." She turned at the bottom of the steps and gave him a quick peck on the cheek.

"Something to build on," he declared.

"An eternal optimist. I like it."

"Good night, Madison. Call me if you want to get breakfast, okay?" He put up his hands defensively. "Just breakfast."

"Good night, Aidan."

THE GIRL who answered the door at Alpha Alpha Gamma seemed in a daze, which was understandable with three sorority sisters dead in one week. She didn't bat an eye when Madison held up her ID. She'd probably seen more IDs in the past few days than the guy working the door at the campus watering hole.

Maybe if Madison looked like a horny frat brother she would have gotten more attention. Like Parker, she thought with a smile.

The light in the hallway outside room six was dim. Madison's hands shook as she slit the police tape and slipped inside.

The windows had been closed, and the room felt hot and stuffy. It was hard to tell if the paint smell still hovered, because the other smells were so strong. Even with the lights on, Madison sensed a lingering darkness. She

had a sudden impulse to turn and leave, to get out of that
room as quickly as possible.

The box of paints was on a bookshelf on the far side of
the desk where Ashley Munroe had died. It was open, the
bottom nesting in the top. Although they looked almost
monochromatic in the dim light, Madison could see that
they were arranged along the spectrum, from blue to violet. Each tube was slightly dented in the middle.

The box was just out of reach, but Madison didn't
want to walk through the area where the bodies had been.
She stretched, her fingertips just hooking the lip of the
box. She leaned a little bit further. It slipped out from under her fingers and fell off the shelf.

Madison cursed under her breath.

The tubes of paint scattered across the floor and under
the table. Crouching down, she started gathering them
up. She put the box back on the shelf and fit the tubes
back into their slots, one by one. She had to reach down a
couple more times, gathering up handfuls of paint tubes,
then straightening up to put them in the box.

She grabbed the last four tubes from the floor. But
when she stood up, she saw that there were only three
slots left in the box. Thinking she must have them lined
up wrong, she took them out and filed them again. But
still, there was one tube too many.

Madison stared at the box, forgetting about both her
desire to get out of that room and the reason she was there
in the first place. These paints were a puzzle, and she took
offense to the fact that she hadn't solved it immediately.

She lined them up one way, then another. Finally, she
tried rearranging the paints along the spectrum, from red to
violet, like they had been when she first saw them. As she
did, she realized she was holding two tubes of cobalt blue.

One of the tubes was slightly crumpled, exactly like
all the others, but the second one was untouched.

CHAPTER 32

AIDAN ANSWERED on the second ring. "I knew you couldn't stay away."

"Wondering if, instead of breakfast, you'd be interested in a late-night snack?"

He sighed heavily. "What do you want?"

"Don't be like that. I went back to Alpha Alpha Gamma. I got all the paints and I want to test them."

He sighed again. "Why?"

"Can we just do it?"

"It's ten o'clock. It's Friday night."

"What if I say please?"

THEY MET at the lab twenty minutes later.

Aidan was already there, waiting at the elevators.

Madison showed up with a large evidence bag in one hand, a cardboard tray with two venti cappuccinos and a bag of biscotti in the other.

"Oh, you think you can buy me off with coffee?"

"It's cappuccino," she sang, temptingly. "And I got biscotti."

"What kind of biscotti?" he asked suspiciously.

"Chocolate hazelnut and anise seed."

He pursed his lips. "All right," he conceded, as the elevator doors opened.

He took hold of the tray as they got on the elevator. "So what are we doing here again? And why?"

"The more I thought about it, the more I kept coming back to the paint. There had to be something in the paint. So I went back to Alpha Alpha Gamma, figured I'd pick up the tubes, call you for breakfast tomorrow, see what we could come up with."

"And yet, here we are. Now."

"Right. Well, I knocked over the box with the paints, and when I gathered them all up, there was one too many. A duplicate. And all the tubes looked opened and slightly used, like they had been squeezed in the middle, but the double one, the second blue, hadn't been touched. It just seemed odd."

"That's why I'm here?"

"No." She took back the bag and shook it. "You're here for the crunchy, delicious biscotti."

He smiled. "Couldn't there have just been an extra tube of blue paint lying around? It would make sense that the second one wouldn't be open yet, if she still had some in another tube."

"Maybe . . ." Madison said slowly, thinking it through. "Only . . . No, the girl I spoke to the day it happened said Beth's brother threw out all Beth's cheap old paints when he bought her new stuff."

"Well," Aidan began, "maybe—"

"No," she cut him off. "I know what you're going to say. Maybe he missed one tube when he threw out her old paints. But it's a different brand." She was starting to get excited. "This is some expensive Swiss stuff, and the old paint was some cheap brand. No, the more I think about it, we might really have something here."

He gave her a look.

"Stop it," she said. "I'm serious."

THEY SIPPED their cappuccinos and munched biscotti as they prepared the tests.

Madison helped him set out his beakers and vials. As he lined up a half-dozen tubes of paint, including both tubes of cobalt blue, Madison leaned against the wall and chewed another biscotti.

"Anything else I can do to help?"

Aidan was already working intently, squeezing out a small amount of green paint into a beaker. He didn't look up from his equipment, even as he sipped his drink. "Nope."

"I still have those samples from under Chirelli's fingernails. I was thinking maybe I'd profile that sample while you were doing this."

"Okay . . ." he said distractedly, picking up the slightly crumpled tube of blue paint and squeezing a small amount into another beaker.

He reached out to pick up the unopened tube of blue, but Madison put her hand on his. "Wait a second."

She picked up the tube and held it under the light. Something protruding from under the cap glinted dully in the light.

Aidan squinted. "What is that?"

"It looks like a human hair."

UNDER THE bright light and the magnifying glass, the hair was so obvious, Madison couldn't believe she had almost overlooked it. She grasped the wisp with tweezers and held it in place while she gently removed the cap from the tube of paint.

Aidan took the tube from her and extracted a dab for his tests. Luckily, the root of the hair was intact—and miraculously free of blue paint, which covered the other half of the hair. Madison snipped off the blue half and put the two pieces in separate bags. She didn't want the paint and whatever else might be on it to degrade the sample.

The unpainted hair went into one tube, and the tissue from under Chirelli's fingernails went into another one. Madison added enzyme solution to each and put them in the thermocycler. When she was done, she went to check on Aidan.

He had his glasses off, standing in front of the gas chromatograph, a blue, cube-shaped machine about a foot and a half on each side. He had a glass syringe in his hand and he was injecting a small amount of blue liquid into a rubber ring in the side of the machine. He looked up as she walked in.

"How's it going?" she asked.

"You might be right about that second tube of blue. Same label, much different smell. Seemed thinner than the others, too. The color seemed a little washed out. I'm doing that one first. How 'bout you?"

"The samples are in the thermocycler. I did the Chirelli sample as well."

He nodded, tweaking a knob and pressing a couple of buttons.

"Biscotti?" she asked.

He grabbed his stomach and winced. "I got pretty busy with them while you were in the DNA lab. There aren't many left."

She took a stool next to him, elbow on the counter, her jaw resting on her hand.

"So what's this all about, really?" he asked.

"What?"

"This whole thing. I mean, I'm not saying there isn't something to all this, and you'll deserve a lot of credit if it does turn out to be something." He fiddled with a few more knobs. "But you're swimming against a pretty strong current here, a lot of political pressure. I'm just wondering why?"

She had asked herself the same question about a thousand times. "Isn't this what it's all supposed to be about? Solving crimes?" It sounded lame, even to her.

"I don't know." She sighed. "I guess I just don't like the idea that someone could murder two women and get away with it, just because some powerful people didn't want a mess. Or didn't want to get caught."

"Yeah, but from what I heard, you had the hots for this case from the beginning. I just wonder why. Is it to impress your uncle? To impress the crew?" He smiled. "Or were you having second thoughts about this whole thing and you figured if you pissed off enough people, you could get out of it?"

Madison attempted an indignant look. Then again . . . he was here with her on a Friday night. The problem was, she didn't have any answers. She didn't know why she wanted this case so badly. All his theories sounded equally valid, and he was probably right on all counts, to one extent or another.

"To be honest, it's probably all those things. And it wasn't that long ago that I was their age. I don't like people just saying, 'Oh, these dumb girls took too many drugs and died.' But you know what else? I really just don't like the thought of someone out there getting away with murder."

Maybe I get it from my dad, she thought.

The buzzer sounded, interrupting her reverie and announcing the samples were finished in the thermocycler.

"That's me." Saved by the bell, she thought as she slid off her stool, wondering if Aidan was thinking the same thing.

She removed the samples from the thermocycler and prepared the gel papers. When they were ready, she put them in place and applied the current.

When she returned, Aidan was at work on the computer.

"Anyway," she said, "whatever my reasons, I do appreciate your help. Especially on a Friday night."

"That's okay," he said, looking up from the screen with a smile. "I kind of like the company."

She put her hand on his shoulder and kept it there. They worked like that in silence for the next few minutes, until he pushed back from the computer and turned to her.

The screen was loading something.

"Here we go."

The seconds dragged on as the screen seemed stuck at 99 percent loaded. A graph appeared on the screen, a y-axis, an x-axis, and a line zigzagging between them.

"Jesus Christ." Right in the middle of the graph was a thick, dramatic spike.

"There," he said, his finger on the spike. "That's your MEK. A lot of it, too. In blue number two. The tube with the hair."

"How much?"

"A lot."

"Enough to fill a large room with enough fumes to kill?"

"Maybe."

"Someone put it there."

"It looks that way."

A loud beep interrupted the silence.

Aidan looked at her questioningly as she stood up.

"Pot roast's done," she called over her shoulder as she turned down the hallway toward the DNA lab.

She took one look at the samples and immediately yelled at Aidan.

"What is it?" he asked from the doorway a few seconds later.

"Look at them," she said, holding up the samples. "They're identical."

"You're sure you didn't mix them up?" he asked.

She gave him a look. "Yes, I'm sure I didn't mix them up."

"Hmm."

"So whoever spiked the paint," she said as she loaded one of the samples into the scanner, "might be the same person who killed Valerie Chirelli."

"It could be," Aidan conceded.

"And I like Vincent Mowry."

A SEARCH of the DNA database came up empty, but so did a search for Vincent Mowry's name. Either one without the other might have cleared him. As it was, the only thing they knew was that they had no proof of his innocence.

"So what do we do now?" Madison asked.

Aidan looked at his watch and yawned. "I don't know. I don't usually handle this side of things. My inclination would be to tell the lieutenant, but even if the mere fact that we are working on this case wasn't enough to get us suspended, it is past midnight. I don't think he'd appreciate a phone call right now." He yawned again.

"If the same person who killed Mowry and Munroe also killed Chirelli, maybe we need to look for some clues from Chirelli. Maybe look at her room again."

"Yup." Aidan yawned yet again. "Maybe we could do that. Tomorrow."

Madison looked put out.

He smiled ruefully and shook his head, putting both hands on her shoulders. "Madison, I'd love to stay up all night with you. But not doing this."

SHE TOUCHED his arm as he left, gave it a little squeeze. The small reservoir of energy that had kept her going evaporated almost as soon as she left. She felt as if a weight had dropped upon her from a great height, and she decided immediately that she was going home as well. She waited a few more minutes, making sure Aidan's car was well out of sight. For some reason, she didn't want him to see her leaving so soon.

Ten minutes later, she dragged herself out to her car. She got about three blocks before the yawning started—deep, whole-body yawns that left her eyes filled with water. During one particularly deep one, she threw her head all the way back. As she leveled her gaze down, she glanced in her rearview mirror and saw a black SUV behind her.

"Oh, for Christ's sake . . ." She squinted, trying to get a look at the driver, but it was no use. At that point, she was so fed up she didn't speed up or turn abruptly or take any measures to lose him. She just kept an eye on her rearview mirror and puzzled over who the hell was following her.

She was so lost in thought pondering their possible identities and motives, she didn't notice the car pulling out up ahead, blocking the road in front of her.

Her tires screeched as her foot punched the brakes. The car skidded and swerved, bouncing hard as it hit the curb, crossed the sidewalk, and came to a stop inches away from the brick wall that ran the length of the block.

Her head had smacked the steering wheel, and as she rubbed her eyes to clear the cobwebs, she saw that two black SUVs had her car hemmed in against the wall. Determined to make a run for it, she threw open her door and took two steps before bouncing off what felt like yet another brick wall, which sent her sprawling to the ground.

But it wasn't a brick wall.

Lying on the ground in the darkness between her car and the wall, she saw the bearded guy with the long hair and shades standing over her. He had a gun tucked in his waistband, and as he looked down at her, expressionless, Madison briefly pictured herself naked on a slab, with Spoons cutting out her organs and weighing them.

"Are you okay?" he asked in a gravelly voice.

Madison tried to say yes, but no sound came out. "Think so," she said on a second attempt.

He stepped back and gestured toward the black SUV parked behind her car. "Get in the car."

"Why?"

"Because you want to talk to Ivan and Ivan wants to talk to you."

THE GUY with the beard was driving and another guy sat up front with him. He was a clean-cut black guy, with short hair and wire-rimmed shades. He had a hard-ass scowl, but there was something else about it, something undefined, something familiar . . .

He was a cop.

Madison looked back at the driver, and she realized he was a cop, too. Somehow, she just knew. Something about the way they moved, the way they looked at the other cars as they drove. She wasn't sure what else, but it added up to cop.

Sitting alone in the backseat, Madison tried to figure

out if that was good news or bad news. It seemed to her that a dirty cop was going to be more desperate than a regular criminal. He'd have more to lose.

She tried to discern whether the back doors had safety locks. Not that it mattered; flying down I-95 at eighty-five miles an hour, the question of whether she could open the doors was pretty academic. Besides, if she was just going to jump out of the car, why had she gotten into it in the first place?

The guy had said, "You want to talk to Ivan and Ivan wants to talk to you." He had it at least half right.

A vague calm settled over her. She had gotten into the car of her own accord. She was at least going to get some answers. And there was really nothing she could do until they got wherever they were going.

A sudden wave of fear did wash over her as they turned toward the airport. She shook her head, chasing away the visions of bodies decaying in marshes and people being pushed out of helicopters.

They weren't headed for the airport.

They were headed for the airport Hilton.

Driving past the front entrance, they curved around to the back and parked next to one of the service doors.

The second cop opened the back door for her. He stood in silence, waiting for her to get out.

They entered through a darkened kitchen, obviously closed for the night, and took a service elevator to the sixth floor.

They stopped in front of an unmarked door. The driver swiped a card through the lock. The little light turned green, and they went inside.

IVAN WAS sitting on the bed, looking at a magazine. At least, Madison assumed it was Ivan; he was the only large black man in the room, and he had a shaved head and a goatee. The only other occupant was a white guy in a dark blue suit that screamed Fed.

The two guys who had brought her stood on either side of the door.

Madison cleared her throat.

"You want to talk to Ivan, talk to Ivan. It's your one and only chance," the guy in the suit said impatiently.

"Are you Ivan?" she obliged, addressing the guy on the bed.

"Why?" he said with contempt. "Who the fuck are you?" He looked up at her, and his expression quickly changed from scorn to lust.

Madison still wasn't quite sure of what was going on. "I'm with the Philly PD."

"Well, you a bit late. They about to move me out to the fucking boonies or some shit, get me a job at Wal-Mart."

She looked over at the guy in the blue suit, who gave her a slight nod.

"Oh." Witness protection. Suddenly, it all started to make sense.

Ivan leaned back on the bed and laughed. "Yeah, that's right . . . 'Oh.'" He laughed even harder, throwing back his head and letting out a throaty, raspy roar. "So bring it on, baby. You got questions, I got answers."

He sat up, looking at her expectantly.

"Okay. Do you know Ashley Munroe and Beth Mowry?"

He started to shake his head, then stopped, snapping his fingers. "Oh wait, Ashley and Beth. All right, yeah, Ashley got the long hair and that body, Beth got that little nose, right?"

"Yes. That's them. Did you sell them drugs?"

Ivan looked over at the guy in the suit. "I got amnesty, right?"

The Fed rolled his eyes. "Immunity. And yes."

"Yeah, all right then. Yeah, I did."

"Did you sell them a drug called methylphenedrine anytime recently?"

He shook his head. "First, if you talking about Ritalin, it's called methylpheni*date,* not . . . whatever you said. Second, they stopped buying that kind of stuff from me a couple months ago. Right after spring break. I just sold them some X after that."

"Do you know why?"

"You ever tried X, you'd know."

"I mean why did they stop buying the other stuff?"

"I know. I'm fucking with you. She said something about getting it from some other brother."

"Did that make you mad?"

He laughed. "I didn't care. It's a free country. Hell, I just sold her the X. So what's this all about, anyway?"

"They're both dead."

His head snapped back. He seemed truly taken aback. "Damn . . . What happened?"

"Looks like an overdose."

Ivan looked a little confused. "So they OD'd. It's an accident. Why you going to all this trouble? 'Cause they rich white girls?"

"Because maybe it wasn't an overdose. Or an accident."

"Wait . . ." He thought intently for a moment. "Damn, was this them two bitches in the sorority? The ones on the news?"

Madison nodded. "Yes."

"Goddamn. Man, that's too bad. I liked them girls, too."

"You did, huh?"

"No lie. The one of them, the fine-looking one, Ashley,

man, she used to polish my knob big time, get that employee discount." He smiled at the memory. "Tell you the
truth, I think she woulda done it without the discount, you
know what I mean. Girl was a freak. And a fine-looking
freak, too."

"What about Beth?"

"Beth?" He laughed. "No, Beth paid cash in full. But I
liked her even more. Sometimes we'd talk, you know
what I'm saying? She a quiet little thing, but once she get
started she just talk and talk. Crazy shit, too. But man,
you could tell that bitch done some thinking . . . Hmm,
that's a damn shame."

ON THE drive back, Madison sat up front with the beard.

As they merged onto I-95, he spoke. "Sorry about all
the cloak-and-dagger shit back there. It's kind of a tricky
situation right now. We had to be sure."

"Don't worry about it. So are you with the Feds?"

"Naw. Me and Jackson are both Philly PD. The uptight
guy back there in the suit, he's a Fed. DEA. My names
Wooten, by the way. Detective John Wooten."

"Madison Cross," she said. "Good to meet you."

"Likewise . . . So this is about those girls at Penn? The
ones who OD'd at the sorority?"

"Yup."

"Pretty big fucking stink for a couple of ODs. So why
were you looking for Ivan?"

"Originally, we thought he might know something.
When we hit all this, you know, resistance—the locked
files and the tails and everything—we thought maybe we
were barking up the right tree."

"You're new, right? First week or something?"

"Yup."

Wooten laughed. "You know you're right in the middle of some major turf shit between the mayor and the commissioner?"

She sighed deeply, which set him off again. "Yeah, I know."

He was quiet for a moment. "So are you really Kevin Cross's little girl?"

She bristled. "Yes, he was my dad." She tried to put a slight emphasis on "was."

He grunted, but let it go.

A few minutes later the conversation was still dead, so he picked up where he left off.

"I worked with him, you know. My first year out of the academy."

Madison waited a second before she looked over, not wanting to appear too interested.

"We were on a task force together," he continued.

"I think it started out as a drug thing. I barely remember, but it just grew and spread, one of those investigations where you just have no fucking idea where it's going to lead, when it's going to end. Man, we scared some big names. Took a few of them down, too. Kevin was fucking fearless, tenacious. Didn't have the slightest goddamn clue about politics, but he had the instincts and the smarts. He was a great fucking cop."

Madison thought she remembered the case Wooten was talking about. She was ten years old, and her father was on a task force, working constantly and the case just getting bigger and bigger.

She would go to bed feeling angry, hurt, and neglected, but sometimes he would come home and wake her up, telling her secrets about his exploits. She was thrilled by the stories, but even more so by the fact that he was telling her all about it, sharing it, explaining his tactics and techniques.

He would tell her about guys he was about to arrest, guys who didn't even know they were under investigation. She was one of half a dozen people in the world who knew it. He would tuck her in and lie with her for a while, until she pretended to fall asleep. Then he'd kiss her on the head and say, "Good night, Magpie."

Maybe the best part was that even though he hadn't been spending time with her, at least he'd been doing real work. At least he hadn't been dwelling on her mother's murder.

WOOTEN SEEMED to be lost in memories of his own, laughing at something in his mind. "I learned a lot from your dad," he said, slowly nodding. "He was a great fucking cop. . . ."

Glancing over, he did a double take. "Oh, fuck. I didn't think you might not want—"

"It's okay," she said, shaking off the spell, feeling the wetness in her eyes. "It's okay. I'm okay. I was just yawning."

Wooten pulled over, and Madison realized they were back at her car.

"Look, I didn't mean to upset you." He turned to face her with an elbow resting on the steering wheel. "I just wanted to tell you that your dad, he knew how to set off some major shit storms of his own. So don't take it too hard when you step into the middle of something." He grinned. "It's genetic."

Wooten waited in his black SUV until Madison pulled away. She looked in her rearview mirror a couple of times as she drove home. But she didn't see any black SUVs.

CHAPTER 33

ONCE MORE, the previous evening's events seemed like
a dream. Only the more Madison woke up, the more real
they became.

She hadn't realized how much the prospect of a corrupt
cop being involved with Ivan was weighing her down. She
was filled with a renewed sense of pride and purpose, a renewed faith in the police force, and she got out of bed feeling invigorated.

The first thing she did was call Rourke, waking her up,
and apparently pissing her off, as well.

"Jesus, Madison, it's not even eight o'clock."

"Look, I just wanted you to know. I got the scoop on
our friend Ivan. He's in witness protection."

"Great," Rourke said with a yawn. "I'll see you Monday." Madison could hear a man's voice in the background,
just before the click.

Apparently, she didn't share Madison's enthusiasm
about the latest development, but at least she seemed to

have a good excuse. She took Rourke's reaction as a cautionary tale and decided not to disturb Parker.

After a jog, a shower, and two cups of coffee, her mind was sharp and awake. When the clock finally read 8:00, she called Aidan.

"You still want breakfast?" she asked when he answered on the fourth ring.

"Do you sleep at all?" he asked, drowsily.

"I slept plenty. Do you still want breakfast?"

"You know, if you were already here, we could be eating breakfast already. Would've made it a lot easier."

She laughed. "Don't want to make it too easy."

"Why not?"

"I'll pick you up in half an hour."

AIDAN'S HAIR was wet and his eyes were still bleary when she picked him up. She handed him a small coffee to tide him over until they got to Silk City, a quirky, retro-cool stainless-steel diner with a nightclub attached.

"Silk City?" he asked as they pulled up across the street. "I don't think I've ever been here before midnight."

"Didn't realize you were such a party animal. This was the closest place I could think of to your place. Had the feeling you didn't want to travel."

"Hey, it's fine by me."

The place was less than a quarter full, with a mixture of artsy types, blue-collar workers, retirees, and one table of late-night partyers who didn't want the fiesta to end.

They took a table between an eighty-something reading his *New York Times* and the rumpled but well-dressed twenty-somethings trying to forestall their inevitable return to Jersey.

Madison looked around and smiled.

"What?" Aidan asked.

"Kind of reminds me of a place in Wardleyville," she replied. As she spoke, a girl with green hair stepped out of the bathroom. "And it kind of doesn't."

While they drank coffee and waited for their pancakes and scrapple, they talked about things other than work.

When Madison asked about his childhood, Aidan told her about his boring, stable family in Cheltenham, just outside the city. He was the youngest of three. Swim team in high school, but mostly a science geek. Undergrad at Penn State, grad school at Drexel.

They talked about his brothers, his sister, his parents, his dog, an uncle who was an inventor, and a cousin who had been on a reality show.

When he asked about her family, she went quiet.

"I know about your mom and your dad," he said softly. "If you don't want to talk about it, that's fine."

She smiled sadly. "No, that's okay. But if you know the story, that's just about it. I don't remember too much from before my mother was killed. I remember being happy, feeling safe. Or at least I remember it enough to compare it to what I felt later.

"One day, Uncle Dave came to get me from school. I didn't find out until later, but that was the day my mom was killed. Someone broke into the house. Robbed us. It's weird, I don't actually remember anyone ever telling me my mom was dead. I'm sure they did, but maybe I just kind of figured it out."

Her eyes went blurry, and Aidan put a hand on hers. She didn't pull away.

"I didn't realize I'd lost my dad as well, you know? Not until later."

"What happened?"

She pulled back, running her hands through her hair. "Well, first he obsessed. He was so driven by the loss of his wife . . . and incensed that he couldn't find the murderer . . . I think he forgot he still had a daughter. Anyway, for the next ten years, all he did was try to find her killer. And he couldn't, you know? Because it was just probably some junkie drifter who was miles away the next day, or dead, facedown in his own filth. But he just couldn't accept that. It ate away at him.

"Eventually, he started to drink . . . I mean, he'd been drinking the whole time, but he started to *really* drink. Things went downhill pretty fast after that. I guess I was fourteen or fifteen. I haven't seen him since my seventeenth birthday."

The lump in Madison's throat made it difficult to eat after the waitress brought their food, but it was well worth the effort to rescue her from telling any more of her story.

After a minute or two of silence, Aidan remarked on how good the pancakes were. Soon they were sharing snide comments about their fellow patrons.

Before they were through their scrapple, Aidan had her laughing, telling her inside stories about the department brass.

After the waitress took away their plates and topped up their coffee, Aidan reached over and patted her hand again.

"You've done very well," he said in a condescending tone.

"If you want," he continued magnanimously, "we can talk about the case now."

She laughed. "You're too kind."

For a moment, they sat there.

"Well . . . ?" he said.

She filled him in on some of what she and Rourke had been up to, including the leads they had been following that led to Ivan.

"A couple of things happened after that. First Rourke

did some digging, did some asking around. All of a sudden people started getting weird on her. She tried to minimize it, but it was obvious she was a little freaked out by it. Then she tries to open the guy's file, and it's blocked on the system. That freaked her out even more, like maybe there's something going on inside the department. I didn't mention it earlier because it seemed like a long shot. And Rourke said to keep it quiet."

Aidan sat forward. "You think some cops are involved? That could explain all the pressure to wrap it up, keep it quiet."

"That's what I thought."

His coffee cup was almost at his lips, but he put it back down without sipping it. "But the pressure has been coming from the top," he said quietly. "Jesus, if this is about corruption, this thing could be huge."

"That's what I was thinking, too, especially when I started being followed."

This time his coffee was at his lips, and he almost spit it out. "Are you serious? You were followed?"

"Yeah, but it's fine."

"Did you tell the lieutenant?"

"No. And I don't want you to, either. Okay, so last night, I'm driving home after you left, and I see the same black SUV behind me that had been following me a couple times before. I almost didn't see the one that pulled out in front of me. Long story short, they took me for a ride."

Aidan looked aghast.

"And guess what?" Madison continued, lowering her voice. "Ivan is in witness protection."

"What?"

"Yeah. He's rolling over on his suppliers. They're whisking him off to somewhere between the coasts."

"So how does all this involve the Munroe/Mowry case?"

Madison shook her head. "Apparently, not one goddamn bit. Ivan said he stopped selling them anything but
ecstasy a couple months ago."

"Hmm."

"So the good news is, the police aren't involved. The
bad news is, the drug-supply angle seems to be a dead
end."

"So we're back where we started," Aidan said with a
sigh, "chasing down the MEK in the paint."

"Right. Someone put it there, knowing Beth Mowry
would use it for her final project. Knowing she would be
in a room with no ventilation. Maybe knowing she'd be
taking methylphenedrine, who knows." Her eyes grew
wide. "Vincent Mowry gave her the paints and gave her
the air conditioner. Hell, he might have even given her the
drugs. I think Vincent Mowry murdered his sister. And
Ashley Munroe."

"Why?"

"Beth Mowry was a trust-fund kid. Her parents died five
years ago, left her a fortune in a trust fund managed by her
stepbrother, Vincent Mowry. Next month, Beth Mowry
would have turned twenty-one. And Vincent Mowry would
have lost control of that trust fund."

Aidan slowly nodded. "That could be why, all right."

They sat there for a moment, pondering the implications. Aidan stirred a creamer into his third coffee. "So
what's your next step?"

"My next step?"

"It's your show, isn't it? I'm a scientist, not an investigator. I'm happy . . . well . . . not happy . . . I'm *willing*
to help you as much as I can, but I'm no investigator."

"I don't know. I'd think the next step would be to search
Chirelli's place, see if that turns up any leads. But . . ." She
grimaced.

"But you don't relish the thought of asking the

lieutenant for a search warrant on an accidental death based on the remote possibility that it's related to a case that he has declared officially closed."

"Something like that."

He hesitated for a moment. "Are you sure you need a warrant?"

"What do you mean?"

"Well, I'm not sure who has legal say here, but I would imagine it's her parents. Maybe you could just ask them if you can look through her stuff. You might not want to tell them you think she was murdered. They'll probably just say yes." He smiled. "And if not, they'll just call the lieutenant and he'll tear you a new one. Another new one."

"A matching set."

"You could get earrings to go with them."

"Right."

VALERIE CHIRELLI'S parents didn't ask many questions. In fact, they asked only one.

Madison had kept things vague, saying they were still trying to figure out what happened to Valerie, and did they mind if she looked through Valerie's possessions?

Valerie's dad said, "No."

"Okay, so you don't have any problem with us searching Valerie's room?" Madison reiterated, wanting to be sure he understood what he had agreed to.

He sighed impatiently. "She's dead, right?"

"Yes."

"Then I don't care what you do."

"Thank you, Mr. Chirelli." He was gone before the words were fully out of her mouth.

Aidan had offered to help her search the room, but he also made it plain that was far outside his area of expertise. Madison felt guilty, because she knew he would do it if she asked him to. But she also knew he really didn't want to.

If she was going to get any further with this, she knew she had to involve some people who knew what they were doing.

Lieutenant Cross was out of the question.

That left Rourke and Parker.

She stared at her cell phone for a full ten minutes, weighing their respective pros and cons.

Rourke might be more sympathetic to her situation, she figured, but she might also be more inclined to worry about the political implications. Plus, she had already pretty much told her to get lost this weekend.

Parker might not be overly concerned about the politics, but he also might not be concerned enough. This was a tricky situation, and Parker had the potential to be . . . loud. Plus, he didn't seem to have completely abandoned his plans to get in her pants.

She called Rourke's cell and got her voice mail. The message said she was unavailable, but the subtext was, "Leave me alone, it's the weekend. And if it's an emergency, you can beep me."

That left Parker.

He answered on the first ring. "Newbie!" he boomed into the phone. "To what do I owe this treat?"

"Hi, Parker. How're you doing?"

"Just calling to see how I am? Ain't you the sweetest thing. I'm fine, Newbie. How are you?"

"I'm fine, too. Look, I was wondering if you could help me with something."

He started laughing. "You just can't let go of this case, can you? I love it. That's what it is, ain't it? What're you up to now?"

She told him what she had learned over the last few days. The only time he interrupted was when she mentioned Aidan.

"You got Veste in on this, too? That poor bastard's got it for you worse'n I do. So, what is it you want me to do?"

When she finished explaining, he grunted again.

"It's not just me, right? This looks like something, doesn't it?"

"Yeah, I guess it does at that. What do you want to do about it?"

She told him about her conversation with Valerie Chirelli's father.

"Wait, wait, wait. You want to go in there with no warrant and search the place without telling the lieutenant? After he's already declared the case closed?"

"Technically, I'm pretty sure we're legally covered with the parent's permission."

"Technically? Well, in a court of law, that might stand up, but in the court of spending the rest of your life at the top of the lieutenant's shit list, it might get thrown out on a technicality."

"Okay, Parker, here's the thing. I've come to terms with the fact that he just wants this case to go away, and that he'll do whatever it takes to make that happen. But it wasn't a goddamned overdose; it was murder. Two murders, and now probably three. It might go away for a little while, but do you really think it's going to stay gone away?"

She laughed bitterly. "I might be new around here, but I just don't see that happening, even if I wasn't around stirring things up. And if it blows up while my uncle is sitting on it, well . . . I can't imagine it's a good thing if something blows up when you're sitting on it. At this point, the only way I see it that he isn't going to get hurt is if this case gets solved despite him."

When she was finished, he grunted again.

"So will you help me?"

To his credit, Parker agreed even before he knew for sure it involved going back to the sorority house, where Madison suspected he'd been hoping to return since the case first broke.

CHAPTER 34

PARKER GRINNED wolfishly when the door to Alpha Alpha Gamma was opened by a woman in a very tight sweater. He didn't seem to notice she had obviously been crying.

As Madison started to explain that Valerie Chirelli's family had given permission for them to search her room, the girl waved her hands indifferently and stepped aside to let them in.

Parker's head swiveled effortlessly as they passed several girls on their way upstairs to room five, Chirelli's room. Door number six, still crisscrossed with police tape, was just a few feet away. Madison and Parker shared a grim look, realizing how close together the two rooms were.

She opened the door.

Valerie Chirelli's room was small and dark. The bed was against one wall with a small table next to it. A desk faced the opposite wall. Even after Madison opened the blinds and turned on the lights, the place still seemed gloomy.

"Okay," Madison exhaled. "So what are we looking for?"

"Hell, I don't know. This is your case. You tell me."

"Right. Well . . . I guess, first off, anything that might tie her to Vincent Mowry. Then anything that might tie her to Beth Mowry or the Munroe girl. Or to the prostitution thing. After that, I don't know . . . Anything, I guess."

Parker poked a pencil into the small hamper in the corner and pulled out a black thong. "As far as the prostitution thing, I guess this would be your homework."

Madison screwed up her face, remembering how much work it had been going through the contents of Ashley Munroe's hamper.

Parker looked under the bed. He lifted the mattress, the box spring, then started taking off the sheets. He glanced up and saw Madison standing idly in the middle of the room.

"I'll tell you what," he drawled. "Why don't you go look through her desk. Start with the top drawer, take everything out and look through each piece of paper. If you find anything, tag it and bag it."

"Okay. Right." She moved to the desk, oddly relieved to have someone tell her what to do.

As she sifted through Valerie's papers, Parker methodically worked his way clockwise around the room: frisking and searching every article of clothing in the closet; thoroughly searching every drawer; fanning and shaking out every book on the bookshelf. He stopped when he got to the desk and resumed on the other side.

By the time Madison was halfway through the second drawer, Parker was helping her, having finished searching the rest of the room.

The fruits of their labor consisted of four scraps of paper with phone numbers on them, a bag of pot, and a shoebox full of sex toys.

"Hey, lookit here!" Parker exclaimed with a grin. He held the open box at an angle so Madison could see inside. He gave it a little shake, jostling the vibrators, dildos, and various other unrecognizable objects.

"Betcha she had fun with these, huh?" he said gleefully.

"Chirelli was a professional, right?" Madison asked, coolly.

Parker nodded, giving the box another shake. "Looks like she used to take her work home with her, huh?"

She shrugged. "Actually, if she was a professional, those were probably for her clients, not for her."

Parker's face fell almost as quickly as the box did when he dropped it. A ten-inch-long rubber penis bounced off the floor, and Parker jumped halfway across the room to avoid it. He stayed where he was, scowling at Madison like it was her fault.

"When you're done playing with those, you should probably bag them. In case there's any . . . evidence on them."

Parker looked ill. He scooped the contents back into the box and put the whole thing in an evidence bag, which he then put into another evidence bag.

"DO YOU think we missed anything?" Madison asked twenty minutes later.

Parker shook his head, sitting back on the bed. "We found her stash, her . . . toys. I don't think there's much else to find here."

As they were leaving, walking down the hallway, they passed the girl who had let them in. "Did you find what you were looking for?" she asked.

Parker grunted.

"Afraid not," Madison said.

"You might want to check her art locker."

Madison pivoted on one foot. "Art locker?"

The girl stopped, too. "Yeah. Her art locker. A lot of the juniors who have studio classes have lockers in the studio building." She shrugged. "Whatever you're looking for might be in there."

Parker bought Madison a meatball sandwich from one of the lunch trucks parked on the street.

"So we're back to square one," Madison said, nabbing some escaping sauce with a few strategically placed bites. "The locker belongs to the school, not the family. We need a warrant and we're not going to get it. Can't even ask for it."

"Not necessarily," Parker replied, taking a more head-on approach and consuming roughly a third of his sandwich in one bite.

"What do you mean?"

"Well," he mumbled, around a mouthful, "if we can spin the request, ask the right people the right way, then hey, the school just might invite us in with open arms."

They agreed that there was no need to let F. Harold Smith know in advance that they'd be stopping by to see him.

CHAPTER 35

SMITH'S RECEPTIONIST reacted differently as they approached this time: a flicker of recognition, a flash of alarm, followed by dread. She looked down at her desk, delaying their interaction until the last possible moment.

Madison cleared her throat, but she didn't look up. Parker elbowed her aside and knocked loudly no more than twelve inches from the receptionist's head. That got her attention.

Parker smiled in a way he seemed to think was charming. "Hi. Thomas Parker and Madison Cross from the Crime Scene Unit. We're here to see F. Harold Smith." He leaned forward and lowered his voice conspiratorially. "We don't have an appointment."

"I'm sorry. Mr. Smith is extremely busy."

Parker winked. "You know what? I think he'll make time to see us."

Huffing, the receptionist reached over and pressed the intercom.

"Hello, Mr. Smith? There's a Thomas Parker and a Madison Cross here to see you—"

She stopped in midsentence as Smith apparently cut her off.

"I—I know, Mr. Smith," she replied, "that's exactly what I told them, but—"

This time Parker cut her off. "Tell him it's about his friend Ashley, but if he's too busy, we can just leave a detailed message."

She looked at Parker with loathing, cupping her hand over the mouthpiece. "He says—" She stopped abruptly. "Okay."

She gently put down the receiver and spoke without making eye contact. "He'll see you in a moment."

It didn't even take that long. Smith came stomping down the hallway almost immediately, his best public relations smile plastered dutifully across his angry red face.

Parker put out his hand. "Thanks for seeing us, Mr. Smith. We were just wondering—"

"In my office, please," he intoned with artificial cheerfulness that masked his gritted teeth. He turned on his heel and stomped back down the hallway, looking over his shoulder after half a dozen strides to make sure they were following him.

Ushering them into his office, he closed and locked the door before taking a seat behind the desk.

"Now . . ." He leaned forward, steepling his fingers. "What are you doing here?"

Parker leaned in, too. "We're trying to help you."

Smith laughed insincerely. "Sure you are. And how's that?"

"We have a job to do, same as you. And we *are* going to do our job. You can help us do it in a way that will make your job a lot easier."

Smith sat back, skeptical but listening. "I can? And how's that?"

"I'm sure you know that another girl from Alpha Alpha Gamma died the other day," Madison jumped in. "You might or might not know that she was in business with Ashley Munroe."

Smith remained impassive, but his eye twitched. "I thought the casé was closed."

"We have to look into that connection," Parker continued. "To see if it's related to Munroe and Mowry. But we don't want to draw anymore unwanted attention."

Madison took a seat on the edge of his desk. "We want to search the contents of her locker in the art studio. But the fact is, if we get a warrant, we can't guarantee there won't be a news crew waiting for us."

Alarm leapt into Smith's eyes at the mention of a news crew. Even after his face had regained its impassivity, he stayed quiet.

"Okay," he said eventually, jabbing a finger on the top of his desk. "But if this does get on the news, I'll deny this conversation ever happened."

Parker shook his head. "No, you won't. We're not going to risk losing the case with an illegal search. And you sure as shit don't want anything to look like a cover-up. Don't worry; there won't be any news crews. But if there are, you'll just say you're cooperating with a routine police investigation. You can smile when you say it, just like the other day."

Smith sighed loudly. "Shit," he said, rubbing his forehead violently. "Okay, but we do it at night."

CHARLES ADDAMS Hall looked plain and boxy from the street: redbrick for the first ten feet and then glass for

the top three floors. But the entrance was off a walkway
and behind a double metal gate studded with black metal
hands, all life-sized, all in poses of creating art, sculpting,
painting, drawing. There were more than fifty of them on
the two gates, behind which was a small brick courtyard
with a garden and a couple of benches.

F. Harold Smith was waiting for them inside the courtyard by the front door, looking nervous and guilty. Standing next to him was a bored-looking security guard who
could not have been any younger than seventy-five.

"As far as Earl here knows, this is a drug search," he
whispered out the side of his mouth.

The guard opened the door and they followed him inside. He led them up a concrete and cinder-block stairwell
decorated with student artwork and plaques thanking
alumni donors. When they reached the third floor, Smith
flicked on the lights and took out a piece of paper.

In the middle of a cluttered hallway was a door
marked "Studio 320."

The studio was a large, plain white room housing half
a dozen unfinished works of what might one day be art.
Windows lined one side, and through them, the traffic on
Chestnut Street was visible in the dark outside. Smith
walked up to a low bank of gray, paint-smudged lockers
lining the wall under the window, and counted off to the
fifth one from the left.

"This is the one," he said, nervously tapping the top.

The security guard fumbled loudly with a large bunch
of keys before selecting one and opening the lock.

Smith opened the door to the locker an inch or two before abruptly stopping and turning to the guard. "You
know, Earl, I don't think I locked the front entrance when
we came in. Can you go check that out for me?"

Earl looked at him skeptically, then he turned and

started back down the hallway. When his footsteps had receded down the stairwell, Smith opened the locker door the rest of the way.

Inside, it was a mess.

Three half-finished bottles of Diet Snapple guarded the top shelf. Behind them was a collage of brightly colored junk-food wrappers: chip bags; Tastykake wrappers; an almost empty bag of Skittles; and half a moldy hoagie.

The bottom shelf was packed with crumpled-up clothing.

Smith made a face. "Lovely," he said.

Parker started taking out the food items and handing them to Madison, who was holding a large evidence bag. "How about one for the perishables and one for the rest," she suggested.

Parker nodded and dropped all the food and food wrappers into the bag. When he was done, he started pulling out art supplies that had worked their way to the back of the top shelf.

He held up a couple of almost-empty tubes of paint. "This the kind of paint like that blue one?"

Madison shook her head and he tossed them into another bag. He followed with a handful of old brushes, a matte knife, a plastic palette, a ruler, some charcoal sticks, and an assortment of rubber bands, pencils, and paper clips.

When the top shelf was empty, Parker looked at Madison with a shrug.

She handed Parker another large evidence bag and he started pulling clothes out from the bottom shelf: a couple of dirty, crumpled T-shirts, a couple of paint-stained socks. But the next garment was tightly twisted, and when he pulled, it resisted. He tugged it again, and it came free—a dark blue hooded sweatshirt. As it unrolled, two small bundles tumbled onto the floor: plastic shopping bags tied tightly with rubber bands.

Smith took a step closer. "What are those?"

Madison picked up one of the bundles and looked closely at it, feeling it through the layers of plastic. It wasn't a single item, but a dozen or so loose ones, all tightly bound together.

She looked at Parker, who nodded his assent.

Peeling off the rubber bands and opening the bag, she jerked her head back as a strong, chemical smell hit her nostrils. Inside the bag was a jumble of paint tubes. Madison took one out and read the label.

"Jesus," Madison whispered. "Lascaux."

"What is it?"

"It. The paints. Lascaux brand, just like the other blue." She pawed through the bag, through the jumbled rainbow. Every color except cobalt blue. When she held the bag out for Parker, he jerked his head away from the smell, just as she had done.

"What?" Smith asked, craning his head but not leaving his post by the door. "What is it?"

Parker started unwrapping one of the other packages. Inside was another bundle, this one wrapped in a thin sheet of some kind of dark gray foam rubber. It was caked with dust that rained down onto the floor at the slightest touch.

Beneath the rubber was a dark gray metal bar. Parker let the dusty foam wrapping fall to the floor as he held the bar up for Madison to see. "What the hell is this?"

Smith was on his toes, trying to catch a glimpse of what was going on. "What is it?"

Parker looked up at Madison. "This stinks pretty bad, too," he said.

As he hefted the bar in his hand, the locker door spontaneously swung to connect with it, making an audible click. Parker pulled the bar away, but the door followed.

"It's a magnet," he said. Three headless nails, each about four inches long, were stuck to one side of it. Parker pulled one off. "Pretty strong one, too."

Madison stooped and picked up the sheet of foam that had been wrapped around the magnet. As she unfolded it, the chemical smell grew stronger.

The foam wasn't a simple rectangle. There were notches cut along the edge, a pair on the top and a pair on the bottom, and a small square hole near one corner. The dust that coated it made a pattern of squares.

"She was in on it," Madison murmured to herself.

"What's that?" Parker asked.

Smith rushed over. "Earl's coming back . . . What's going on? What did you find?"

Madison grabbed the magnet from Parker, rewrapped it in the foam, and dropped everything into an evidence bag. "Come on, Parker," she said, quietly but urgently. "Let's go."

Parker put a hand on his knee and heaved himself up. "Whatcha got there, Newbie?"

"What is that?" Smith demanded frantically. "What did you find?"

He turned to Parker. "What did she find?"

Parker walked past him, ignoring his pleas.

"Oh, come on, you guys, goddamn it! I arranged this! I need to know what's coming my way next." Earl appeared at the doorway, shaking his head.

"Thanks for your help, Mr. Smith," Madison said as they walked toward the door. "And thank you, Earl."

CHAPTER 36

MADISON WALKED briskly down the hallway, Parker keeping pace right next to her. When they reached the door, he looked over his shoulder to make sure no one was following, and as the door closed, he turned to her. She didn't slow down.

"Hold on just one second there, Newbie. I don't care what you tell him or not, but I don't know what the hell's going on and I don't like it one bit."

"She was in on it. Chirelli. She was the one who was in the room before Donna LaMott." Madison held up the bag with the paints and shook it. "These are the paints she took from Beth Mowry's room. The ones Vincent Mowry gave Beth."

Parker thought for a second. "What about the magnet? What's with that?"

"I don't know about the magnet. I mean, that could be some art thing for all I know." She pushed open the front door and paused. "But the foam wrapped around it?"

"Yeah?"

"That's the filter from Beth Mowry's air conditioner, the one her brother just bought her. I'd bet anything that's the filter someone replaced before we got there that morning. It was Valerie Chirelli."

Driving back to the lab to pick up Parker's car, they agreed not to tell the lieutenant just yet.

Madison pulled out her phone. "I should let Aidan know about the paints and the filter."

"Aidan," she said when he answered, "it's me, Madison."

"Hey," he replied, his voice sleepy.

"We got it."

"Got what?"

"Evidence. The filter from the air conditioner, I think, for one. Reeking of MEK, or some kind of chemical."

"Where?" He sounded suddenly awake.

"In Valerie Chirelli's art locker. Along with a set of paints just like the ones from Beth Mowry's room, only get this—"

"No cobalt blue."

"Bingo."

"So what does that mean?"

"Well, for one thing, it suggests pretty strongly that Valerie Chirelli was in on it—that she was the one who tampered with Beth Mowry's room. It explains where the MEK came from, or it will once we get these paints tested. It explains where it all went. And why the air conditioner filter was so clean. It explains how Beth and Ashley were killed. It explains everything."

"Wow. That's great." The tiredness was seeping back into his voice. He yawned. "Congratulations."

"Thanks . . . Anyway, I just wanted to tell you."

"Right. Thanks . . . I'll talk to you tomorrow."

As soon as she put down her phone, she could sense Parker staring at her.

"What?" she asked defensively.

"That was good police work, and that's some good evidence. It is. But, sweetheart, it better not be everything."

"Why not?"

" 'Cause if that's everything, we got nothing."

She looked at him indignantly. "What do you mean?"

"What've we got, really?"

"What've we got? We got the paints. We got the filter from the air conditioner. What do you mean?"

"Well, lookit. What is it that you're saying happened?"

"What am I saying?" She looked out the windshield and growled in frustration.

"Calm down, calm down, just timeline the crime for me. Tell me what you want the lieutenant to believe happened."

She took a deep breath. "Okay. Beth Mowry is about to turn twenty-one. Vincent Mowry doesn't want to hand over the trust fund. He knows she's taking the methylphenedrine to study, knows its finals time. He comes up with the paint idea, gives her the new air conditioner with the broken vent switch, gives her the spiked paints . . . It kills her."

"Then what happens?"

"Then Valerie Chirelli sneaks in the next morning, switches the paints, switches the filter in the air conditioner, and opens the windows. And waits for someone to find the bodies."

"I know that sounds like a lot, and I think you might have it pretty close to the way it went down. But legally, it's shit."

"Why!?"

"You got a great motive for Vincent Mowry, but all your physical evidence points to Valerie Chirelli. You see? There's nothing to connect them."

"No, wait, there's the tattoo. Some of the people in

Wardleyville said they saw Vincent with someone who looked like Beth, but who had a tattoo just like Valerie's."

"No. As I recall, they said it was Beth, but she had a tattoo. They've already identified her as someone else, with or without the tattoo."

"Well . . ."

"Look, Newbie, I ain't saying you don't have a case, but it ain't close to finished. You want Vincent Mowry? You think Vincent Mowry was behind it all? Then you got to get something on him."

They drove in silence for a minute.

"I bet I do have something on Vincent Mowry," she said softly. "I just can't prove it yet."

"What's that you say?"

"I said I think I do have something on Mowry, I just can't prove it."

"What do you think you have?"

She told him about the match between the hair from the paint tube and the tissue from under Valerie Chirelli's fingernails.

"So if he set up the paints and the air conditioner . . . got Chirelli to help him clean up the crime scene, that would fit, all right . . ." Parker blew out a breath. "But that air conditioner was in the window for at least a week. Anybody could have tampered with it in that time, including Chirelli. Same thing with the paints. What proof is there that somebody else didn't taint the paint, or even that the tainted ones were the ones he gave her in the first place? He could have given her the other ones. And here's another thing . . . we have no way of proving those samples came from Vincent Mowry. Could be anybody. And without that, it's all just circumstantial."

Madison let out a long, low exhale to match his.

"Couldn't we just . . ." She drifted off, lost in thought. "No, no. Surely if we just . . . tell him . . ."

Parker laughed. "Yeah, I know. I just painted myself the same mental picture. You going in to see the lieutenant, after having been all but suspended for doing pretty much what you're doing now, working on a closed case he has specifically told you is closed. A case he got a ton of shit for letting drag out as long as it did. And you go in there telling him you've been at it again, only this time, you really can prove it was murder, kind of . . ."

He started laughing harder. "You just need him to get you a court order so you can scrape some flesh off the brother of one of the victims." He slapped his thigh. "The rich, well-connected brother, who . . . who you're already in trouble for harassing before."

Madison touched her forehead to the wheel of the car.

Parker was still laughing. "I honestly think he might just take out his service revolver and shoot you right there."

They pulled into the parking lot of the Roundhouse.

"So then what do we do now?"

Parker was wiping his eyes. "Well, if you want to finish this thing, you got to bring him a better case. Bring him a complete case."

"And how do I do that?"

"Well, first off, you gotta get your friend Aidan to come in and test those paints and the filter, make sure we have what we think we have."

MADISON DROPPED Parker off at his car, then brought the evidence bags inside and secured them in a locker. When she returned to her car, she punched Aidan's number into her phone. He answered on the first ring.

"Hi, Madison."

"Hi, Aidan."

"I'm guessing you want some analysis on the paints, and on that filter, right?"

She laughed. "You're so clever."

"I was surprised you didn't ask when you called before."

"Yeah, well, I didn't want Parker to hear me getting all giggly on the phone."

"Can it wait until morning?"

"It's almost eleven now."

"That's kind of my point."

"Yes, of course it can wait until morning."

"I'll meet you there at eight."

"Great."

"One request though."

"Yes?"

"Bring along some more of those biscotti."

CHAPTER 37

MADISON BROUGHT in some decent ground coffee and got to the lab early enough to brew a pot before Aidan showed up. The cappuccinos were starting to get a little expensive. But she bought a few extra biscotti so she wouldn't feel cheap.

When she heard the elevator ding, she poured a coffee, added some cream, and put a couple of biscotti on a napkin. She turned to present it to Aidan, and saw Parker walking into the room.

"Ooh! Cookies! Don't mind if I do." He crunched one of the biscotti in half. "These are hard," he said through a mouthful of hazelnut and chocolate.

"I thought you were Aidan."

He washed the biscotti down with some coffee. "Yeah, I figured that, but if you're offering cookies, who am I to argue, you know?"

"What are you doing here?"

He popped another half in his mouth. "Figured you'da had Veste down here testing those paints and stuff by now. I figured I'd come down and see what we actually got. Where is Veste anyway?"

"I'm here," he said, walking up behind them. "And don't eat all the biscotti, either."

"The what? Oh, the cookies. Yeah, well you better hurry up if you want some. These bad boys are awesome."

Aidan took the second biscotti just as Parker's hand was about to fall on it, earning him a scowl.

Madison handed Aidan a coffee. "Thanks," he said, and promptly dipped his cookie. "So what do we have here?"

She placed the bags onto the table. "We found these in Valerie Chirelli's locker in the art building. They were both tied tight with rubber bands."

He opened the bag with the paints. "Sure does smell like something," he mumbled, as he laid the tubes of paint out in a neat line. "What's in the other one?"

Madison handed him the second bag. "It's the filter from the air conditioner, I'm pretty sure. It's wrapped around some kind of big magnet."

Aidan looked up at them as he reached in. "A magnet?"

Parker shrugged and nodded.

Aidan pulled out the bundle and gently removed the sheet of foam, sending a small cloud of dust into the air. Almost immediately he started sneezing, once, twice, three times.

"Bless you."

"You okay there, buddy?" Parker asked, concerned but amused as well.

"Allergies," he said, wiping his nose with a tissue. "If that thing is a filter, it's probably loaded with pollen, along with whatever else."

He picked up the magnet, weighing it in his hand. "It's heavy." He touched it to the table and it pulled hard, making a solid clunk as it connected. "Yeah, that's a magnet, all right."

He left it stuck to the tabletop and gently spread out the foam sheet, nodding to himself. Without speaking, he got up from his chair and left the room.

A moment later, he came back with a large evidence bag and pulled out the other filter, the one he had removed from the air conditioner. He unfolded it and held it over the one on the table, lining the edges up. The one from the locker was much paler.

"They're identical," he said, looking at Madison first, then Parker. "Or at least, they were once.".

"Is that discoloration from age?" she asked.

Aidan shrugged. "Age, dirt. Maybe a chemical reaction with whatever was in the air." He clapped his hands and rubbed them together. "Okay, let's test these. I'm just going to start with a few of the paints, no need to test them all just yet. Then I'll get the filter sample ready."

Aidan set Madison up cutting out a small section of the filter. She dipped it in distilled water, then squeezed it into a small beaker.

Parker made a considerable dent in the bag of biscotti while Madison and Aidan got a few samples ready, then Aidan loaded the first sample from one of the paints into the chromatograph. There was a second chromatograph in another room, and Aidan got the sample from the filter started there.

As the machine started to hum, Parker asked how long it was going to take and wandered off to work at his desk. He came back a couple times for more biscotti.

Madison brought her personnel papers into the lab.

"You've been working on those papers all week," Aidan teased. "What, did they add an essay portion or something?"

"I know. I just can't seem to get it done."

"Second thoughts?"

"Seventeenth and eighteenth."

Aidan laughed and tweaked a knob.

Putting her papers down yet again, Madison picked up the magnet. "So what do you suppose this is about?" she asked, turning it over in her hand and playing with the nails stuck to it.

"What's that?" He looked over at her. "The magnet?"

She nodded.

"It's a window lock."

"A what?"

"A window lock. Here." He held out his hand, and she passed the magnet to him. "Remember those holes we saw in the window frames in room six?"

"Yeah?"

Aidan plucked a nail off the magnet with one hand and curled the fingers of the other hand into a loose fist. "You drill a hole through the bottom sash and into the top sash." He slid the nail into the middle of his fist until it was completely hidden. "You take the head off a nail, slide it into the hole, through the bottom sash and into the top, and the window is locked. Even if someone broke the glass, there's no way to get the nail out, unless . . ." He picked up the magnet and held it close to his upraised fist. The nail slid out and clicked against the magnet. "See?"

"I've never seen those before."

"You don't see them much anymore. Cool idea for its time, though."

"But if the holes were in the windows in room six, why were the magnet and nails in Chirelli's locker?"

"Don't know."

"I guess she needed the magnet to open the windows when she went in there."

"She might have even taken the magnet some time

earlier," he said. "So they couldn't open the windows."

Madison thought about the two girls in their room, feeling sick from the fumes, unable to open the windows, maybe looking for the magnet until it was too late.

"What's that about the windows?" Parker asked, fishing the last biscotti out of the bag.

Madison explained the magnet window lock and the possible explanations as to why Chirelli had it.

"I had an aunt used to have a setup like that. Used to get all bent out of shape when I'd play with the magnet, because I'd always lose it and then she couldn't open her windows. So I guess that ties Chirelli into it even more."

"Yup." Madison said, grinning.

"I guess so," Aidan said unenthusiastically.

"Hey, come on, that's like the icing on the cake."

As Aidan was about to reply, the chromatograph dinged. He whistled as he turned and looked at the computer screen, pressing the print button.

"What is it?" Madison asked.

As the printer shuddered to life, the chromatograph in the other room issued a similar ding.

"Hold on," Aidan called as he ducked into the other room.

A few seconds later, he returned with a printout. "Off the charts for both of them. Methyl ethyl ketone out the wazoo."

"We got her," Madison said.

Aidan bit into a biscotti.

Parker's head shot up. "Hey! Where'd you get that?"

"Stashed it earlier," he said, sipping his coffee. "The way I see it, all this stuff is great." He shifted his gaze to Madison. "And I mean that, it is. I can't believe you've been able to dig all this stuff up. But . . . right now, everything you have is just about enough to get a dead girl into court."

Parker nodded. "That's what I told her."

"There's nothing here that really connects Vincent Mowry with all this. I know he had a motive, and I know he bought her the paints and the air conditioner, but anybody could have spiked those paints and anybody could have broken the air conditioner. Especially Valerie Chirelli. Right now, it stops at Chirelli. If you want Mowry, you've got to find something to tie him into it."

"I might have something already," Madison said quietly.

"You might have what?" Aidan's eyebrows rose.

"She's got some DNA," Parker said.

"From where?"

"Remember? The samples from under Chirelli's fingernails and the hair from that tube of paint."

Aidan nodded. "But we don't know whose that is, right?"

"Well . . . no."

He shook his head sadly. "You got a lot here, and I agree; it looks like you're right, Vincent Mowry probably did kill his sister. He knew she was taking the methylphenedrine, somehow figured out that the MEK would interact with it, brought her the paints, and waited. Actually, it's a pretty clever plan. But even with this, I just don't see the lieutenant going to bat for a court order to get a sample from this guy."

Madison slouched against the wall. "So, what, that's it?"

Aidan raised his eyebrows and opened his mouth, but Parker cut him off.

"Maybe, maybe not."

A dubious expression flickered over Aidan's face. "You think you can get a court order?"

Parker laughed. "Well, I don't know about that . . . But there might be other ways as well."

"Like what?" Madison said, perking up.

"Well, you might be able to get one of his hairs some other way."

Aidan shook his head. "How are you going to prove it's his?"

"Well, I don't know. But if you think about it, it doesn't necessarily have to stand up in court."

"How do you mean?"

Aidan pushed himself away from the table. "I already don't like the sound of this." He started packing up his equipment.

"Well, if we could get a sample that we knew was from Mowry, we could take that to the lieutenant, tell him it's airtight but not admissible. Maybe then he'll go to bat for the court order."

Aidan sighed loudly and shook his head, preparing his samples for storage.

"Yeah, but what kind of sample can we get from him that we know is his?" Madison asked. "We can't sneak up and stab him with a needle, or break into his house and steal his hairbrush."

Aidan picked up the dirty filter and started slipping it back into its bag. "This is . . . is . . . ." He froze, then let out an explosive sneeze.

"Sorry. It must be that pollen again."

"Bless you," said Parker.

Madison looked at Parker with a gleam in her eye. "Bingo."

CHAPTER 38

AIDAN WAS adamantly opposed to the plan from the start.

It wasn't safe, he said. It wouldn't work and it probably wasn't legal.

Parker listened to his concerns and insisted he didn't think any of that would be a problem.

Madison was torn. She trusted Aidan's advice, but she desperately wanted to be able to tie things up. And the way Parker described it, it didn't sound like it would be that difficult.

"I know you want this to work," Aidan said, slightly condescendingly. "But it's just not a good idea. Too may things can go wrong."

"So what do we do then, just let him go? Just drop the whole thing and let him get away with it because too many things could go wrong?" She shook her head. "That's just not good enough."

Parker leaned against the wall, arms folded, looking on with a wry smile on his face.

"Okay," Aidan said quietly. "You do what you think is best. But I don't want to have anything to do with it."

With that, he packed up and left.

In the quiet that followed Aidan's departure, Parker walked up beside Madison. "Why is it you don't bring cookies when I come and help you?"

THE DRIVE to Wardleyville felt shorter this time. Maybe because Parker was driving, but more likely because of Madison's apprehension about what would happen once they got there.

After Aidan left, Madison and Parker had stayed at the lab, fleshing out their plan. When they were satisfied, Parker went out to get the equipment they needed, and Madison went home and switched her denim jacket for a vinyl windbreaker. As she left, Parker suggested again that she pick up some more of those biscotti.

She sat quietly as the scenery flashed by, staring out the window. "You know, a lot of what Aidan said back there was pretty close to the mark. He had some good points." Parker's voice interrupted her reverie. "No one's saying you have to do this, or even asking you to. You can back out at any time."

"No. I know what I'm getting myself into. This is something I want to do."

Parker nodded slowly. "And what I said before, about this being a job for the detectives, that still holds true. The only reason we're doing this, or the only reason *I'm* doing this, is because they're not."

She turned to him, perplexed. "Okay . . ."

"I'm just saying, I don't want you to think this is actually the way things are supposed to get done. Because it's not. Remember that, Newbie."

Parker volunteered to be the one who went in, but they

both knew it made more sense for it to be Madison. They had decided early on that whoever went in would wear a wire, and Parker had used the receiver many times. Plus, since Madison had already been out to see Mowry once, she'd raise less suspicion. And although neither of them mentioned it, the potentially career-ending repercussions of the plan were obvious, and Parker had a lot more invested in the job.

The idea of the wire initially came up for Madison's protection more than anything else. But the more she thought about it, the more she wanted to catch Mowry in a lie on tape. Something that would incriminate him.

They also agreed Madison would carry a gun.

She was glad Aidan had left before that decision was made. She was a little unsure about it herself, but she told herself she'd had plenty of shooting practice at the range with her uncle. She knew how to handle a weapon.

Parker got her a .22. It was small, but still heavy. She checked the clip when he gave it to her and nonchalantly slipped it into her jacket pocket, but the longer they drove, the bigger and more obtrusive it felt. When they were getting close to Wardleyville, she took it out of her pocket and repositioned it in her handbag, in an interior pocket where it would be accessible but less visible.

"Shit," she said, reaching around in her bag. "I forgot my cell phone."

Parker pulled his out. "You need to make a call?"

"No. Just thought it would make sense to bring one, you know?"

He held up his phone and squinted at the display. "Actually, my battery's just about out. I'll turn it off until we get there. Save the battery."

* * *

A COUPLE of miles from Mowry's house, Parker pulled off to the side of the road and turned to Madison. "Time to unbutton your shirt."

For a fraction of a second, she went through her list of maneuvers to disable an assailant in close quarters. Then she saw Parker unpacking the listening device she would be wearing.

He saw the look on her face and let out a guffaw. "Son of a bitch, you really do think highly of me, don't you? Jeez. Don't worry, Newbie, if I was going to pull something, I sure as shit would have done it before I gave you the fucking gun."

She blushed. "I'm sorry, I just . . ."

"Yeah, all right, all right. That's going to earn you some extra fucking tape, I'll tell you that. Goddamn." He had a roll of duct tape in one hand and a small, flat black box in the other. "All right, c'mon. It's not like I ain't seen a bra before."

Madison's color deepened. She could picture the heavy-duty, no-nonsense white cotton bra she *wished* she were wearing. It was sitting at home in her underwear drawer. If she had known how the day was going to progress, that's the one she would have on.

But she hadn't expected to be opening her shirt in front of Tommy Parker. She had been expecting to be working in close quarters with Aidan. Somehow, she had ended up wearing a sheer, satin-and-lace number from Victoria's Secret.

She closed her eyes and unbuttoned her shirt.

"Hmpf." Parker took a deep breath. "You know, that's not making it any easier."

"Just tape the damn thing on me," she snapped.

To his credit, when she opened her eyes and looked down, Parker was focused solely on the task at hand. He positioned the box under her left breast, with the microphone attached to the bottom of her bra. He crisscrossed it with tape, checked to make sure it was secure. "There."

He started up the car and pulled onto the road as Madison buttoned her shirt.

"We really should do this more often."

"Parker!"

"Well, I know my day is going downhill from here."

"I have a gun," she reminded him.

Parker chuckled. "All right, all right." He put the earpiece in one ear and covered the other one. "Give me a test."

Madison counted to ten.

"Loud and clear."

They rode in silence after that, Parker occasionally snickering to himself. A couple of times, Madison had to look out the window so he wouldn't see she was laughing, too.

But when they drove through the center of town, past the Wardleyville Diner, it started to sink in that she was about to confront a murderer, in his own house. Alone.

There was a distinct chance that things could go very, very wrong.

Parker looked over and smiled reassuringly. "Don't worry, Newbie. This'll be fine. I'll be real close, listening in. I'm not going to let anything happen to you."

"I know," she said without conviction.

"You sure you want to go through with this? It's not too late to change your mind. I won't think anything less of you."

"Yeah, because that's what I'm worried about."

Parker grinned.

"No, I'm fine," she said.

Wardleyville's main drag passed behind them, and before long, the wall around the Mowry estate rose up on the left. Parker pulled over about thirty yards from the gate. He parked on the grass, between two of the oak trees evenly spaced along the wall.

"Okay," Parker said. "I guess this is it."

Madison nodded. "Yup."

"And just remember, I'll be right here, so nothing's going to happen."

She smiled bravely. "I know."

They were quiet for a second.

"All right then," he said. "Off you go."

Madison put her hand out. "Okay."

He looked confused.

"The keys," she said. "Give me the keys."

"I thought I'd be waiting in the car."

"I can't just walk up there. He'll know something's up immediately."

"Right . . ." Parker handed over the keys. "So then, what am I going to do? Where am I going to be?"

"I don't know. But you better be someplace close."

Parker turned around in his seat, craning his neck as he looked for a place to hide. Twenty or so yards past the gate, a rhododendron grew alongside the wall. Parker pointed to it. "I'll be in there . . . I guess." He smiled ruefully. "In that bush."

Madison couldn't hold back a grin. "That's okay. I'll be in there . . ." She hooked a thumb at the wall. "With the murderer."

With a wink, Parker hopped out of the car and jogged up the street to his hiding place. Madison got out and walked around to the driver's side. As she waited for Parker to get settled, she adjusted her seat and the steering wheel.

"Okay," she said aloud in the car. "Shake a branch if you can hear me loud and clear."

One of the branches began shaking.

"Okay. I see you." She closed her eyes briefly. "I'm going in."

She pulled at her collar and looked down her shirt at

the small black nub of the microphone taped to her bra. It didn't make her feel much better.

She took a deep breath and drove through the gate, winding her way to the circle at the top of the driveway.

A dark green Jaguar was parked by the front door, and Madison pulled in behind it. She picked up a stack of plastic folders she'd brought with her, and gingerly placed her notepad on top, hugging the stack against her.

"I'm getting out of the car," she mumbled.

Looking around, she walked up the stone steps and rang the doorbell. The seconds dragged by. Madison felt like she was suffocating in her plasticky nylon windbreaker. The sky was overcast and the air was heavy and still.

When a minute had passed, she rang the bell again. "I'm ringing again," she said quietly. "I don't think he's home."

Just as she said it, Vincent Mowry opened the door.

His eyes narrowed when he saw her. "Hello?"

"Hello, Mr. Mowry," she said, trying to sound polite and upbeat, but routine.

"Yes?"

"I'm Madison Cross from the Philadelphia Police Crime Scene Unit. We're just trying to close your sister's file and I was hoping you could answer a few questions to help us do that."

Recognition registered on his face and he frowned. His back straightened and he looked down his nose, exuding an air of superiority. "I was under the impression it was already closed."

Madison smiled nonchalantly. "It pretty much is, sir. This is just a formality."

He looked at her with his head to one side.

"This should only take a few minutes," she added.

Mowry bowed his head. "Okay then. Come in."

CHAPTER 39

AS SHE stepped inside the house, Madison wondered if the wire would be unable to pick up anything over the pounding of her heart.

The doorway opened into a large central hall with a stairway running up the right side, curving into a second-floor balcony. It was cooler inside, and it felt somehow subterranean.

Mowry motioned for her to follow him. "This way," he said, disappearing down a hallway to the left.

Madison had to fight a sense of panic as her means of escape became more and more remote with every step. She felt like a deep-sea diver getting lost inside a sunken ship.

The hallway ended in a large sitting room with a massive fireplace. It was comfortably furnished in expensive traditional furniture, dark wood, and Persian rugs.

Mowry led her to a corner of the room where a pair of Queen Anne wingbacks bracketed a delicate, tile-topped pedestal table. He motioned for Madison to sit in one and he took the other.

Madison spread her plastic folders out on the table, pretending she was looking for something. Then she held up her notebook and flicked through the pages, creating a visible cloud of dust.

Mowry jerked his head back.

"Sorry," she said apologetically. She took out a pen and wrote the date at the top of the page. The dust in the air was already tickling her nose.

When she looked up to ask her first question, Mowry raised his eyebrows in bored anticipation.

"Sorry," she said again, flicking her pages back and forth at random, raising more dust.

He sighed wearily.

"Okay, just a couple of questions . . . When I was here before, someone in town said something about Beth having cosmetic surgery on her nose." She looked up. "Did she ever have a nose job?"

Mowry tensed at the question, giving her a hard stare. She noticed his nose just starting to twitch.

Madison's nose twitched as well, and she succumbed, shattering the silence with a loud sneeze. She looked around, helplessly, expectantly, until Mowry sighed and got up. He brought a box of tissues from across the room and put them down on the table.

"Thanks," she said, wiping her nose and mouth. "Now, where were we? Oh, right, Beth's nose . . ." She crumpled the tissue and put it in her pocket.

Mowry looked more confident now, settling back into his chair. "I assume they were referring to the bandages on her nose last year." He smiled. "Beth had a reaction to a minor cosmetic procedure. As I recall she wore a bandage briefly to hide it."

"Oh." As she scribbled on the pad, she snuck a peek and saw his nose twitching again.

Mowry sighed and then sniffed. His eyes were pink around the edges.

"Did Beth come and visit a lot after she went to school?" She looked up at him brightly.

It was hard to resist smiling. No matter what he said, she could catch him in a lie. If he said she didn't, then who had the locals seen him with? If he said she did, then why did her friends say she never went home?

Mowry sniffed again. He looked unhappy and uncomfortable. A vein was pounding in his temple, and his eyes were now red. He opened his mouth to speak, but paused, and in that instant he let out an enormous wet sneeze.

Madison felt a few droplets of moisture settle on her cheek. "Bless you," she said, repulsed but overjoyed.

"Excuse me." He pulled a tissue out of the box and blew his nose into it.

Mowry looked around, then got up and dropped his tissue into a small wastebasket next to the sofa, a few yards away.

Madison cleared her throat loudly and coughed. As he was about to sit, she asked in her sweetest tone of voice, "I'm sorry. Could I trouble you for a glass of water?"

Eyeing her coldly, Mowry sniffed again.

"Of course," he said finally. He walked across the room and through a doorway.

Madison tensed in her seat, listening as Mowry's footsteps receded behind the door. She counted fifteen steps. When she heard the squeak of a swinging door, she dashed across the room to the wastebasket and scooped Mowry's wet tissue into an evidence bag.

The door squeaked again, and she quickly folded the bag and stuffed it into her back pocket. As Mowry's footsteps grew louder, she plucked her own used tissue out of her pocket and dropped it into the wastebasket.

She turned on her heel, starting back to her seat, but as the tissue drifted down, she noticed in horror that her lipstick had left a pink smear.

She froze, flat-footed, midway between the wastebasket and her chair. The box of tissues was on the table just a few feet away, and Madison tried to calculate how long it would take to switch her tissue with a clean one. She had lost count of the footsteps, but she knew he was too close.

As it was, she got back into her seat just as he entered the room. He carried a cut-glass tumbler of water, which he placed on the table in front of her.

"Thanks," she said meekly.

She took a sip of the water and started carefully assembling her folders into a pile.

Mowry looked slightly confused.

"Well," she said apologetically. "I'm sure I've taken up enough of your time."

"Well . . . okay. Fine. I *am* rather busy. And I'm sure you can understand this entire ordeal has been quite trying."

"Well, I appreciate your help, Mr. Mowry. Hopefully this will all be over soon."

"I certainly hope so."

As the front door closed behind her, Madison hurried down the steps to her car.

"I'm outside the house, walking down the steps to my car," she said quietly for Parker's benefit.

Once inside, she immediately pulled a large evidence bag out from under her seat. "I'm inside the car," she said quietly as she opened the bag and slid the folders into it. "And I got the goods."

As she held up the key and moved it toward the ignition, she noticed movement out of the corner of her left eye. Looking over, she caught a glimpse of Vincent Mowry charging down the front steps toward her, a fireplace poker raised in his hand.

The side window exploded and a cloud of razor-sharp shards of glass filled the car, ricocheting in every direction, biting into Madison's face. She screamed, more from shock than from fear or pain.

She was still screaming when a hand closed on her throat and squeezed hard, then lifted her out of her seat. As she scratched and clawed at her attacker, she looked up and saw Vincent Mowry's face, contorted with anger and hatred and the effort of crushing her windpipe.

Her nails dug into his flesh, but the pressure on her throat didn't waver. His hand lifted her up, pulling her out of the car. She was starting to feel faint, distantly noting how the door lock was scraping painfully across her ribs. Then she remembered the gun in her handbag.

The moment she let go of his wrist, she could feel herself being dragged out of the car more quickly. Her hand groped blindly but found the handbag, somehow found the gun inside. She tugged it out and brought it around, trying to aim at Mowry's face.

He snarled and ripped it from her hand, then drew it back and slammed it across her forehead.

The blow stunned her, and as her world started to go dark, she heard Parker's voice in the distance shouting, "Freeze!"

She twisted her head just enough to see Parker, huffing across the lawn, maybe thirty yards away.

Without relaxing his grip on her throat, Mowry aimed and squeezed off a shot. The sound was deafening in her ear. Almost immediately, Parker went down.

Mowry returned his attention to Madison, dragging her through the car window and slamming her to the asphalt, pinning her to the ground by the throat.

"You stupid bitch," he snarled through gritted teeth. "You couldn't just let it go." He held the gun against her jaw.

Through the fog that increasingly permeated everything, she could feel pieces of glass digging into her back. Looking to one side, she saw broken glass sparkling like diamonds, scattered everywhere.

In desperation, she curled her fingers around the largest shard of glass she could feel, feeling blood well up in her hand.

Just before the blackness washed completely over her, she saw Vincent Mowry looking away, looking off to one side. She flailed her arm blindly, slashing with the piece of glass.

The sound of blood rushing in her ears was deafening. As she slipped out of consciousness, she heard one last distant bang.

CHAPTER 40

THE FIRST thing Madison saw when she woke up was Aidan's face.

"So I guess I'm not dead."

Aidan smiled and shook his head. "Not yet, anyhow. I'm still not sure what the lieutenant's reaction to all this is going to be."

"Where's Parker?" she asked, suddenly alarmed.

"He's okay. He's right over there. Flesh wound to the thigh. A couple dozen stitches and they'll send him home."

"Ouch."

"Yeah, that's what he said. Then he said some other stuff. That man has a very impressive vocabulary."

She laughed and then grimaced, holding her head.

He delicately brushed a hair away from her face. "Yeah, you lie still. They'll be over here for you in a second."

"So, how did you know we were here?"

"You might not have noticed, but I am extremely clever."

"Actually, I had noticed. Now, come on. Tell me."

"Remember when Spoons gave the cause of death, he said there were a couple lawsuits against manufacturers of methylphenedrine and MEK?"

"Yeah?"

He smiled. "I did some digging. One of the plaintiffs was a division of Mowry Chemicals."

Madison's eyes widened. "That's how Vincent Mowry knew."

"They won the lawsuit by proving the kid who died inhaling their chemicals was also taking methylphenedrine. That's how he knew. And that's how I knew. I tried to call and tell you."

"I left my phone at home."

"Yeah, you should try not to do that when pulling crazy, ill-advised stunts. I tried Parker's phone, but couldn't through."

"Dead battery."

Aidan nodded and looked up away from Madison. She turned to see an ambulance pulling up next to them. A second one was already parked twenty feet away.

"All right," Aidan said. "They're going to take care of you now, okay?"

"Wait!" Madison raised her hands and looked at her fingernails. "Aidan, I came here to get a DNA sample from Vincent Mowry. I have it here, under my nails. I need you to clip them. The kit's in the car."

Aidan sighed and stood up. "You know," he said as he fished out the clippers, "I think at this point we have enough on Mowry to get a court order."

She held out her hands like she was waiting for a manicure. "Humor me," she said. "And I need you to get the evidence bag on the passenger seat. There's plastic folders in there, sprayed with Mowry's . . . mucus."

He clipped her nails into a small evidence bag. "Is this really necessary?"

The paramedics walked up and put a stretcher down next to her.

"I came all the way out here to make this guy sneeze on me. Yes, I want you to collect the result of it."

"Okay, okay," he said as he finished up.

The paramedics were growing visibly impatient.

Aidan gave her a warm smile. "I'll see you at the hospital, okay?" As he turned to leave, the paramedics took over.

She started to tell them she was fine, but when they lifted her onto the stretcher, she felt suddenly woozy. Her lids were starting to droop when she saw Parker rising up on a stretcher near the other ambulance, his leg heavily bandaged.

She smiled when she saw him. He looked over and grinned back at her.

As the paramedics wheeled him over to the ambulance, he gave her a big thumbs up. "Looks like we're going stateside, Newbie!" he shouted. "How 'bout that?"

"Don't bet on it, Parker," she shouted back feebly. "I'll see you Monday morning!"

"Bring in some more of them cookies!" he shouted back as they slid him into the back of the ambulance.

She laughed, even though it hurt her head.

This time, when her eyes started to close, she let them. A gentle breeze swept across her face, lulling her even more. She felt a slight lurch as they lifted her up, and another as they moved her toward the ambulance. When she heard the doors opening, she opened her eyes.

One of the paramedics gave her a reassuring but impersonal smile as they rolled her inside.

She realized she'd been sleeping when the ambulance

lurched a few minutes later. As her eyes opened partway, she saw a familiar figure stepping out of the daylight.

"Daddy?" she said, struggling to open her eyes further, to bring them into focus.

He was bent over, sidling closer in the cramped confines of the ambulance. Madison struggled to make out his face.

"Oh. Uncle Dave. Hi."

"Maddy girl," he said, stroking her hair. "How're you doing?"

She cocked her head sideways and her eyes finally aligned themselves. "I'm fine. Bit of a headache, but apart from that, I'm fine. I'm sorry for, you know, for all the trouble and everything."

He put up a hand and gazed out the door. "Shush. None of that now." He looked back at her with a fond, wistful smile on his face. "I'm the one who's sorry."

He picked up her hand and folded it in his. "I'm sorry about your father, Madison, and about your mom, of course." He paused. "The tragedies you suffered as a child, we suffered them as well, your aunt Ellie and me.

"Those were dark, dark days." He slowly shook his head at the memory. "Anyway, I'm sorry you had to come to us that way, but I want you to know how much you've always brightened our lives. How much you mean to us. I just want you to know how glad we are that you're back, and how much we've missed you."

He stopped to blow his nose and sneak a quick wipe of each eye, then cleared his throat and settled back into Lieutenant Cross mode. "As far as the case goes . . . well, damn good job. Highly unorthodox, obviously, and . . ." He gave her a stern look. ". . . bordering on insubordinate. But you showed a firm grasp of the job, Madison, and courage of your convictions, which fortunately this time were well placed."

He relaxed again after having delivered his official review. "Truth is, Maddy, you saved my keister."

"That's bullshit, Uncle Dave."

He gave her a stern look. "Potty mouth. And no, it isn't. There was a lot of pressure from upstairs. A lot. One side wanting me to sit on it, the other side wanting me to milk it. Just my luck, I ended up in the middle."

"Yeah, because of me."

He shook his head stubbornly. "You were right, Madison. It was murder. And if that had come out after I sat on it, regardless of whatever pressure there was, I'd have been shit canned."

"Potty mouth."

"Sorry."

"Uncle Dave?"

"Yes?"

"Did you sit on it?"

He smiled sadly. "That's a tough one. I let it be rushed, I did do that. I didn't think it was anything but an accident, so I let it be rushed. And I let it be known that I wanted it rushed. So maybe I didn't sit on it, but I didn't do my job. If you hadn't stuck to it, Madison, I'd have been up a creek. You're tenacious . . . a lot like your father that way, you know that?"

"I wish people would stop saying that."

"Your father was a good man, Maddy. He was. It's a damn shame what happened, but it's not all his fault." He sighed. "He loved your mother so much. He loved you the same, you know. It just . . . when he lost her, the way he lost her . . . It was just too much for him, that's all. It was just too much."

CHAPTER 41

"So MOWRY confessed, huh?" Madison asked, picking out a jelly doughnut from the box on Parker's desk. The lieutenant had brought them in, a little Monday-morning treat for the troops.

Neither Madison nor Parker were supposed to be there, but while they had spent the weekend recuperating, the rest of the crew had been tying up loose ends on the Mowry case.

There were details to be shared.

"Yeah, he confessed," Lieutenant Cross replied. "But he didn't need to. We had everything we needed once the samples from Madison's fingernails and those plastic folders matched the hair from the contaminated paint tube and the tissue under Chirelli's fingernails. They also matched the sample we obtained with the court order. Confronted with that, Mowry confessed about the paints, the air conditioner, everything."

"So what did they charge him with?" Madison asked.

"So far, three counts of first-degree murder," Lieutenant Cross replied. "There may be some more."

"Plus he got a little wear and tear on him." Rourke smiled. "You guys weren't the only ones in the hospital, you know. Between the bullet Lieutenant Cross put in his shoulder and the really nasty-looking piece of glass Madison jammed into his thigh, he's going to be hurting for a while. And they're not real generous with the pain pills where he's going."

Parker chuckled and winced as he moved his leg.

"So, okay, I know how the evidence pieces together," Sanchez said between bites, cupping a hand under her chocolate glazed, "but I still don't get what the whole thing was about."

"When Mowry's parents died a few years ago, they left the family business to him and a trust fund to Beth, his stepsister," Madison explained. "The business was a bit iffy to start and now it's in the tank. So Beth was about to turn twenty-one and get control of this trust fund worth $2.2 million, and all Vincent had left is a business that's a million dollars in the red."

"There's more," Aidan added around a mouthful of apple spice. "I did a little more digging. Turns out not everybody believed Mowry's dad died accidentally."

Madison raised an eyebrow. "I actually wondered about that . . ."

"Nothing ever proven," he went on, "but Mowry senior was on his deathbed, presumably with a will that left most if not all of his estate to Beth's mom. This was about four months after the doctors had said he had two months, so it was pretty late in the game."

"And . . . ?"

"The wife was driving him down the shore for the weekend, they went off the road, crashed, and burned. Both killed. Investigation was inconclusive—where have we heard that before, right? But there were some concerns that the brakes had been tampered with, some possible traces of industrial lubricant and some suspicions about how the fire started."

"Did anybody suspect Vincent Mowry at the time?" Rourke asked, dropping sprinkles on Parker's desk.

"Do you mind?" Parker scolded, brushing them onto the floor. "If I gotta live at this desk for the next two weeks, I don't want you trashing it." With his leg in a cast, he was resigned to the desk duty ahead of him.

Aidan shrugged. "Some did. Not enough proof though."

Madison shuddered as she thought about how close she had come to being his next victim.

Parker bit a cinnamon doughnut in half, dusting his desk with sugar and crumbs. "You guys learn anything else about the whole 'sex' angle?"

Everybody stopped chewing and gave him the same reproachful look.

"What?" he asked defensively, taking another bite. "That's a legitimate question."

"Actually we did," Rourke said, washing down some doughnut with a gulp of coffee. "Madison had it pretty much figured out. Chirelli was Munroe's partner in prostitution. They were even friends, in a willing-to-kill-you-for-money kind of way. She met Vincent Mowry at a student art show; he was the purse-string-controlling stepbrother that Ashley's rich roommate was always complaining about. Chirelli used the same approach Munroe used with Smith: coming on hot and heavy until the last second, then the awkward news that anything else would require payment." Rourke smiled wryly. "On the advice of his closest advisors, Mowry said yes."

"But how did Chirelli become his accomplice?" Madison asked.

"Here's where it gets good," Rourke replied mischievously. "Mowry and Chirelli soon developed a special relationship. His business might have been tanking, but he still found enough to pay Chirelli's tuition and other bills, in addition to her regular fee. In exchange, Mowry got sex, plus something else."

Rourke looked around, making sure she had everyone's attention. "Chirelli wasn't just selling her body. She lost ten pounds, changed her hair, she even had surgery to make her nose look just like Beth's. Vincent Mowry wasn't just paying for sex; he was buying himself a fantasy that state law, cultural taboos, and Beth Mowry's disgust would have otherwise made impossible."

"What are you talking about?" Sanchez asked, her hand hovering over the doughnuts.

"Vincent Mowry wasn't just paying Valerie Chirelli to have sex, he was paying her to have sex while she pretended to be his stepsister."

Sanchez's hand withdrew from the doughnuts, her expression making it clear she had momentarily lost her appetite. "Eww."

"Damn," Parker said with a laugh. "And I thought I was a sick bastard."

"That part actually contributed to the rest of it," Lieutenant Cross added. "The money that made their whole relationship possible was running out, and at the same time the clock was ticking on Beth assuming control of the trust fund."

"I think Beth was openly contemptuous of Vincent," Madison added. "And it must have really pissed him off. Maybe once he found a replacement for her, he could finally act on his resentment. All those gifts that couldn't buy her affection must have seemed like the perfect cover. And Valerie Chirelli, in the room next door, must have seemed like the perfect accomplice."

"At least, until the prostitution story hit the news. Chirelli lost her cool and started to panic," Rourke added. "Then, she had to go, too."

Lieutenant Cross smiled grimly. "Apparently, Vincent Mowry's other fantasy was not spending the rest of his life in prison. Doesn't look like that one's going to come true, either."

The phone rang in the lieutenant's office, but before he turned to answer it, he raised his coffee. "Anyway, thanks, everybody." He gave Madison a wink. "That case was a pain in the ass, but sweet Jesus, it could have been a hell of a lot worse."

They all raised their coffees in assent and resumed the assault on the doughnuts, Madison and Parker answering questions about their injuries.

Half a minute later, the lieutenant returned, holding a slip of paper at arms length, narrowing his eyes as he read it. "Well, it's back to business, I guess. We got a gunshot victim at a Chinese take-out in Tioga." He looked around the room. "Parker's parked; that leaves Rourke."

She plucked a napkin from the stack and wrapped it around another doughnut. "I'm on it," she said, licking her fingers.

"Madison? You feel up to tagging along?" the lieutenant asked, "See what a normal day is like?"

"Love to," she said, gingerly rising from her chair.

She had a couple of stitches in her back and hand from the broken glass, and a headache lurking nearby that felt like it could return at any moment. But she was anxious to get to work.

Rourke eyed her dubiously. "You sure you're okay?"

she asked, quietly enough so the lieutenant wouldn't hear.

Madison waved dismissively. "I'm fine."

"All right. I'll bring my car around, okay? Meet you in the lot."

Outside, the sun was blindingly bright, already blazing high in the sky. The knot on Madison's head was throbbing by the time she got outside, and she made a detour to her car for some Advil.

The sun glared off her windshield, making it difficult to see, but as she put her hand over her eyes, she saw what looked like a parking ticket under the wiper blade. She laughed to herself; maybe it didn't look so much like a cop car after all.

But when she tugged the paper out, she saw it wasn't a ticket—it was a note.

She read it once, and then spun, catlike, forgetting her headache and her stitches. Scanning the parking lot, all she saw was the gaggle of smokers at the entrance.

She'd been inside less than forty minutes. He could easily still be around. Without hesitating, she bounded across the parking lot and out onto Eighth Street, then up Arch. She stopped halfway up the block and doubled back toward Seventh.

The running felt good at first, loosening her muscles, clearing her head. Part of her wanted to just keep running away, anywhere, but when she paused, she felt woozy. Shaking her head to clear it, she turned the corner, but the street seemed oddly uninhabited. She doubled back toward the Roundhouse, but ran out of steam when she reached the parking lot.

The wooziness returned and she grabbed onto a post for support, trying to catch her breath.

The note was still crumpled in her bandaged hand, and when she looked down at it again, a droplet landed right in the middle of it. For an instant, she thought it was a tear, until a second drop fell, and she realized it was perspiration dripping from her face.

"Hey, you okay?"

Madison looked up and saw that Rourke had pulled around next to her.

"What is that?" Rourke asked, a concerned look on her face as she glanced at the note in Madison's hand.

Madison looked down again and smiled wearily. She'd recognized the writing immediately, though years had passed since she'd seen it. The letters were shakier, but it was the same blocky, up-and-down print she would never mistake.

Good job, Magpie.

"You okay?" Rourke asked once more.

"Yeah, I'm okay."

Madison slipped the note into her pocket and got in the car. "Let's get to work."